THE TOWN
THAT BUILT US

What Reviewers Say About Jesse J. Thoma's Work

Hero Complex

"Thoma (*Data Capture*) delivers another rousing, high-heat lesbian take on classic sci-fi tropes. ...The fascinating, queer-normative worldbuilding focused on powerful female characters adds appeal and the push-pull romance will keep readers turning pages. Anyone looking for queer paranormal romance should snap this up."
—*Publishers Weekly*

"[*Hero Complex*] is a good dip into the super hero genre for people who do not want to have to watch 19 movies to get up to speed. ...The book was pleasant to read, the world building was light but the snarky banter between Athena and Bronte as their romance grows was entertaining. You should pick this one up if you are a fan of romance, superheroes or both."—*Paper Phoenix Ink*

"For me, the characters are what makes *Hero Complex*. Bronte and Athena are joined by two other 'superheroes' Spero and Galen. I loved the way everything sort of fits together, the nanobots and technology ideas, and the emotional manipulation that Spero and Galen utilised (in different ways and to different degrees). The four have a really nice slow-build found family dynamic which I really enjoyed. ...*Hero Complex* kept up a good balance of action and character moments. The 'training montage' section was well done, and it was a lot of fun to see Bronte's abilities gradually come to the fore. Fun and futuristic, *Hero Complex* is a great superhero adventure."—*Foxes and Fairy Tales*

Wisdom

"I like Jesse J. Thoma's writing style and the topic of drug addiction and health problems she addresses is interesting and still an actual problem all over the world. ...Drug use, addiction, and in this context safety and health are perennial issues that every mayor of any city has to deal with. Obviously, this is an important topic for the author, and she writes it very well. All in all, this was an entertaining political story."—*Lez Review Books*

"Every time I read a book by Jesse J. Thoma, I remember how much I enjoy the way she combines heavy topics and light writing. Despite being book 3 in a series (after *Serenity* and *Courage*), this book can be read as a standalone. ...This book is an interesting blend of instalust and slow burn. Sophia and Reggie start flirting on their first meet and almost never stop. The sparks are everywhere and it's all very exciting. All the edging and sexy talk are pretty damn hot too."
—*Jude in the Stars*

Courage

"Thoma writes very endearing characters, extraordinary people in normal lives. ...A slow burn romance with plenty of sparks and chemistry."—*Jude in the Stars*

"Set in the same universe as *Serenity*, Thoma has again done a great job of exploring difficult, relevant topics in an accessible way, whilst also managing to include a believable romance and some much needed elements of humour."—*LGBTQ+ Reader*

"I love a serious police procedural. Add in an enchanting romance with beautiful characters, and you have the perfect novel. That is

exactly what I found in *Courage* by Jesse J. Thoma. I was hooked on page one, and was sad to leave this tale when I reached the end."
—*Rainbow Reflections*

"*Courage* is a slow burn romance with plenty of sparks and chemistry. You can always count on Jesse J. Thoma to write solid but tender stories."—*Rainbow Literary Society*

"I LOVED that Thoma addresses the issues of police reform, Black Lives Matter, and 'defund the police' in a non-political way. She brings these issues into the story in a way that makes SO MUCH sense."—*Love, Literature*

"Jesse J. Thoma brings two stories to life in parallel, one being the work and dynamics of the new ride-along program and how the two protagonists deal with it, and the other the romance between the two. I loved both parts. …Highly recommended for anyone looking for a good cop/social worker story who enjoys angst and tricky situations."—*Lez Review Books*

Serenity

"*Serenity* is the perfect example of opposites attract. …I'm a sucker for stories of redemption and for characters who push their limits, prove themselves to be more than others seem to think. This lesbian opposites attract romance book is all that, and well-written too."
—*Lez Review Books*

"I really liked this one. I liked the pace, the stakes, and the characterizations. The relationship builds well, there are likeable supporting characters, and of course, you're rooting for Kit and Thea even as your heart breaks for both of them and their situations. It's a sweet romance, and I appreciated that a lot of the issues Kit faces have nothing to do with her sexuality in a predominately male-driven, sexist profession.."—*Kissing Backwards*

The Chase

"The primary couple's initial meeting is a uniquely amusing yet action-packed scenario. I was definitely drawn into the dynamic events of this thoroughly gratifying book via an artfully droll and continuously exciting story. Spectacularly entertaining!"—*Rainbow Book Reviews*

Seneca Falls—*Lambda Literary Award Finalist*

"Loneliness and survival are the two themes dominating Seneca King's life in Thoma's emotionally raw contemporary lesbian romance. Thoma bluntly and uncompromisingly portrays Seneca's struggles with chronic pain, emotional trauma, and uncertainty." —*Publishers Weekly*

"This was another extraordinary book that I could not put down. Magnificent!"—*Rainbow Book Reviews*

"...a deeply moving account of a young woman trying to raise herself from the ashes of a youth-gone-wrong. Thoma has given us a redemptive tale—and Seneca isn't the only one who needs saving. Told with just enough wit and humor to break the tension that arises from living with villainous ghosts from the past, this is a tale woven into a narrative tapestry of healing and wholeness." —*Lambda Literary*

Pedal to the Metal

"Sassy and sexy meet adventurous and slightly nerdy in Thoma's much-anticipated sequel to *The Chase*. Tongue-in-cheek wit keeps the fast-moving action from going off the rails, all balanced by richly nuanced interpersonal relationships and sweet, realistic romance."
—*Publishers Weekly*

"[*Pedal to the Metal*] has a wonderful cast of characters including the two primary women from the first book in subsidiary roles and some classy good guys versus bad guys action. ...The people, the predicaments, the multi-level layers of both the storyline and the couples populating the Rhode Island landscapes once again had me glued to the pages chapter after chapter. This book works so well on so many levels and is a wonderful complement to the opening book of this series that I truly hope the author will add several additional books to the series. Mystery, action, passion, and family linked together create one amazing reading experience. Scintillating!"
—*Rainbow Book Reviews*

Visit us at www.boldstrokesbooks.com

By the Author

Tales of Lasher, Inc.

The Chase

Pedal to the Metal

Data Capture

The Serenity Prayer Series

Serenity

Courage

Wisdom

Romances

Seneca Falls

Hero Complex

The Town That Built Us

THE TOWN THAT BUILT US

by

Jesse J. Thoma

2023

THE TOWN THAT BUILT US

ISBN 13: 978-1-63679-439-6

This Trade Paperback Original Is Published By
Bold Strokes Books, Inc.
P.O. Box 249
Valley Falls, NY 12185

First Edition: July 2023

Credits
Editor: Cindy Cresap
Production Design: Susan Ramundo
Cover Design By Tammy Seidick

Acknowledgments

Thank you to Sandy and Rad and the BSB team. Getting to write and publish in such a supportive environment is a gift.

To Cindy, thank you for your editing guidance. I appreciate your insights and your knowing exactly the small tweaks to make the story shine. A writer is only as good as their editor prods them to be and I'm glad I get to work with you.

To my kids, thank you for being exactly who you are and letting me love you and be your parent.

To my wife, every day I think I couldn't love you more, but then I wake up the next morning and my love grows a bit more. I'm one lucky duck.

Finally, to the readers, thank you for picking up this book. I'd write even if no one read a word, but it's so much more fun to write for all of you.

Dedication

To Alexis, Love rocks and I only want to rock with you.
To Goose, Bird, and little Purple Martin, I love you
yesterday, today, and tomorrow too.

CHAPTER ONE

Grace Cook was gasping, sure she was about to die, when she made it to the entryway. She yanked open the front door to the house she'd known her entire life and stumbled onto the porch. She sucked in mouthfuls of air, but the heat and humidity provided no relief for her dry mouth, racing heart, and clammy skin.

She sat heavily on the porch swing and lowered her head to nearly between her knees, cradling it there between her hands. When she no longer felt the need for an ambulance, she raised her head and looked toward her rental car. Her large pink suitcase stood perkily next to the rear passenger door, waiting to go inside.

"Fuck you. You can wait in the sun."

Her tears flowed freely, and unlike every other time they'd arrived, Grace didn't try to keep them at bay. There was no one to judge her for her emotions, and besides, if she couldn't have an ugly cry on the porch she grew up on, where in the world could she?

Grace didn't keep track of how long she cried, but it was hard enough and long enough that her eyes felt puffy and empty and she had a headache when she was done. Although she was exhausted, she'd not yet completed the one task she needed to do. She stood on unsteady legs and faced the front door again.

"You're a grown ass lady, you can do this." Grace patted her cheeks to give her words some oomph. She took a deep breath, pulled open the front door, and once again slipped inside her family home.

As it had before, the stillness hit her in a part of her heart reserved for the deepest grief. This time she was ready for it or perhaps she was emotionally spent. Whatever the reason, she was able to feel her way past how wrong it felt to be in this house in its current, stagnant form.

She went to the living room first. Someone had cleared out the hospital bed and medical supplies her father needed the last two months of his life. She appreciated not having to see them and be reminded of what he'd gone through.

The furniture, the stains on the carpet, the decorations on the mantel were all as familiar and comforting as an ice-cold Popsicle on a blazing summer day. Grace wandered to the mantel and took down the picture she'd looked at for as long as she could remember. Her parents had taken her to the local department store to get a Christmas photo the year she turned two. They all looked so happy. She loved the way her parents looked at her in that picture, like there was nothing they'd rather be doing and no one they'd rather be with. As she grew, she knew those looks weren't plastered on for the camera.

Grace gently touched both her parents' faces before putting the picture back and looking at the others. Her heart felt as though it skipped a beat or two when she came to the picture of her and Bonnie Whitlock, arms thrown around each other, looking very much in love. Her father had taken the picture Grace's senior year of high school and had for some stubborn reason refused to take it off the mantel when they'd broken up. No amount of pleading on Grace's part, or pointing out that Bonnie had broken her heart ever got through to him. The picture remained.

"I know you still love her and so do I," was his standard response. As if love mattered one lick to Bonnie. If it had, Grace might not have moved across the country. She might not be here alone now. She gently placed the picture facedown on the mantel. "What ifs" and "should haves" didn't do anyone any good in the present.

The longer she wandered, through the kitchen, her old bedroom, the three-season room, the more comfortable she felt. She knew this place, where the floorboards squeaked underfoot, and the doorframe where her height was carved out inch by inch as she grew. What she didn't know was the lifelessness. The soul of the house was missing.

More tears fell as she approached her parents' bedroom door. This was the door she'd passed through when she'd had a bad dream in the middle of the night and crashed through on Christmas morning. When she peeked in now, there was no laughter, no comfort. Only a pair of her father's dust-covered slippers at the bedside and silence greeted her.

She pulled the door closed and walked quickly down the stairs and out the front door. Her exit was less frantic than before, but this time she was clear; she couldn't stay in the house tonight. She walked back to her rental, threw her perky suitcase back in the trunk, and sped out of the driveway. Now that she'd made the decision, she didn't feel like she could get away fast enough.

What sounded like a revving engine sounded to her left, but she was in the country. Farm country, so engines of all sorts revved constantly here. She had other things to worry about than a noisy tractor.

Grace drove the rural roads at a much more reasonable speed than she had as a teenager. Through adult eyes, the recklessness of her younger self terrified her. Were all kids so stupid? How did parents survive?

As she drove, she contemplated her options. She could drive back to Providence and stay in one of the many hotels there where her privacy and anonymity would be preserved. Here, in Garrison, there was one option, and it was owned and operated by Ms. Babs. Not only was she the grandmother of Grace's high school rival, but she knew everyone in town and seemed to talk to all three hundred and eighty-two residents daily. If Grace stayed at Ms. Babs' bed-and-breakfast, she assumed the whole village would know about it by morning.

Grace sighed and made the turn to the village center. She was too tired to drive back to Providence. Maybe it was better if Ms. Babs spread the word she was back. Would anyone care? Every other time she'd returned to Garrison she'd barely seen or spoken to anyone in the village. She'd come to see her father and no one else. Most people probably didn't even remember her name.

Gravel crunched under her tires, and she pulled into one of two empty spots in Ms. Babs' parking lot. The large colonial-style home was a cheerful yellow and the landscaping around the house was colorful, neat, and inviting. Ms. Babs used to do it all herself. Grace thought of her father and how much he'd slowed over the past five years. Maybe that was true for Ms. Babs too.

"Are you going to stand out there admiring my roses or are you coming inside for a room, Grace Cook?"

Grace smiled despite herself. Every kid in Garrison knew Ms. Babs' voice. It was a sound of sneaked candy bars and cabinets after school on hot days. Grace had asked Ms. Babs why milkshakes were called cabinets in Garrison and Ms. Babs had winked and told her it made them taste better.

Still lost in memories, Grace walked through the door. She remembered a split second before the screen door slammed to stick her foot back and catch it. Ms. Babs nodded and smiled.

"Come here, child."

Before she had a chance to weigh her feelings on the matter, Ms. Babs pulled Grace into a full body, grandmother hug.

"Your father was one of the best of us. We all miss him deeply." Ms. Babs squeezed tighter.

"I couldn't stay in the house alone tonight." Grace had to fight to get the words out the side of her mouth since her face was smooshed into Ms. Babs' ample bosom.

"Of course not, child. You should stay here, with your people. I don't know why you've stayed away so long, but I'm glad you're here now." Ms. Babs ejected Grace from her chest and the hug and held her at arm's length. "I saved the best room in the house for you hoping you'd come by. Get your things and head on up. Let me get to work. Grief has clearly done a number on you. Look how skinny you are. You're going to be okay now. I'll fatten you up again." Ms. Babs gave her a little shove toward the stairs and pointed upward.

Grace looked down at herself then up at the ceiling as if she would magically be able to see the mystery room Ms. Babs had saved for her. Was that sweet or creepy? She couldn't decide. She mumbled something unintelligible she hoped conveyed the need for her suitcase still in the car. Outside, she was again assaulted by the hot humid air.

"Third floor, dear. It's the only room up there. You'll have plenty of privacy. Unless that's not what you're looking for this time back around." Ms. Babs smiled knowingly and shooed Grace toward the stairs.

It took all the reserves she had left, but Grace managed to not inquire what the hell Ms. Babs was implying. It certainly couldn't be about Bonnie. No one knew about what they'd had unless Bonnie had been more open over the last fifteen years. Besides, Bonnie couldn't turn her head anymore, right? In fact, she'd prove Bonnie meant nothing to her the first time she saw her. Dear God, please make it true. There was only so much pain her heart could take.

CHAPTER TWO

Bonnie couldn't remember the last time she'd cried, but losing Lionel Cook had torn her heart to shreds. She nearly embarrassed herself during the funeral service by loudly ugly crying in the last row.

Losing him had been more of a blow than when her own parents had died. He'd never held her history with his daughter against her. Quite the opposite in fact. He seemed to hold her closer after Grace left for college, and annoyingly, he would stare at the picture of her and Grace on his mantel anytime she was around. He never said a word, but Bonnie got the message. He thought she screwed up and she and Grace had been perfect together. Tell her something she didn't already know.

She debated whether she should go to the after-funeral luncheon. It would seem weird if she didn't. Everyone in the village would notice and ask her about it, but it would probably be more uncomfortable if she did go. What would she say to Grace? I'm sorry about your father and breaking your heart back in high school? Grace would do her a favor if she slapped her in front of everyone and put her out of her misery. Then at least Bonnie would know Grace still hated her and she could stop torturing herself with "what-ifs."

"Hi, Bonnie. Thanks for coming today."

Bonnie nearly jumped out of the nicest pair of boots she owned. She didn't need to turn around to recognize Grace's voice. The years hadn't changed the sweet sound. It was more mature perhaps, but still warm and smooth and went straight through Bonnie's bones. Her heart clenched at the sadness she could hear squeezing the edges of Grace's niceties.

She turned. "Hi, Grace. I wasn't sure you'd want me here, but I needed to say good-bye. He and I…well, we stayed in touch and I truly loved him." Bonnie wrung her hands.

Grace looked surprised. "He never mentioned that, but I'm glad you came. Dad never seemed to want us to be apart and I'd certainly not keep you from saying good-bye. Are you coming to lunch?"

Bonnie nodded even though up until that moment she was going to bow out. She wasn't sure how much longer she could keep up this conversation. She wanted to reach out and tuck the stray strand of hair behind Grace's ear. She wanted to cup her cheek and tell her everything would be fine. She wanted to pull Grace into a hug and breathe in the scent of her citrus shampoo. Except that was her Grace from years ago. The woman in front of her wasn't someone she knew anymore, and neither of them were those carefree kids so deeply in love.

Grace gave her a funny look, probably because she'd been staring without saying anything for too long. "Okay, I'll see you over there. It's nice to see you, Bonnie."

It sounded like Grace meant it. That was something. If only she could stop getting pulled into the past and make conversation like everyone else in the room, she should be okay.

She flagged down her friend Duck. "You going to the lunch?"

Duck tugged at his necktie and unbuttoned the first button of his dress shirt. "Yeah, Candace says we have to. I offered to take the baby home for a nap, but she said her mom's going to do it when Avery gets tired. You need a ride?"

"I'll sit in the back with my favorite person in the world. And I don't want to hear even the slightest grumbling about Candace. You worship the ground that woman walks on. You have nothing to complain about. You were a feral man-child before you met her." Bonnie gave Duck's shoulder a shove.

Duck threw his arm around Bonnie and they went in search of Duck's wife and daughter. "Not a word of a lie. When are we going to find a lion tamer for you, Runt? Grace is back in town you know."

"Oh, gee, I hadn't noticed when she gave the eulogy at the funeral we just attended. Give me a break, man. I tripped all over my ass trying to have a conversation with her. I need a second." She tried to pinch Duck in the ribs, but he pulled her tighter to him so she couldn't get where she was aiming.

Before they got to Candace, Bonnie was wrapped up from the other side by another towering tree trunk of a man. "Grace's back, Runt. Whatcha gonna do about it? Finally going to grow a pair?"

"Carl, let go. Both of you lay off." Bonnie slipped away from the two guys, two of her three best friends, and stomped over to Candace.

"They giving you a hard time?" Candace handed Avery, her six-month-old daughter, to Bonnie.

"When aren't they?" Bonnie cooed at Avery, her annoyance with Duck and Carl far from her mind. "You'll never give me a hard time, will you, baby girl? Because I'm yours forever."

"Oh. I didn't mean to. I mean I didn't know about the three of you...Anyway, I wanted to say hi, Candace. Thank you for coming."

Grace's voice once again seeped into Bonnie's pores and sent a shiver along her spine. She looked up and caught Grace's eye, but she quickly looked away. Grace looked flushed and embarrassed and maybe disappointed? Was that possible?

"It's so nice to have you back, although the circumstances are terrible. Did you know my husband, this amazing little baby, and I are living in my parents' house now? Your dad and I were neighbors these past few years. He was such a sweet man and he loved you something fierce." Candace gave Grace's hand a squeeze. "Bonnie, can you take Avery over to Roy and have him change her diaper before we head over to the restaurant?"

Bonnie looked quickly between Candace and Grace before taking the diaper bag from Candace and walking the twenty feet to Duck and Carl. "Candace said you're on diaper duty."

"You're her godmother, you do it." Duck teased her.

"If she pees on you, you get to take off your tie." Bonnie handed Avery and the diaper bag to Duck and shooed them toward the bathroom.

"Why'd Candace send you over? What's she talking to Grace about?" Carl looked suspicious.

"Me, I think. Grace looked flustered when she saw me holding Avery and standing by Candace. Now they're talking and Candace made a big deal of mentioning Duck was her husband." Bonnie ran her hands through her short-cropped hair. It was probably now sticking up in all directions. After a stressful day at work she was always amazed at the exciting hairstyles she managed.

"Candace's got your back. Keep that door wide open in case you need to drive right through." Carl winked.

"Enough already. Don't let Stumpy get going too. I can't take all three of you after me." Bonnie rolled her eyes for effect, but she couldn't forget the look in Grace's eyes for the brief moment when she seemed to think Candace, Bonnie, and Avery were a happy family.

"All right, poopy pants have been changed and Avery and I are hungry. Let's get going. You coming with us too, Carl?" Duck headed for Candace who was now standing alone.

Bonnie and Carl trailed after Duck and his family. They all piled into the large SUV Duck insisted on when Avery was born. Duck couldn't park it to save himself so Candace was the only one allowed to drive it.

"Can you come pick me up Friday for boys' night, Duck?" Carl cupped his hand behind his ear like he was listening intently. "What's that? Oh, you don't know how to drive your own truck. Well, shit, maybe Candace can drop you off if she's not too busy."

Duck turned from the passenger seat and flipped him off. "Says the man sitting in my back seat. Why don't you come pick me up, Carl?"

"Runt, can we stop by and pick up Duck after you get me?" Carl laughed harder than anyone.

"Why is Bonnie the only one who has a car that works and she knows how to drive?" Candace looked to the back seat through the rearview mirror.

"She's the Dude of boys' night so she has to drive. Unwritten rule." Both Duck and Carl pointed at Bonnie and snapped their fingers. They'd been doing it since elementary school, but no one could remember why it started.

Candace parked the large SUV perfectly and killed the engine.

Bonnie leaned forward and high-fived Candace. "Duck, that's how you execute a parking job. Now, no more acting like fools once we're inside. We're here for Lionel."

"And Grace." Duck raised an eyebrow.

"Your ex-girlfriend that you regret breaking up with and still love."

Carl attempted to give Bonnie a hug, but she shoved him away and got out of the truck. She stomped toward the restaurant entrance, leaving the others behind. They'd be a few minutes getting Avery out of her car seat and she'd have time to settle down before facing their teasing again. Why didn't they know when to leave well enough alone? Grace was a scab she picked enough on her own.

Before Bonnie could open the door and decide whether continuing to stew alone was preferable to having people to talk to, Stumpy, the fourth member of her tight group of friends, stepped out of the restaurant.

"I'm going to warn you before you say anything, if you mention Grace, I will beat on your nuts until you no longer have the ability to speak." Bonnie crossed her arms and waited for Stumpy to say something.

Stumpy stared at Bonnie a few beats. "Carl and Duck making jokes about Grace that are pissing you off?"

Bonnie nodded. Stumpy was the only one who knew the whole story behind her breakup with Grace. Since he was little, he'd always been a caretaker and a great listener. No one was born to a career more naturally than Stumpy was with his clinical psychology practice.

"Before you ask, no, I don't need you to talk to them. It's an emotional day is all. They don't mean anything by it." Bonnie kicked nonexistent dirt off her boots and climbed the stairs to join Stumpy at the restaurant entrance. "Ready to go in?"

Stumpy nodded cautiously. "I'll get my jock from the car if I need it, but I'd prefer if you'd leave my balls alone and hear me out. Grace is inside and she asked me if I'd seen you yet. It seemed like she was looking for you." He covered his junk protectively.

"Okay. Thanks. I think." Bonnie smoothed out her shirt front and checked the collar of her button-up dress shirt. The others finally caught up, but Stumpy engaged them in conversation before they could mention Grace again. Not that they probably would after she'd stormed off.

Once inside, Stumpy led them to the function room reserved for the funeral guests. Since most of the village was in attendance the rest of the restaurant was nearly empty. Someone had hung a huge "RIP Lionel" sign above the bar and taped a smaller "pour one out for Lionel" sign on the bar top. A full shot glass sat on top of the sign. Bonnie knew it contained whiskey, Lionel's favorite indulgence.

Bonnie only made it halfway to their table before she felt a tap on her arm. "I'm sorry to catch you on your way in the door, but I was hoping I could talk to you before things get going." Grace looked shy and uncertain.

Bonnie tried to smile and put her at ease. She wasn't sure how effective it was since her insides felt as unsteady as Grace looked. "Of course. Anything." Grace sat at an empty table. Bonnie followed her lead.

"I wasn't sure I wanted to see you, much less have an entire conversation with you." Grace paused and looked down at her hands. "But I need to know, you and my dad were close?"

Now it was Bonnie's turn to squirm and look down at her hands folded on the table. She silently cursed Lionel for putting her in this position. She'd begged him for years to talk to Grace about her relationship with him.

"I didn't seek him out or run to him the minute you left, if that's what you think. I own the hardware store in the village center and do handyman work. He had some shingles come off the side of his house in a storm and needed a couple of balusters replaced on his porch railing." Bonnie dared to look at Grace. She was crying.

"I almost came home after that storm. He called me pissed off his back was acting up and he couldn't get on the ladder himself to fix the shingles. I was homesick and that was nearly the nudge I needed to drop out of school and run home."

"I guess I should have turned down the job. Then I could have apologized and maybe things would be different." Bonnie moved her hand a smidge in Grace's direction.

Grace pulled her hands off the table and crossed her arms. "Please don't say things like that. If you'd had anything to say to me then, you knew where to find me and how to get in touch."

Bonnie pulled her hand back and rubbed her hair, likely making any style that remained impossible to salvage. "Okay, got it. Sorry. Anyway, after your dad hired me that first time, he kept calling anytime something needed fixing. Then he'd give me a call to swing by just to say hi. After a while, I'd swing by on my own to check on him or stop and chat for a while. We became friends and I loved him deeply. You know what my relationship was like with my parents. I'm not saying he filled that void, but we seemed to fill a role for each other."

"Why weren't you at any holidays and why didn't you come by when I was in town in the past fifteen years if you two were so close?" Grace narrowed her eyes and squeezed her arms tighter around herself.

"Because of how you reacted just now to my mentioning us. Your time with your dad was special to both of you. Neither of you needed me mucking it up with reminders of our past." Bonnie pointed between the two of them, then looked away again. What she wouldn't have given to spend one Christmas with the Cook family.

"How did you spend your holidays, Bonnie?" Grace's voice was softer and warmer.

The tenor made Bonnie look up. She wished she didn't because she could see glimmers of her Grace shining in this older version's eyes.

"Do you really want to know that? I screwed up and never made it right, remember?" Bonnie sighed heavily.

Grace stood without saying a word. She put her hand on Bonnie's shoulder and gave it a gentle squeeze before walking off into the crowd. Bonnie leaned down and put her head in her hands. She'd known seeing Grace would be hard, but she hadn't expected the repeated sucker punches of emotions.

But she should have known. She should have seen this coming as soon as she'd laid eyes on her at Lionel's house and saw how beautiful she was. She'd seen the strange car pull into the driveway and had gotten nosy. She'd been on Duck's four-wheeler fixing fencing and couldn't help but take a peek. When she saw it was Grace, her heart shattered all over again. Grace had aged but grown more beautiful with the passing years. Bonnie should have seen the emotional turmoil coming, she'd had plenty of warning, but she didn't and now she was reeling.

Bonnie had always known that mistakes as large as the one she'd made with Grace always came back to get you eventually. Her time ignoring Grace and their past was up. If only she knew what to do about it.

CHAPTER THREE

Grace looked around the kitchen of her father's house and gave herself a figurative pat on the back. The now dated cabinets were clean and the green Formica counters that reminded her of her childhood were as spotless as counters that had a decade on her could ever be. She'd been at the house since the early morning, cleaning, throwing out expired food, old newspapers, and unidentifiables under the sink. She'd left the dishes, glassware, and other donatable kitchen items for another day. Her heart wasn't ready to start giving things away yet. Trash was easier to part with.

Although she hadn't actually seen his will, Grace assumed she was his heir and the house was now hers. Even if the universe pulled a cruel joke and he left the house to the cat across the street, no need for the new owner to get his paws dirty prying up the cleaning product her parents had probably bought the year after she was born and was determined to become a permanent part of the cabinets.

She thought about inheriting this house. Owning a home was on her to-do list, once she figured out where "home" was, but she'd never considered owning this one. That was silly of course since she was an only child and no one lived forever, not even people as magical as her parents. She'd have to make a decision whether to keep or sell the place. Her life was after all in Los Angeles. She'd assumed the decision would be easy, but logic was no match for sentimentality. She glanced into the living room where the picture of Bonnie and her from high school still rested facedown. Was sentimentality why her father had always kept it?

The idea of Bonnie having a relationship with her father had unsettled her. She couldn't put her finger on why. Was it because she wasn't involved? Was she jealous? Upset she'd known nothing about it? The more she tried to sort out her feelings, the more tangled they became. Tangled was how she'd felt about Bonnie for the past fifteen years, why should this be any different?

The fact Bonnie was a part of her father's life but not hers felt like a rewriting of history. It certainly wasn't the way things were supposed to have turned out. All of this would be easier if Bonnie didn't still have the hint of mischief in her voice and she didn't look like a barely aged version of the beautiful girl Grace had fallen in love with. In fact, the laugh lines around her eyes and the few gray hairs in her short hair made Bonnie sexier than the mystical creature Grace held close in her memory. None of that mattered now though. What Bonnie looked like didn't matter. Grace certainly wasn't the same person she was in high school. Bonnie likely wasn't either. Now they were nothing more than two women who used to know each other, just like any other high school exes.

Grace's eyes burned as she thought that. It's what she wanted, but it was hard to name all the same. She'd been trying to stop comparing every woman she met to Bonnie since she graduated high school. Maybe this trip would finally set her free. If she stopped living in the past maybe she could start building a future in California, where her entire life was. She sighed. Nothing in California felt worthy of building around and that didn't have anything to do with Bonnie. Except she had friends there, which was more than she could say about Garrison, which now that her father was gone, had nothing for her anymore.

She tossed the final moldy take-out container in the trash, washed her hands, and brought her lunch out to the porch. While she ate she tried her father's lawyer again. She'd left a few messages with no response. This time she picked up and Grace was promised a copy of the will within the hour.

The sun was shining brightly against a clear blue sky and the wildflowers were in full bloom along the side yard. Even the front lawn that chased the long narrow driveway to the road was impossibly green. It was neatly trimmed, which her father certainly hadn't done.

Solving the mystery of the generous lawn mower wasn't worth her brainpower on such a beautiful day.

"Hey, neighbor. Mind a few minutes of company?" Candace waved from halfway across the yard, close to the property line between their houses.

Grace only hesitated a second before waving her over and patting the well-worn wooden boards next to her. "Pull up a porch rail." She'd fallen out of touch with Candace when she'd left for college in California and regretted it. They'd been close friends since kindergarten.

"How you doing?" Candace sat and examined Grace intently. "Really doing, not the bullshit 'I'm fine' to get old ladies to leave you alone at the grocery store."

Grace laughed. "I've missed you. I don't know why I never wrote or called. I'm sorry."

"Now you know to do better. I could have called you too, so I've got my own apologies to make. Now answer my question."

"I don't know if this makes sense, but I'm fine and I'm not fine. Sometimes nearly at the same time. I miss him. That's the long and the short of it. I miss him, and right now it feels like that will never stop being the first thing when I think about him." Grace squeezed her eyes shut to try to prevent the tears she could feel threatening to cascade down her cheeks.

"Oh, honey. It will get better, but it's so recent. Two weeks ago, he was still with us. You don't have to rush through any of this." Candace pointed to the house. "And you don't have to do it alone. You're still one of us whether you want to be or not."

"Why does everyone say 'one of us' like it's a secret society you're born into and can't ever leave?"

"Because it is and you can't." Candace gave Grace's shoulder a squeeze. "You get something special in your bones from growing up in a village like Garrison. There aren't even four hundred of us, we have to stick together and we don't let our own go easily."

"You all raised money to send me across the country. That's hardly fighting to keep me." For the first time since she arrived, the pit of sadness eased and Grace laughed.

"We send the best of us out into the world, show them what we're made of, but we always reel them back in. You watch." Candace winked.

Grace was working on her comeback when she got a ding on her phone notifying her of a new email. It was from the lawyer and contained an encrypted copy of her father's will. She skipped the lawyer's explanation of the probate process and opened the file. She was nervous, which seemed ridiculous.

She scrolled until she found the section detailing his wishes for the house. Grace needed to know. She needed her father's guidance to help her decision-making process. She read the paragraph, then read it again. No way that was correct. She read it a third time to be sure. When she was done and the words hadn't magically transformed, she threw her phone as far from the porch as she could. It landed with a thud on the lawn.

"Whoa, what just happened?" Candace stood up and took Grace by both shoulders. "You look like you're ready to lose it. What did that email say?"

Grace slammed her fist on the porch rail. "He left it to her. Can you believe it? To her. Was this his idea of a joke? I'm not laughing." She didn't try to stop the tears now. They streaked down her cheeks and she let them fall.

"Left what to who?" Candace looked baffled.

"The house. He left it to her. To her and to me. To share. My house. The first and only place that's ever felt like home, and now I have to share it with her. He knows what she did to me and how much I want to move on from her." Grace paced the porch wiping away the tears as soon as they fell.

"He left the house to you and Bonnie?" Candace looked like a cartoon character with her mouth open wide. "What was he thinking?"

Grace stopped pacing and considered. "Maybe he wasn't. What if she suggested it and he was too weak at the end to say no?"

"Come on, Grace. You know Bonnie well enough to know that's not something she'd ever do." Candace looked alarmed.

"I did know her, but that was years ago. Now I don't know her at all." Grace couldn't get the image of Bonnie's joyful expression the night they'd first kissed as teenagers out of her mind. That night

Grace would have sworn Bonnie wasn't capable of hurting her. But then things changed. Now years had passed. Maybe Candace was wrong.

"If you doubt her, then I'll vouch for her. Bonnie's not capable of what you're accusing her of." There was fire in Candace's voice now.

Grace was a little embarrassed. She shouldn't have been so quick to assume the worst of Bonnie because of her own past hurt. "Can you call Bonnie and ask her to meet me at Ms. Babs' tomorrow? I don't have her number and there are things we need to talk about." Grace smiled weakly.

Candace nodded and stepped off the porch to make the call. While she did, Grace retrieved her phone from the lawn and plopped back down on the first step. She reread the email from the lawyer.

Some of this might come as a shock to you. These were your father's wishes. I'm sure he had his reasons.

"A bit of a shock? That's the understatement of a lifetime." Grace looked skyward hoping her dad was getting a good laugh about all of this.

What was he playing at and now that the game had begun, had he written enough rules that she could participate safely without getting hurt?

CHAPTER FOUR

Bonnie sat in her truck in the parking lot of Ms. Babs' bed-and-breakfast. She'd been staring at the front door long enough that the temperature in the cab was reaching unbearable. If she stayed much longer she'd be in danger of heatstroke and that would be worse than whatever Grace wanted to talk about inside. Probably.

The truck door squeaked when she opened it. She'd been meaning to oil it for the past six months. Before slamming the door, she grabbed a letter Lionel had given her the day before he died. It was addressed to Grace. He'd asked her to deliver it once she was sure Grace had read his will. Candace had mentioned the will, so the letter had ridden shotgun on the ride over. Bonnie was jealous that it knew its contents and had no reason for nerves.

Bonnie had one foot on the front porch when Ms. Babs intercepted her. "She's around back at the picnic table." Ms. Babs narrowed her eyes and looked closely at Bonnie. "You're going to scare her half to death showing up in the state you're in. Take some deep breaths, do some push-ups, or phone a friend to burn off some of that energy. And for the love of the contents of that letter, unclench those fists." Ms. Babs pointed at Bonnie's hands.

The middle of the envelope was indeed crumpled in Bonnie's tense hand. She tried to even it out as she walked around to the back of the house. Before she rounded the corner, she took Ms. Babs' advice and took some deep breaths. What was the worst that could happen? Why was she so nervous? All she was doing was meeting with Grace, someone she'd known most of her life, to talk about Lionel, a man she'd loved as if he were her own father. She tried desperately to ignore the intrusive thoughts asking why Grace summoned her, what the will had to do with her, and what the hell was in the letter?

Grace was facing the sunflowers lining a quarter of the lawn when Bonnie entered the yard. She took a moment to really look at Grace, something the emotions and formality of their other encounters hadn't allowed. She was beautiful, perhaps more so than even in high school. That had been apparent the first time Bonnie saw her again. But now, unguarded, Grace looked sad and a bit lost. Grief could certainly do that, but the emotional topography of Grace's face looked older than her father's death.

Bonnie looked away and cleared her throat. Seeing Grace in that unguarded moment didn't feel like her right anymore. She was sure Grace wouldn't want her as witness. Grace's sorrow, loneliness, joy, and excitement were not Bonnie's to share unless Grace invited her in. She respected the boundaries that her youthful mistake and time had created even if it jolted her more than she expected.

As soon as Grace was aware of Bonnie's presence, her face lost its openness and her expression became pleasantly bland. "Thanks for meeting me, Bonnie. Sorry to have Candace call. I didn't know your number."

Bonnie sat at the picnic table across from Grace. Now that they were face to face, she could see how nervous Grace was too. Something about Grace's display of nerves calmed Bonnie's. Whatever was happening here today was stressful to Grace on top of significant emotional upheaval. No matter the reason Grace asked to meet, it couldn't be worse for Bonnie than what Grace was going through. She could make it easier on Grace and get herself under control. Exactly like Ms. Babs had tried to tell her.

"Why did you have Candace call instead of asking for my number? I would have answered if that's what you were worried about." It wasn't the softball she'd meant to lob in for Grace, but she did want to know.

Grace shook her head, a small smile on her lips. "No, I wasn't worried about that. I asked Candace to call you because I'd thrown my phone across the yard."

"That doesn't seem like you." Bonnie felt heat rising up her neck. "I meant, that's not what I remember of you."

"I'm still not an easily angered phone thrower, but I was mad at my dad for something he did in his will. I guess he inspired me." This time Grace smiled a full smile.

"Speaking of Lionel and his will." Bonnie slid the slightly less wrinkled letter across the table. "He asked me to give this to you after you'd read the will. I have no idea what it says. I'm only the messenger, so please don't throw anything at me."

"No promises. He handpicked you and he's not here to receive my wrath." Grace tapped the letter, looking thoughtful. Finally, she pushed it half an arm's length away. "Let's talk first, then we can get to that."

Bonnie nodded, looking between the letter and Grace. The butterflies were threatening to return. Reading the letter was about Grace and Lionel. Whatever Grace was about to say was between Grace and her. To top it off, it was too important to be said in an email or over the phone. She tried to find her calm again, but damn it, she was nervous.

"Did my dad ever talk to you about his will? What he was going to do with money, the house, his things, that sort of chat?" Grace folded her hands on the table and looked intently at Bonnie.

Bonnie laughed. Was that a serious question? Grace didn't share her laugh and Bonnie's caught in her throat. "Of course not. Why would he talk to me about that? What's there to discuss anyway? You're an only child, he adored you." Bonnie shrugged.

Grace looked like she was an inflatable pool toy and someone pulled the plug. Her shoulders sagged and she looked close to tears. "I thought he might have warned you or told you why."

"Warned me about what?" Bonnie had to spit the words out through a suddenly desert-dry mouth.

"Apparently, he adored you as much as me." Grace looked at Bonnie, her eyes pleading as if asking Bonnie to understand.

"I don't know what you mean. Did he leave me some tools or something? I always teased him he had a nicer mower than I did. Is that it?" Grace needed to hurry up and get to the main event. Or maybe she should keep it to herself and they could both pretend they'd never met up tonight. She wasn't sure she could handle whatever Grace was about to tell her or the look of pain in Grace's eyes. What had Lionel done?

"He left you the house. And he left me the house. He left us the house. To share."

Bonnie stood up so quickly she almost tripped over the bench. She needed air that the yard didn't seem to have enough of. She needed to think, but all her brain seemed capable of was repeating "house to share." "Why?" was the question that bubbled to the surface over and over. From the look on Grace's face, she wouldn't be able to provide an answer.

She returned to the table and sat down again, next to Grace this time. "I had no idea. He never said anything to me. You have to believe me."

Grace put her hand on Bonnie's shoulder. "I do. You're not that good an actor. At least your poker face used to be awful. You looked as shocked as I felt when I read it."

"I guess I know why you tossed your phone."

Grace smiled ruefully. "I'm ashamed to admit I first thought maybe you had convinced him to do it somehow."

Bonnie pulled away. That hurt. "You must not think very much of me. You know, people don't change that much. Once upon a time you knew me better than to ever think something like that."

Grace looked down at her hands in her lap. "Candace said something similar, but less politely. That's why I'm telling you. So I can apologize. I'm sorry. We apparently own property together so I don't want to get off on the wrong foot."

"About that. You can buy me out. It's your family home. I'll sell my half for a dollar. I'll sign whatever papers are needed." Bonnie glanced at the letter. Did it say anything about Lionel's decision on the house?

Grace looked at the letter too. "Let's hold on that for now. My dad made the decision he did for a reason. How about I open this and see if there's an explanation. I want to honor his wishes. Maybe there's a way to do that that will work for both of us? Besides, if anyone should sell, it's me. I don't even live on this coast."

The words looked hard for Grace to force from her mouth.

Bonnie got up again and put her hand on Grace's shoulder. She gave it a friendly squeeze. "After you've read the letter, let me know how you want to move forward and if Lionel gave any explanation.

I'll follow your lead on this. I want to do what's best for you." That was easy for Bonnie to say since she was still too shocked to know how she felt about it all. It also seemed like the right thing to do. "Please stay." Grace patted the bench next to her. "You should be here when I open this too."

Bonnie nodded weakly and sat down heavily. She wanted to take the cowardly way out and run. The letter was for Grace, not her, and they didn't have any relationship anymore. That didn't feel right and she'd never leave anyone in distress, much less Grace, no matter their history.

Grace held up the letter and slid her finger under the seal. "Here goes nothing." She ripped across the top and pulled out the handwritten letter. Grace quickly wiped away the tears as they fell. "It's his handwriting but it's so shaky. It's not the bold, strong printing I remember from my childhood."

Bonnie put her arm around Grace's shoulder and Grace leaned into the embrace. She rested her head on Bonnie's shoulder and moved the letter between them. In that moment, all that seemed to exist was the two of them and that letter. There was no past hurt or future problems. Bonnie was there with Grace in her arms, and they were reading a prophecy about what lay ahead.

Grace inched closer, sniffled, and read:

Dear Grace and Bonnie,

Grace, if Bonnie's not with you while you're reading this, stop now and go get her. Or go to her if you've already flown back across the country. You know I hate that you live all the way over there. You never seem happy when I talk to you. You never seem like you've found "home."

Anyway, that's what I want for you both. I want you to have a home. I know you both quite well, and I've watched you searching for something you can't name. I know what it is because, Grace, you're like me. We're wanderers who are easily untethered. That's a scary thing to be in a chaotic world, until you find your anchor point and can roam safely.

Bonnie, you've cared for me for years. That's your nature. You're grounded and steady, and by my observation, you need someone to look after. Now, my Grace doesn't need looking after and you wouldn't be served babysitting her, but I saw you both in high school. You fill a need for each other that perhaps only an old man can see.

I waited fifteen years for you two to figure it out, but finally I had to take matters into my own hands. I'm sure you're furious, but I'm dead so it's not my problem. I don't care if you get married, become best friends, or tolerant roommates, or use the house as an office for a sanctuary for abandoned and injured kookaburras. The point is to give each other a second chance.

With that in mind, please don't buy each other out or sell the house at your first chance. Grace, don't leave all the work and upkeep to Bonnie. Keep an open mind, for me. Do it to prove me wrong. Consider this a dare you can't own the house together for a year. I've hidden ten dollars for frozen lemonade next summer somewhere in the house. If you work together for a year, toast me or curse me, up to you.

I know since you're reading this that I'm gone. It's hard to write that sentence even though I know it won't be long now. Grace, I may not think California is home for you, but I'm so proud of all you've done out there. There isn't a day that's gone by that I haven't loved you. And, Bonnie, I was furious with you after you broke Grace's heart, but I now know why you did what you did, even if I don't agree. I think I would have been in the ground far sooner if it wasn't for your company and helping hand. I've come to love you like a second daughter.

Please take care of each other and take some time to think over my request. Most people would say what I've done is crazy and maybe it is, but I love you both too much to see you staying away from each other.

Love,
Dad

After they read the letter, Bonnie pulled Grace closer. Bonnie didn't try to hide her tears, nor did she make any effort to wipe them away. She was not ashamed of her grief.

Grace wrapped her arms around Bonnie's waist and buried her face in Bonnie's shoulder. Bonnie felt her upper body begin to shake with the herky-jerky movement of a wild, out of control cry.

She turned so she could pull Grace closer. As she did, Grace seemed to let go of any control she was still clinging to. Bonnie held Grace until she was crying so hard she was gasping for breath. Bonnie wanted to comfort her or say something to stop Grace's sorrow, but she knew that wasn't what Grace needed. The tears and the hiccupping and the gasping were what she required. Even though she wished she could do more, Bonnie could be here for Grace while she went through this.

As Bonnie was settling in to hold Grace all night on this bench if needed, Grace pushed out of Bonnie's arms and stood quickly.

"I shouldn't have put you in that position. I'm sorry." Grace's words were punctuated by big, heaving breaths. "I hope your shirt isn't ruined." She reached her hand halfway to Bonnie's shirt before pulling back as if Bonnie was toxic all of a sudden. "I'll be in touch and we can go over the details of the house."

Before Bonnie could tell Grace she hadn't done anything wrong or put Bonnie in an awkward position and to hell with her shirt, Grace was gone. The screen door barely slammed behind Grace as she raced inside, but Bonnie jumped all the same at the anticipated noise. She'd spent too many summers out in this yard listening to the bang of that screen door and the accompanying scolding from Ms. Babs not to react instinctively.

But now, there was no bang of the screen, no admonishment from Ms. Babs, and no Grace. Maybe Lionel had gotten it wrong and she was the one lost. It certainly felt that way now. How was she supposed to navigate home ownership with Grace? They could barely navigate an average conversation. Not that anything had ever been average between them.

Bonnie picked up Lionel's letter which Grace had left on the table in her haste to depart. Bonnie reread it, tracing her fingers across Lionel's unsteady print. She'd watched him writing many times in the last few weeks of his life. Had she watched him pen this letter?

She stopped on the passage where he described her. Was she a caretaker? She remembered the look on Grace's unguarded face when she'd arrived earlier. Bonnie thought she looked lost. Could Lionel actually be right about the two of them? She shook away the thought.

Bonnie traced her finger over Lionel's signature. He hadn't signed it with his name or broken out a signature for Grace and one for her. He'd signed it "Dad." Her chest felt full, not of the grief that had been renting space, but of serenity and joy. She'd always wondered if she meant as much to him as he meant to her. This felt like all the confirmation she needed. She raised the letter to her lips and kissed the precious word. "Dad." That was hers for the rest of her life.

"I still don't know what you were thinking, old man, but I'll give it a try. I make no promises that it won't blow up in our faces, but I'll try."

She turned so her back was to the table and she had a view of the same sunflowers Grace was admiring earlier. Their overt cheerfulness made her smile. She looked to the sky. If Lionel was up there looking down he better be ready to lend a helping hand. He'd gotten them into this mess, it was no time for his ghostly spirit to sit on the sidelines.

After a few minutes of quiet contemplation, Bonnie returned to her truck and pulled out of the drive. She looked in the rearview mirror and saw a light in Ms. Babs' reserved third floor room. Was that where Grace was staying? When would Grace move back to her house? To their house? Bonnie swallowed hard. Would there ever be a day when Lionel's house would feel like home?

CHAPTER FIVE

Grace's mind wandered while her best friend, Madison, explained her blast of a weekend at some club or party or what was it Madison had said? It wasn't that Grace didn't care what Madison was saying. She loved Madison. They'd been friends almost since the moment they'd seen each other in Marketing 405 junior year of college. Madison wasn't the problem, Grace's life in California was.

The parties at expensive houses, soirees on the beach, dinners, hangouts, and events, events, events, had always been too fast-paced for Grace, but now, hearing about them from three thousand miles away, it was shockingly obvious how aversive they were. How had she fallen into a life that drained instead of nourished her? What would a fulfilling life look like? It was a question that should have an infinite number of answers, but so far Grace hadn't been able to uncover a single one that felt right. Part of the problem was her job. She was a marketing consultant for a large public relations firm in Los Angeles. Being seen as part of the cool crowd at the hottest social events was close to the top of the roles and responsibilities in her job description. It might be unwritten, but everyone knew the expectations. She loved the creativity, helping clients, and seeing her projects come to life, but the rest of it exhausted her.

"Did you hear me, Gracie?" Madison's voice was well above a library whisper, and there was an edge to it that Grace knew was the first stage of annoyance.

"I'm sorry, what did you say?" Grace pinched the bridge of her nose. "It's been a long couple of days. My mind wanders easily."

"Oh dear me, you need to get out of that clown car village and come home already. There's probably too much fresh air or cow manure out there. You need some good old-fashioned city pollution to get your brain working again and a giant tub of ice cream and reality TV with your bestie to put your heart back together."

Grace could picture Madison gesturing wildly as she got more animated speaking.

"How is it though? Being back I mean? There are what, like one hundred of you all there in the village? Are you on an island? How do you keep everyone else out? Why are there so few of you?"

"I'm not on an island." Grace laughed. "And the village isn't in the middle of nowhere. It's actually in the middle of a larger town. That happens a lot in Rhode Island. Technically we're part of the larger town, but don't tell anyone in Garrison that."

"Wait, the smallest state in the union has the balls to take their tiny towns and put villages smack in the middle? You grew up in a weird-ass place." Madison was teasing now, no longer annoyed.

"I did." Grace tried not to get lost in memories of racing her bike next to Mr. Calluccio's tractor, planting the garden every year with her mom, or taking the bus to the beach all summer to watch the sunset with Bonnie. "I guess you have to live here to appreciate it." Did she appreciate it? After she'd left for college, as fast as she could, she'd only seen Garrison as a place to stay away from. Her father lived there, but she'd never revisited her relationship to the land and community that helped shape her.

"Not for me. I survive on tourist traps, ten-lane highways that are always snarled, smog, and vapid humans. That's my lifeblood. I've never known anything else. Would I even like wide-open spaces?" Madison was selling her burning desire for the worst of LA so aggressively she sounded like she was trying out for a low-budget porn. Madison could market anything and was the best part of LA.

"Easy on the moaning or I'll never be able to look at you at work." Grace held the phone away from her ear.

"You're lucky we're not on FaceTime." Madison made a kissing noise but stopped all the other nonsense. "You will tell me if there's anything I can do for you, right? I'm only a phone call or a flight away. I'll be there as fast as our traffic jams could shepherd me to the airport."

Grace assured Madison she was fine before they hung up. She flopped on the bed and stared at the ceiling. What did she know about Garrison? Everything she knew for certain was contained within the property lines of her father's house or she'd learned in dribs and drabs over the past couple of days. Maybe it was time for her to reacquaint herself with her hometown.

Before she changed her mind, Grace got to her feet, gave herself a quick once-over in the small mirror surrounded by intricate tile work, and went to look for Ms. Babs. To call it a search would have been disingenuous. Even in her short time staying with Ms. Babs, Grace had come to understand Ms. Babs could almost always be found in her kitchen or her garden.

Today she was in the kitchen, scalding two enormous stainless steel pots burbling on the stove. She smiled when she saw Grace and motioned her into a chair. "Just in time. I need your opinion. You have to promise to be honest though or you're fired."

Grace sat down where she was directed. The kitchen smelled divine. She wasn't in a hurry to leave even if she hadn't wanted to talk to Ms. Babs. "What do you need my honest opinion about?"

"Jam, dear. These two batches are misbehaving and I need an objective taster." Ms. Babs dipped a spoon into one of the pots and handed it to Grace.

The fiery red gelatinous substance on the spoon smelled amazing but looked like actual lava. Grace was leery of trying it given how much steam was wafting into the air.

"Oh, blow on it, child. You were tougher than this when you were a kid. I know it's in there still." Ms. Babs had a hand on her hip and was watching Grace expectantly. Clearly, she took her jam seriously.

Grace did as she was told and licked the spoon, hoping to still have the use of her taste buds when all was said and done. As soon as the flavor hit her senses she didn't care what it cost her. It was the best raspberry jam she'd ever tasted. Whatever Ms. Babs was worried about was unfounded.

"Well, I guess your face is all the answer I need. Here's the next one." Ms. Babs handed Grace a second spoon from the other pot.

After not burning her tongue to ash and discovering her new favorite jam the first time around, Grace was less hesitant about this one. "Is there mint in here?" She took another bite from what was left on the spoon.

Ms. Babs looked delighted. "Yes. Is the flavor strong enough? It will fade after it cools."

"It's perfect." Grace wanted to ask for more, but Ms. Babs was already busy with whatever else she needed to do with these incredible concoctions, and Grace hadn't come down to talk about jam. "Ms. Babs, if I wanted to explore Garrison, where should I start?"

"You grew up here, child. What is there left to explore?" Ms. Babs turned around and gave Grace an inquisitive stare.

Grace hadn't considered how to explain what she was asking for. Of course it sounded silly to anyone not in her head.

"Ah." Ms. Babs' eyes lit up with understanding. "You're not talking about the shrubbery. The Penalty Box is a good place to get you started. Sit at the bar, not in a corner booth. From there, you might need a tour guide. I could recommend a few of your old friends, but it might be better for you to choose, depending on what you're looking to get out of all this."

"Penalty Box and a tour guide, got it." Grace nodded like that plan didn't sound awful and awfully silly. What was she thinking asking Ms. Babs how to explore somewhere she'd known her whole life. Except she didn't know it. Not now. Not anymore.

"A lot's still the same around here. You'll recognize most of the good. I like to think we've evolved away from some of the bad. I hope you find what you're looking for. I'm always here if you need me." Ms. Babs turned back to her jam work.

Grace debated a moment before running with what small motivation she had. She was out the door and on her way to the Penalty Box before she came up with any one of a hundred excuses not to go.

The parking lot was jammed when she arrived. The place used to have a different name when she was in high school, but from the outside it looked the same. Even a fresh coat of paint couldn't hide the long years of fisticuffs by the dumpster, spilled beer and stubbed out cigarettes, and the emotional Richter scale of love found and lost in and around the building.

Grace took a long, steadying breath before getting out of the car and walking to the front entrance. She'd been to bars of all shapes, sizes, and level of swank in LA, but she was nervous to walk into this one. She'd avoided anyone and everyone in Garrison for so long, how would they treat her now?

The smell of the place pulled Grace back years, all the way back to the few times she and her friends had been able to sneak in here during high school, long before they were of legal drinking age. Jeb, the youngest of the owner's three sons, chased them out every time, but they'd still made it in the door. Once, Grace and Bonnie had lasted long enough to steal a few kisses in the hall to the bathrooms. Grace had been terrified of getting caught since the village wasn't very open-minded about gay people, but Bonnie had told her she'd never let that happen. Bonnie had kept that promise. No one outside of their closest friends knew they were dating, and no one suspected Grace was gay before she left for college.

"Grace Cook, is that you?"

It seemed as though an image from her memory had appeared before her. Although he was older, Jeb Duncan was unmistakable standing in front of her.

"Jeb, you're still here. At the bar I mean." Grace winced. That sounded rude and judgmental.

"Hazard of owning the place. I'm here way more than my wife would like." Jeb's eyes softened and his mouth crooked in a small smile at the mention of his wife.

How could Grace get someone to look like that anytime a thought of her crossed their mind? She used to smile like that when she thought about Bonnie. Grace shook off the thought. They were young and dumb and it was firmly in the past. Bonnie and the past had no bearing on the present. Unless you counted joint home ownership, but in this moment, Grace was not.

"Ownership looks like it suits you." Grace wasn't lying. Jeb looked like she felt when she slipped into her favorite pair of jeans. The fit was perfect.

"Thanks. It does suit me. And as owner, I'm not responsible for chasing all the high schoolers who sneak in the door right back outside." Jeb winked. "I'm real sorry about your dad. He was a regular here. He'd come tell everyone stories about you and how you were doing in LA. But now we've got the real deal. Come have a seat at the bar. I'm sure you'll be popular tonight."

Popular? That didn't sound good. And what kind of stories was her father telling? Grace sat at the corner of the bar, only one seat available next to her, and ordered a glass of wine even though she really wanted a shot of whiskey. The shot would be gone too quickly though and then she'd be sitting at the bar with no drink and plenty of nervous energy.

It turned out she needn't have worried. Jeb wasn't lying when he said she'd be popular. Almost the moment she sat down, two people she didn't recognize came by to say hello and thank her for representing Garrison so well. After those two, a steady stream of people stopped by to chat. Some were old classmates, some the parents or grandparents of kids she knew growing up. A few she didn't know but they said they were relatives of someone who had donated to her fund. They wanted to say how proud they were of all she'd accomplished. A large number were content to shake her hand and talk about her dad. It felt like speed dating, and it was exhausting.

"Anyone sitting here?"

Grace barely managed to stifle a sigh. Who was she to be ungrateful for a warmer welcome than she would have dreamed of receiving? "All yours." She looked up to see if she recognized who she was paired up with this time. She did a double take. "Eugene? That can't be you. You are so…you were so much less." Grace made nonspecific hand gestures toward Eugene, trying to convey her thoughts on his physical changes without making things weird. Of course all her flailing and stuttering did exactly that. "You were so much smaller the last time I saw you."

"You were so much younger the last time I saw you." Eugene smiled a big, welcoming, winning smile and took the barstool next to her. "Everyone still calls me Stumpy. It would be strange if you and my grandmother were the only two who called me Eugene."

Grace choked on a sip of her wine. "Stumpy it is." Stumpy had always been one of Bonnie's best friends. Grace had no idea if that was still true, but she had seen them chatting together at the luncheon after her dad's funeral. This was the first time Grace was truly frustrated with not understanding Garrison anymore. Candace, Stumpy, Bonnie, and a few others had been her friends. They were people she'd known since toddlerhood, and she'd given all of them up. She'd walked away so completely she had no idea what was happening in any of their lives. That sacrifice made sense at the time, but she was reevaluating now. Was the life she had in LA worth what she had lost here?

Stumpy waved Jeb over, ordered a drink, and asked for a couple of food menus. "Seemed like you'd had enough of Garrison's curiosity for one night. I'm hungry so it seemed like a good time to sit at the bar and have dinner. I hope you don't mind I chose the seat next to you. I don't expect a conversation partner if you're not interested."

"You wouldn't mind the two of us sitting silently next to each other? Wouldn't it be awkward?" Grace squirmed in her seat.

Stumpy shrugged and took a sip of his drink. "I'm a therapist. I love a good uncomfortable silence."

Grace scrunched up her nose. "I don't. They make me nervous and then I start babbling." She looked around the room thoughtfully. Not much had changed since high school. The old jukebox was still aging in the corner, the pool tabletop was a different color, but the same leg was still made of a different wood than the other three. The floor was sticky and the lights were dim. "Ms. Babs suggested I come here to see what Garrison is today, but being in here makes me think the Garrison of the past and present are one and the same. I bet the boob drawing I did on the back of the bathroom door in high school is still there."

Stumpy nodded. "Probably, but just because something looks the same doesn't mean nothing's changed. Do you know what happens here on Thursday nights?" Grace didn't answer and Stumpy continued. "Trivia night. I know you probably think, who cares, that happens in thousands of bars around the country, but this one is hosted by our very own, very famous, drag queen."

Grace put her wine glass down hard on the bar. "Garrison has a drag queen?" It felt like her eyes were bulging out of her face.

"There are a lot of things about the village that have changed since you lived here. Things change. People change."

Was there deeper meaning to that statement? Grace wasn't sure what Stumpy was trying to convey. Or was there no secret meaning and she was reading way too far into his innocent word choice?

"I know things with you and Bonnie are complicated."

"Are you referring to house or historical?"

"Yes." Stumpy raised his eyebrows and took a bite of fries. "No matter what the issues are between you, if you want to know Garrison, she's the one to show you around."

"Why not you?" Grace took a chance and stole one of his fries.

Stumpy slid the plate between them. "I'm a therapist. No one wants to see their shrink unexpectedly playing tour guide to the most interesting person to show up around here in years. Bonnie knows everyone from the shop, she's worked on nearly everyone's house, and everyone likes her."

They finished the fries in silence. Grace pondered Stumpy's advice. She'd come to Garrison to say good-bye to her dad, settle his affairs, and to avoid Bonnie. So far she was failing miserably with the latter. On the flight here she was so confident seeing Bonnie would be the end of her, but now that it was happening regularly that was far from the truth. Was there still a place for Bonnie in her life, albeit one far different than what she had once assumed? Her stomach churned. Perhaps she was jumping the gun, but maybe Stumpy's idea wasn't awful. Bonnie knew the Garrison from Grace's memories because she'd been there with her. Who better to show her the village as it was today? Besides, they owned a house together, things couldn't get much more intimate or downright weirder than that.

CHAPTER SIX

Y ou did what?" Bonnie looked at Stumpy with her burger halfway to her mouth. "What were you thinking?" They were meeting Duck and Carl at the bar for lunch, but as usual, they were running late.

"I was thinking she wants to see Garrison how it is today and you're the best person of any of us to show her around. Duck can't drive his own car, Carl's Carl, and no one's overly excited to chitchat with a psychologist." Stumpy crossed his arms and frowned. "I'm not asking you to talk about the past, the house, anything. She wants to see how things have changed around here, and you can show her that."

Bonnie put her burger down and wiped her fingers with her paper napkin. She looked at Stumpy carefully. She'd never considered whether his profession created difficulty in his social life. She knew most of his clients were from outside Garrison and assumed that was all that mattered.

"People here really don't like talking to you?"

"That's not the point, Runt." Stumpy shook his head and pointed at her. "The point is you need to woman up and do this."

"It's the point to me." Bonnie heard her voice raising higher than was necessary. She lowered it. "What's wrong with people?"

Stumpy laughed. "Nothing's wrong with people. They're worried I'm psychoanalyzing everything they say. They'll remember it's just me. It takes a little time."

"Stump, it's been five years since you opened your practice. How long are you going to give people?" Bonnie put her hand on his shoulder. "I can see it bugs you. You don't have to hide that from me."

"What do you want me to do, Runt, wear a sign?" Stumpy looked down at the table, sadness in his eyes.

"That's not a bad idea."

"It's a terrible idea. Can we get back to talking about you, please?"

"I'd really rather not." Bonnie looked to the ceiling and sighed. What was she about to agree to? "But in the interest of getting you off my back, I'll call Grace. Happy?"

"Eminently."

Before they could continue, Carl and Duck arrived and their quiet conversation turned loud and boisterous as it always did when the four of them got together.

"What'd we miss?" Duck threw his arm around Bonnie's shoulder.

Bonnie shrugged him off. "Well, Stumpy's upset that..." She saw Stumpy shake his head subtly, his eyes pleading. "That you two are late, as usual."

"Candace had to drop Avery off at her sister's house. Took a little longer than we thought." Duck took Bonnie's uneaten half burger and finished it in three bites.

"I wasn't done with that." Bonnie punched him in the shoulder. "Does Candace do all the driving in other parts of your relationship?" She looked pointedly at his crotch.

Duck grinned, ketchup stuck to the corner of his mouth. "Sure does and it's hot as fuck."

"Good thing she's in charge given your parking issues." Carl tried to steal a pickle from Stumpy but was rejected. "I want to talk about Runt. I didn't know anyone liked you enough to leave you even half a house. Do you get to pick which parts are yours? I'd choose the roof and basement."

"What good does a roof and basement do you? What if you have to pee? Or eat?" Stumpy shook his head.

Bonnie cocked her head at Carl, not sure if he'd been kidding. "The house was a shock to me too. Although not as much as for Grace. Lionel had his reasons, but I'm not sure I agree with them." Bonnie waved to Jeb so she could get another burger.

"Let the league decide. Present the facts." Duck, Carl, and Stumpy leaned back with their arms crossed and waited.

When they were kids they'd all been fascinated with superheroes. In first grade they'd formed their own league of superheroes and since then had convened the league when large decisions needed to be made, opinions needed to be rendered, or a group member had done something stupid and needed to be counseled. The league had been all over Bonnie when she'd abruptly ended things with Grace.

Bonnie hesitated. These were her best friends and she told them everything, but it didn't feel right to share the contents of Lionel's letter. On the other hand, no one had ever rejected a request for judgment from the league. She settled for middle ground. "Lionel thinks Grace and I are better if we have each other in our lives. He didn't think we'd do it on our own, so I guess this is his way of forcing the issue."

The only sounds for a few minutes were the clinking of bar glasses, muted conversation from the few other patrons in the bar, and the sizzling of the grill in the kitchen.

Duck broke the silence. "Didn't you kind of"—he made a slashing motion across his throat—"back in high school when you sent her to California like an idiot?"

"Come on, Duck, that's harsh." Stumpy came to Bonnie's defense.

"We're all thinking it." Carl drummed his fingers on the table.

"She owns a house with Grace. What's she supposed to do, never interact with her? No matter what you say, she can't pick part of the house for her own and never let Grace in. They're not in kindergarten." Stumpy sounded angry. "I told her she should show Grace around Garrison and help her know the village again. No one knows it like Bonnie."

"To what end? What do you want from her, Runt?" Duck's tone was more even than before.

"I don't want anything from her. I didn't ask for any of this." Bonnie pushed her chair back, the legs protesting the abrupt motion loudly. She tossed some money on the table to cover her food and headed for the door. Maybe she could have dealt with Duck's questions if she had any clue what the answers were, but as it stood, Grace, the house, and their intertwined future was like staring Medusa in the eye, it paralyzed her as if she were made of stone.

Once outside, Bonnie opened the tailgate on her truck and hopped up. She sat with her feet dangling, taking in the orchard across the street. The trees were heavy with the end of summer peaches. Plenty of birds and squirrels were enjoying the bounty despite the best efforts of the farmers. Near the road was a family picking their own to take home. Bonnie's breath caught. Was that something she'd ever have? A wife, a family, a happily ever after? She was desperate for it, even if she'd not shared that with her friends, but the dream faded a little more each year. Hadn't she met all the single lesbians in her corner of the state by now?

Bonnie was settling into a good wallow when her phone rang. She nearly fell off the tailgate in surprise. It had to be Duck calling to patch things up. He could never wait much longer than this when there was tension in the group.

"Duck, I need more time to feel sorry for myself and be annoyed. Can you call back later?" There was silence on the other end of the line. "Duck?"

Finally, a woman on the other end spoke. "I'm not a duck, goose, quail, or swan. Is this a bad time? It sounds like you're in the middle of something."

Bonnie took the phone away from her ear and tapped it against her forehead and grimaced. She put it back to her ear. "Grace, no, I'm free. Sorry, I thought you were my friend Duck. I should have checked the caller ID. What can I do for you?"

"Your friend Stumpy said you could show me around Garrison. I feel a little silly now that we're talking. I grew up here. I shouldn't need a tour guide." Grace sounded wistful.

"You haven't lived here in years. Places change in all kinds of ways. Some are obvious and some are harder to spot. Of course you need someone to show you around. I'm happy to help." Did adults still have to cross their fingers behind their back when they weren't being completely honest?

"I'd really love that. It became clear to me I don't know much about the village anymore. I'm basing my assumptions off fifteen-year-old data. That's not fair to anyone." Grace sounded relieved.

Bonnie had an insane idea, knew she would probably regret it immediately, and plowed ahead anyway. "I know it's last minute, but

I have a few stops to make this afternoon to provide quotes to folks for house repairs. Would you like to ride along and meet some of your new neighbors?"

"I'd love to." Grace sounded buoyant. "When do you start?"

"Why don't I pick you up in an hour?" Bonnie couldn't back out now. She didn't want to if she was honest. Despite the fraught circumstances, Bonnie enjoyed Grace's company. Was it possible to leave their past exactly there and move forward as something resembling friends?

Bonnie hung up after confirming the pickup time and location. She looked back to the bar. Her friends hadn't exited yet and they weren't the types to sneak out the back. She slid off the tailgate, slammed it shut, and grumbled her way back to the bar. Damnit, why'd she have to lose this round of apology chicken?

Once inside, she slid back into her seat between Stumpy and Carl. Her soda had sweated a large puddle onto the table, but everything else was about the same as when she'd stormed out. Someone, probably Stumpy, had tried to keep her burger warm with a paper cup, a stir stick, and four napkins.

"Did you take bets on how long I'd be gone?" Bonnie carefully removed the marvel of bar engineering and took a bite of her burger. Still warmish.

"Of course not." Carl looked offended.

"So who won?" Bonnie held a fry out like a sword pointing at each of her friends.

"Stumpy. He always wins when it comes to you. Are you sure you two aren't twins separated at birth or something?" Duck crossed his arms. He looked like a grumpy toddler. "I'm sorry I hit a nerve. I'm not on her side, Runt. I was only asking a dumb question."

"There are no sides, Duck. This isn't capture the flag or pickle ball. It was a fair question. I'm sorry I stomped off. That was an overreaction and shitty. My answer's the same though. I don't want anything from her. I don't know what I want from this situation, from her, from myself. It's easy to laugh at the fact that I own half a house, but it's really fucking hard. Especially since it's with her." Bonnie had to make an effort to unclench her jaw.

There was awkward silence broken only when one of them shifted in their chair or twirled their glass on the table.

"Guys, you've been able to talk to me about anything our whole lives. Why is this different?" Bonnie looked at each of them in turn.

"Well." Duck made an exploding motion with his hands and then mimed walking away with two fingers. "You're usually the calm one. You and Stumpy. What are we supposed to do when you freak out?"

"I'm not freaking out." Bonnie considered. "Not that much. And what you're supposed to do is treat me like you always do. I'll freak out even more if you three start acting weird. We're screwed if you and Carl decide you're the calm ones from now on. Now, what did the league decide?" She folded her hands on the table, sat back, and awaited judgment.

"It was not easy to come to consensus." Stumpy leaned forward like he was delivering the final elimination on a mega-popular reality TV show. "But the league has decided being a decent human being is more important than running from your past."

"There are rules though." Duck interrupted Stumpy. "You can't ever think with your little dick head, only this one up here." Duck poked Bonnie in the forehead.

Bonnie slapped Duck's hand away. "Gross, man. I'll do very painful things to your dick if you mention Grace and—"

"Easy, Runt. Just a colorful reminder not to lose your head." Carl put a hand on both Bonnie's and Duck's shoulders. "The other rule is to get out if you could get hurt."

That was the great unknown Bonnie was facing. Could she spend time with Grace without one of them getting hurt? Her own wounds from the past still felt open and raw, even if they were self-inflicted. Why else would she stomp out of the bar to pout alone for a while outside?

But what if she now had the chance to let the past rest so she and Grace could forge ahead with a clean slate? What if she hurt Grace again or Grace hurt her? Bonnie wasn't afraid of very many things, but she was terrified of Grace Cook and the emotional minefields hidden everywhere waiting to blow up in her face.

CHAPTER SEVEN

Grace waited nervously outside the hardware store Bonnie had recommended as a meeting point. Her impulsive phone call had seemed like a brilliant idea when she'd made it, but now she was more inclined to run away than wait for Bonnie to arrive. Before she could act on her anxious desire to flee, Bonnie pulled her pickup to the curb and Grace was obligated to ride with her as agreed.

"Grace, I only need a minute to run inside. You're welcome to come along if you'd like. We could count this place as the first stop on your tour." Bonnie unlocked the door to the hardware store and let herself in.

"The owner won't mind my being here when the shop's closed?" Grace took a tentative step inside. As expected, the store was filled with tools of all shapes and sizes, but many of them Grace didn't immediately recognize.

"You are always welcome in my store." Bonnie reappeared, startling Grace.

"This store is yours?" Grace realized too late that she sounded more shocked than was probably polite. "That's amazing." Was that enough to cover her surprise?

"Sometimes I can't believe it either."

Apparently not. Shoot. Luckily, Bonnie didn't seem offended.

"What are all these tools?" Grace pointed at a few that seemed especially obscure.

"Those are how I stay in business against the larger box stores and the enormous internet shopping options." Bonnie pointed at the tools around them. "I know this community and what they need, whether it's farming, building, fishing, you name it. I even keep track of preferred makes and models. Why shop online when you can get exactly what you want same day right here? Plus I have very loyal customers." Bonnie made her way down the aisle toward the door. "I'll be happy to tell you more about the shop on the way if you'd like, but if we're late to Branch Tucker's appointment I'm going to get an earful. I'll blame it on you of course so he'll have some fresh blood to yammer at."

Grace quickly followed Bonnie and climbed into the passenger seat of her truck. "Branch Tucker as in Branch, Branch?"

"One and the same. He celebrated his ninety-fourth birthday last week." Bonnie smiled fondly.

"Wasn't he one of the leaders of the anti-gay factions in Garrison?" How could Bonnie have affection for Branch Tucker of all people?

"At the time, yes. But times change, people change, minds change." Bonnie shrugged.

"But they're the reason we had to sneak around when we were in high school. They're why we couldn't hold hands in public and we prayed we never got caught." Grace's words caught in her throat. How was Bonnie so nonchalant?

"Grace, he is the guy who was part of what made Garrison unsafe for us. He's also the guy who punched an eighty-year-old six months ago because the guy dared question whether trans women are women." Bonnie glanced over, her eyes were soft and open. "How or why he made that transition, I don't know. You wanted to see Garrison as it is today. He's one of the examples of how under the surface, not everything has remained stagnant for fifteen years."

The rest of the drive to Branch's house was made in silence. Grace attempted unsuccessfully to reconcile her past experience with the present that Bonnie described. The emotional experience was so deeply ingrained in her memories of Garrison. This project of learning Garrison anew might prove harder than she thought.

Bonnie pulled into the driveway of Branch's house. It was well kept, if showing its age.

"You can wait in the truck if you're uncomfortable around him. I shouldn't be long."

Grace shook her head. "I'm never going to get to know Garrison sitting in the cab of your truck."

A funny look crossed Bonnie's face, but Grace couldn't decipher it. It was gone as quickly as it had arrived, and Bonnie turned and walked to the front door. Grace wanted to ask her what she'd been thinking but instinctively knew Bonnie wouldn't share.

Branch was waiting for them at the door. "You're ninety seconds late, Bonnie. You can make it up to me by telling me you found yourself a wife and are busy making babies that I can claim as my grandchildren before I'm too old to play with them."

"I'm still a disappointment. Not a wife to be found." Bonnie held out her hands as if a wife might be hiding behind her or in her pockets.

Before Bonnie could say anything else, Branch spotted Grace. He trundled down the steps and right up to her. "I don't believe we've met. I'm Branch Tucker. You're stunning if that's not too forward of me. I'm trying to marry off my Bonnie. Any interest?"

Grace could feel her cheeks warming. What color must they be?

"Leave her alone, Branch. She's a friend and she's riding along with me today. Get your nose out of my business and tell me about the job you need me to do for you." Bonnie looked a little flustered herself.

Branch listed his needs while Bonnie took notes. "These won't take long, Branch. How about I take care of them right now. Do you mind, Grace? Shouldn't take more than thirty minutes. You can take the truck for a drive if you'd like or you can enjoy the view here." Bonnie pointed to the farmlands stretching out in front of Branch's property.

"If I promise not to inquire about marriage, would you do me the pleasure of keeping an old man company?" Branch leaned on his cane, looking hopeful.

Grace wasn't interested in taking a drive and she couldn't say no to Branch. She fetched two lawn chairs from his garage, and they sat with their backs to the sun while Bonnie got to work. Branch regaled her with a steady stream of stories from his youth, adventures he'd had, his travels, and the best memories he had from different places on his property. By the time Bonnie finished and came to collect her, Grace was thoroughly charmed by Branch and could have spent another few hours in his company. Before they left she promised to return before she departed Garrison. To her surprise, it was a promise she intended to keep.

"You were right. He's wonderful." Grace wrung her hands. "I should have been more open-minded."

Bonnie reached over and put her hand on Grace's before pulling away like it was made of porcupine quills. "I don't blame you. I'm sure he was charming and wonderful to talk to back then too. The devil's always in the details. Are you okay making a couple more stops?"

"Of course. I'm in it for the full tour. Why do you do this if you have your store?" Grace turned in her seat so she could see Bonnie better. That proved to be a mistake because in profile she looked so much like her younger, teenage self it took Grace's breath away.

Thankfully, Bonnie turned toward her, breaking the spell. Not that Bonnie wasn't beautiful as she was now, because she was stunning, but the Bonnie of today didn't suck Grace to the past the way the glimpse of her profile had.

"I love the store. I work as many hours as I can, although I think that annoys my staff. They've got everything down to a system and then the boss comes and mucks it all up. The store pays my bills and allows me to meet people from all over who happen upon us." The look in Bonnie's eyes gave away her deep love of what she'd built.

"And yet, here we are, driving around Garrison so you can change lightbulbs for the Branch Tuckers of the world. Did you even charge him?" Grace shifted further in her seat so she was facing Bonnie. She leaned her head against the seat.

"Nah, I put it on his tab. He needs me to do things his age and neuropathy prevent him from taking care of himself. I wouldn't charge him if his pride wouldn't be wounded so I opened a tab for him." Bonnie grinned like she was letting Grace in on a secret.

"How high has he run his bill?" It was thrilling to feel a part of Bonnie's insider club again, if only for the afternoon.

Bonnie stroked her chin in thought. "Well, he's called me out regularly over the past couple of years, so he's probably up to close to two dollars and thirty-five cents."

Grace laughed. "How much do you charge him each visit?"

"A nickel." Bonnie scowled at Grace. "I'm a small business owner, I get to set my own prices. No judgments from the passenger seat."

"I'm not judging. I think it's very sweet." Grace laughed at the sour look on Bonnie's face. "Let me guess, sweet doesn't match your manly self-image?"

Bonnie turned into a long, narrow driveway. "Not so much. You'll be happy to know, I charge this family full price. Husband's a banker. He'd catch on quick if I was under-charging. You'll probably recognize Nadine."

"Nadine Zlotnick?" Grace searched her memory, trying to put a face with the name. They hadn't spent a lot of time together in high school, but they'd had quite a few classes in common.

"She's Nadine Stanley now, but yes, one and the same. Come on, I'll introduce you."

Bonnie was out of the truck and rummaging in the bed before Grace collected herself. There was no reason for her to be surprised she'd encounter former classmates and yet she was. Bonnie had been treated terribly in high school. How was it so easy for her to work with her tormentors now?

Grace followed Bonnie to the house. She chided herself for being nervous. This visit wasn't about her. Before they hit the first step of the porch, the door burst open and an enormous, furry dynamo on paws shot past them quickly followed by two small humans moving at roughly the same speed as the dog.

"They'll loop back around. Bend your knees in case Tank clips you." Grace couldn't see who shouted the warning.

"Nadine, meet you out back?" Bonnie hollered into the house and started toward the back. "She's not kidding about Tank. The dog sometimes loses her footing too, and she weighs a ton so keep a sharp eye out when the three of them are nearby."

Grace looked at the two boys and the dog wrestling in the grass on the other side of the yard. "Which one is Tank?"

"The smaller one. He's the older by eighteen months, but his younger brother grows like a corn stalk. Tank's name is actually Albert Fredrick Stanley the fourth, but no one calls him that." Bonnie waved to Nadine as they rounded the corner of the house.

"Was Garrison always full of so many nicknames?" Grace didn't expect an answer.

"Yes, but I always liked that you never called me Runt." Bonnie looked shocked at her admission. She quickly turned and focused her attention on Nadine.

Grace stopped walking for a beat or two. What was she supposed to do with that? She heard her name and rushed to catch up. Now was not the time to slip into thoughts of the past. There was never a good time for a stroll down that particular lane.

Bonnie facilitated the reintroductions as soon as Grace caught up. Nadine's smile was open and genuine. "After high school I bet you didn't expect this to be in my future."

Was she that easy to read? Grace made sure her face was as neutral as she could make it. "I try not to make assumptions about people, especially based on who we all were in high school."

Nadine nodded. "A diplomatic answer. I'm sorry about your dad. He kept us all up to date on how you were doing. It sounds like you've been doing what everyone expected of you since high school. Does that make you happy?"

The air felt too thin and her stomach raged against her. How many people were on her dad's update list? What was Nadine implying?

"Leave her alone, Nadine. She's out for a drive around Garrison, not an inquisition, and I'm here to take a look at the shingles you need replaced on your studio and show you for the third time how to replace the faucet in your slop sink. If I come out for that again I'm going to have to do it myself." Bonnie put her arm around Nadine and steered her away from Grace. She looked back as they walked away.

Grace could see the concern written deep within each worry line. She was thankful for Bonnie's rescue. She didn't want to answer Nadine's question, nor did she know how. If she did, maybe she wouldn't feel so lost every time she called LA "home" especially now that she and Bonnie owned the house together in Garrison.

Bonnie looked back once more. She mouthed something Grace couldn't make out. She pointed back toward the truck and Bonnie nodded. She had nothing to contribute to Bonnie's work and she didn't want to be under Nadine's microscope again. Waiting in the truck, alone, was preferable.

On the way she narrowly avoided getting mowed down by the rumpusing trio of joy and drool. She couldn't help the pang of longing that accompanied the sight of the boys and dog. She'd never been one to actively plan every year of her life, but seeing the kids made her question some of the winding paths her life had taken. Would a different path have led her to a house full of scenes like this?

Despite her initial misgivings, Grace was glad she'd come today. Not even Nadine's questioning swayed her opinion. Even though there was no chance of rekindling any of what she and Bonnie once had, she was surprised at how much she enjoyed her company. After spending time with Bonnie today she couldn't believe she'd entertained the idea that Bonnie was capable of tricking her dad into leaving half the house to her. Someone who charged a nickel for handyman services wasn't after money.

There was still part of her though that couldn't forget the hurt Bonnie had caused her. Not without an explanation. Learning Bonnie anew, seeing the best of her, including many of the characteristics that made Grace fall in love with her years prior, was a reminder of how much she'd lost and the pain that came with it. Was a friendship, a true unguarded friendship, possible with Bonnie? And with the complications and entanglements in their lives, what was she going to do if the answer was no?

CHAPTER EIGHT

Bonnie didn't know what she was doing. Not only had she gone from renter to half homeowner, but now she and Grace were meeting with a Realtor at Lionel's house, well, their house. They'd agreed it was only to get a sense of what the house would sell for so they had all their options on the table, but it still felt icky.

She climbed the steps that were so familiar and knocked on the door like she had hundreds of times before. She had a key and knew that technically she had every right to walk in without knocking, but she wasn't ready for that step. She might never be. This should be Grace's house. She was the interloper here, Lionel's wishes be damned.

Grace opened the door with a smile. It didn't reach her eyes and it looked forced. She looked sad beneath her put-on facade.

"Would this be easier if I wasn't here?" Bonnie hesitated in the entryway.

"The only reason I have a chance of getting through it is because you'll be here. I don't want to call Ms. Babs or Candace or Branch Tucker so I don't have to be alone. Please don't go." Grace looked close to tears.

Bonnie held out her arms and Grace tumbled into her embrace. Bonnie hesitated a moment, surprised more than anything, before she wrapped Grace in a hug. She'd impulsively offered Grace her comfort, but hadn't expected her to accept. Now that she was safely tucked in her arms, sobbing, she was glad she had. Whatever the baggage from their past and whatever their future might bring, right now Grace was in the thick of grief and too much responsibility. She needed a friend and whether or not Bonnie qualified, she was more than willing to be a shoulder to cry on.

"I know this is hard. We don't have to do it if you're not ready. There's no rush." Bonnie made no move to shift Grace from her arms.

"I think I need to, just to know." Grace took a big shuddering breath.

"Okay, then we plow forward. I'm with you every step of the way. Remember, we're not committing to anything today. We're getting information, nothing more. We never have to talk to her again when we're done. Okay?" Grace wrapped her arms more tightly around Bonnie's waist and Bonnie held her close.

Grace's crying slowed and she took some deep breaths against Bonnie's chest before releasing her grip and pulling away. "Thank you for that. I'm not sure why, but I didn't expect today to be a big deal." She wiped her eyes and cheeks. "I'll be right back." Grace turned and quickly retreated toward the half bath tucked behind the stairs to the second floor.

Bonnie stepped fully inside and looked around. She saw Lionel everywhere. Every corner contained a memory, every piece of furniture held a story, and the soaring ceilings were filled with years of joyous laughter. So many of her fondest moments had happened in this house, first with Grace, then later with Lionel. It was hard to think of the house separate from the history it held, but that was exactly what they both needed to do today. Bonnie knew how dreadful it was going to be, especially for Grace. Who was she kidding? It was going to be painful for her too.

Before Grace returned, the doorbell rang. Bonnie glanced at her watch. The Realtor was ten minutes early. She looked over her shoulder toward the bathroom, but Grace didn't appear. She loudly announced the Realtor's arrival. She hoped Grace heard her.

Bonnie opened the door and swallowed her instant reaction which was a mix of amusement and disbelief. The Realtor was a recommendation from one of her high school classmates. He'd recommended his aunt who worked out of the part of the state that was stereotyped for being in your face and over-the-top, especially when it came to hair, personality, and personal style.

The woman standing on the porch was a perfect embodiment of that stereotype. Her bleach-blond hair should have been outfitted with aircraft warning lights. Her makeup and clothing complemented each other beautifully, and combined, she had leaned so fully into the stereotype, consciously or not, that Bonnie wanted to give her a round of applause.

Bonnie quickly introduced herself. It gave her something to do that didn't involve staring open-mouthed at the woman's teased to death bouffant.

"I'm Mimi. I'm so sorry for your loss. Estate sales are always some of my most difficult." Mimi patted Bonnie's hand soothingly.

"Thank you, although my father wasn't the one who passed. Grace will join us shortly. Her father owned the house." Bonnie stumbled over her explanation.

"I'm Grace Cook." Grace appeared at Bonnie's side and shook Mimi's hand. "Bonnie and I are co-owners and are hoping to get your thoughts on the house *if* we decide to sell."

Bonnie could tell Mimi had questions, most likely about the co-ownership and Bonnie and Grace's relationship, but she managed to keep them to herself. Bonnie wasn't sure she'd have been so restrained.

"I'm happy to help you both. I'm not one who's shy to share an opinion, but in this case, I've been in real estate for twenty-five years. I've come to understand the market pretty well." Mimi held out her hand like she was a waitress leading them to their table at a fine dining establishment.

It took Bonnie three steps into the house before she remembered Mimi wasn't leading the tour. Bonnie snuck a look at Grace as they moved into the living room. If Bonnie hadn't already known, she'd never have guessed Grace had very recently been crying. Mimi probably had no idea.

Not only had Grace hidden her previous tears, but she was talking to Mimi about the house, its charm and flaws, as if this wasn't one of the hardest things she'd ever done. Grace was amazing.

They meandered toward the fireplace and the mantel. Bonnie hung back, letting Grace take the lead since she knew the house and should have the final decision on whether it was sold. It wasn't until

Bonnie saw Grace flinch, subtly, but enough to catch her eye, that she tuned back into the conversation.

"You'd be best served if you reworked this entire fireplace area. Gas inserts are popular these days, and a stone surround would change the entire feel of the room. Remember, people buy houses based on how they make them feel, so it's not always about paint color or fancy upgrades. They need to picture themselves sitting in this room in front of the fire, comfortable and warm." Mimi turned and walked toward the kitchen, seemingly unaware of the impact of her words.

Bonnie quickly moved to Grace's side. She looked like an animal unsure where to run. "Hey, stay with me. We're only gathering information, remember? She can tell you to paint the ceiling with yellow and green stripes, but it doesn't mean we're going to do it." Bonnie risked taking Grace's hand and giving it a squeeze.

It was a mistake. The feel of Grace's hand in hers was both familiar and wrong. Grace yanked her hand away. She looked at Bonnie sheepishly but put both her hands in her pockets before following Mimi into the kitchen.

Bonnie wanted to slap herself on the forehead. It had been an instinctive reaction to comfort Grace, but that wasn't her place anymore. What was she thinking? She didn't want to take that place. She'd given up that chance years ago and made peace with her decision. Well, eighty-four percent peace. Okay, maybe seventy-one. Or perhaps sixty-eight percent, but if she rounded, she was one hundred percent at peace.

"Bonnie, will you be joining us?" Mimi poked out from the kitchen door looking confused.

"Yes, sorry." Bonnie took a deep breath, put her own hands in her pockets, and joined the other two in the kitchen.

"Bonnie, I was telling Grace I think the kitchen could be a showstopper if you were willing to make some changes. Prospective buyers love updated kitchens with all the bells and whistles, even the ones who never cook. The layout in here is great, but I'd suggest pretty much starting from scratch with cabinets, appliances, the sink." Mimi moved around the room pointing out places she'd tear out and start new. "Of course this is assuming an unlimited budget, which most people don't have. We can talk smaller upgrades if you want to improve your sale price but don't want to put in a lot of work or money."

Grace looked ready to vomit, but unlike before, Bonnie didn't rush to her rescue. If Grace needed her, she knew Bonnie was available, as a friend. This entire situation was strange enough without trying to unpack all the interpersonal baggage on the fly, in front of Mimi. Bonnie hadn't expected to see much of Grace at all, much less be making life-altering decisions with her and seeing her multiple times a week.

The rest of the tour proved to be more of the same. Mimi offered her opinion on ways to increase the value of the house, Grace looked more and more distraught, and Bonnie's stomach began to churn uncomfortably. She was worried about Grace, but the idea of changing so much about Lionel's house was unsettling to her as well. It didn't feel right. If Grace wanted to gut the whole house, she'd argue, but in the end, it was Grace's family home, who was she to say no? Thankfully, it looked like the two of them were on the same page.

Before Mimi left, she took Grace's hand. "I know I asked you to consider changing a lot of what makes this house a home to you. I'm speaking to you as a Realtor giving you advice on selling a house. That doesn't mean I don't recognize that this is not any house and that this isn't hard for you, for both of you." Mimi reached out and took Bonnie's hand as well. "Take all the time you need to talk it over and make a decision."

As soon as Mimi's taillights were no longer visible, Bonnie turned from the driveway to Grace. "It's your decision in the end, but I can't imagine doing what she's asking. I don't want to sell the house." Where had that come from? How would it work? Bonnie didn't care about the logistics. She didn't want to see this beautiful house stripped of its charm and history so another family could pay a few thousand dollars more.

"I don't want to sell either." Grace scuffed her shoe along the porch wiping away dirt or some unseen imperfection. "I don't know where that leaves us. If it's okay with you, I don't want to try and figure it out just now. I know we need to talk, about a lot of things, but I don't have it in me right now." Grace still didn't look up at Bonnie.

Bonnie couldn't help but feel her impulsive clasping of hands might be one of the things they needed to talk about. Why had she been so stupid? "I'm not in the mood for serious conversation either. We can kick that can down the road a day or two."

Grace looked relieved.

"Hey, you two." Candace waved from her property line across the expansive lawn. "Why wasn't I invited to the party? I could have done up my hair and stomped all around your house too."

"Come on over now so I don't have to shout at you." Grace waved Candace over.

"Since we live next-door, I get to be the nosy neighbor. Who was that woman? I loved her hair. It'd look good on you, Bonnie." Candace joined them on the porch.

Grace looked at Bonnie with a funny look on her face. Bonnie assumed she was picturing her with Mimi hair.

"Realtor." Grace sounded like she had trouble getting the word out. "We wanted to get a sense of the house's value if we wanted to sell. Turns out neither of us can imagine it. So now we're stuck."

"On what?" Candace looked confused. "Why don't you both live here?"

Bonnie was sure Grace's confused look mirrored her own, but she could have done without Grace's slight look of horror. It wasn't that terrible of an idea, was it?

"Well, I don't live on this coast, so that makes it tricky for one." Grace sat on the porch swing and rocked slowly. "And Bonnie and I aren't, you know, a domestic unit."

"Grace Cook, you've always had a way with words. Someday you're going to knock some girl's socks right off her feet with sweet talk like that." Candace joined Grace on the swing and slung her arm over Grace's shoulder. "You don't have to be sleeping in the same bed to share a house you know. Roommates is a word you may like to look up in the dictionary when you have some time this evening."

Bonnie and Grace both started to protest the suggested arrangement, but Candace held up her hands to stop them.

Bonnie couldn't help entering one thought into the record. "Grace and I have only gotten reacquainted over the past couple of weeks. I don't think either of us are ready to move in together. Besides, as Grace said, she lives across the country."

Candace shrugged as if that wasn't her problem. "Come on, you two, let's go on over to my house. I've got dinner going. The least I can do is feed you before I send you on your way. Roy will be happy to see you, Bonnie. He has some project out in the garage he's always saying he needs you to look at."

Bonnie wanted to talk to Grace, alone, but she'd never turn down Candace's cooking. She showed up around dinner time as often as she could come up with an excuse. Halfway across the lawn, the delicious smells from Candace's house wafted their way. Bonnie's stomach growled loudly. She put her hand over it as if that would somehow quiet the noise.

"I'm going to run ahead and stir the pot. Come on in when you get over." True to her word, Candace jogged to her back door and let herself in.

Bonnie slowed her pace, hoping Grace might mimic her. Luckily, she did. "I'm sorry about earlier. I shouldn't have taken your hand. Instinct I guess. I have to hold Stumpy's hand for everything so I saw you upset and my hand shot out all on its own."

Grace nodded, the hint of a smile pulling at the corner of her mouth. "I'm sure it had nothing to do with anything you and I used to be to each other. I'll tell Stumpy he got you in trouble today. But I should be thanking you for helping me get through that meeting. It was an instinctive reaction to pull away. I'm sorry."

Bonnie shook her head. "No more apologies. Let's enjoy Candace's hospitality, and if we're lucky Avery will be up late and we can enjoy baby time. If not, Candace and Duck are fun too. Maybe tonight's the night they tell me they finally made the second baby they've been teasing me with for months."

Grace smiled and nodded. They resumed their stroll across the yard. As they walked, Bonnie thought about what it meant that they didn't want to sell the house. Could she afford to buy Grace out? Would Grace go for that? Would she try to buy Bonnie out? It seemed impossible that the current arrangement was sustainable. Maybe a solution would still present itself. She could only hope. However, the question became, what solution was she hoping for?

CHAPTER NINE

Grace pulled into the parking lot of one of the many state parks Rhode Island had to offer. She loved this one for the beautiful hiking trails and paved path encircling a large lake. The lake froze in the winter, but today was hot without a cloud in the sky.

It was Sunday morning so the walking path was busy with joggers, dog walkers, and families out enjoying the beautiful weather. She also passed groups of men or women, clearly friends, walking together, laughing or deep in conversation. Grace turned away every time she passed a group like that. She didn't want the tickle of jealousy she knew was lurking beneath the surface.

She had friends though, right? LA sprang, fully realized, to mind. No, she had Madison. She had Madison and rotating members of the chorus, bit players in her life, even if they were the stars of their own. She served the same role for them which was a comfort and disheartening. Why weren't there lasting connections? Why hadn't she bothered to make true friends in all the years she'd lived there?

Or was it that she'd tried but hadn't been able to? Her industry wasn't one that rewarded lasting friendships. She wasn't asked to form attachments; she was asked to be seen with the newest, shiniest influencer, entertainer, or sports star. Since those individuals changed constantly, so did the people in her orbit. What the hell kind of life was that? Spending all her nights at a bar would've provided more stability. At least bars had regulars.

Grace sat heavily on a bench overlooking the lake. It sparkled as the sun reflected off the surface. There was little wind so the water was still, resembling a depthless sheet of glass. She felt closer to her father here than she had since he died. He'd loved places like this, full of nature and contemplation, more than almost anywhere else on earth.

The acute sadness that had gripped her any time she thought of him was absent. It was the first time she'd been able to think of a happy memory without spiraling into thoughts about his final days, how much of her life he would miss, why him, and regrets about the things she hadn't done or said. Being somewhere he loved so much felt like permission to remember him, without all the rest. She savored the feeling.

The tears still came but they tasted sweeter as they trickled to the edge of her mouth. The feeling of contentment was short-lived though. She hadn't cried since the morning the Realtor came to assess the house. She was still horrified she'd broken down so completely and sought comfort in Bonnie's arms. They were close to strangers now and she didn't want to give Bonnie the wrong impression. It was a moment of weakness, one that she'd be careful not to repeat.

Grace's phone rang before she could fall too far down the Bonnie rabbit hole. It was Madison. Grace stared at the phone for two rings before answering. It was early on the West Coast, especially for a Sunday.

"Why are you up so early? Is everything okay?" Grace could hear the worry in her voice.

"Up early? I haven't gone to sleep. But I figured you'd be up and I miss your face. At least with a phone call I get your voice. I'm not up for walking and FaceTiming. Too tired. How're you holding up?" Madison sounded sober even though she'd probably been partying all night if she was just getting home.

"Maddy, am I happy there?" Grace dropped her forehead to her hand and stayed like that, head in hand, while she waited for an answer.

There was a long pause on the other end of the phone. "What kind of question is that? Of course. You would have loved last night. So much fun."

Grace shook her head even though Madison couldn't see her. "I don't mean do I have fun. That's an obvious yes. I mean, am I happy there? You know, deep in your soul kind of happy."

Another long pause. "You know I haven't slept in thirty-six hours. These kinds of existential questions should be illegal in the code of friendship, but I'm here for you, always. Every last cell in my body wants to say yes, you're the happiest person I've ever seen, but I'd be lying. The last time I saw you really happy was junior and senior year of college."

Now it was Grace's turn to pause. "I didn't realize until I was back here."

"Is this about her?" There was an edge to Madison's voice.

"No. It has nothing to do with her." Grace spoke a little more quickly than she meant. The feel of Bonnie's arms wrapped around her popped into her head unbidden. She shooed it away. There was nothing left between Bonnie and her. There couldn't be.

"So if you had a chance to play kissy face you'd walk the other way and not regret it at all?" Madison made kissing sounds through the phone.

Grace couldn't help but laugh. "Who uses 'kissy face'? We're not in junior high."

"Not an answer, Gracie."

If given the opportunity, would she kiss Bonnie? Based on looks alone, if Bonnie was a stranger in a bar, hell yes. But she and Bonnie had too much history that was impossible to ignore. "We had our chance. Didn't work out. We've both moved on." What was that pang in her chest? Regret? Longing? Indigestion?

"You've assured me that's true a lot of times so I guess I have no choice but to believe you."

Grace didn't appreciate the sarcasm. "Don't you have to go to bed?"

"We're talking about you right now, and I'm not home anyway. It would be rude to sleep on these nice strangers' lawn." Madison must have pulled the phone from her ear because her voice sounded far away. "You wouldn't want me sleeping on your lawn, would you?"

A muffled "keep walking, lady" was easy to pick out in the background.

"See, they don't want a lawn tenant." Madison was back. "We have plenty of time to talk about your happiness and sex life."

"That's not what we were talking about." Grace knew Madison was messing with her, but she fell for it every time.

"It wasn't? Well, now that you brought it up, getting any action over there?"

"Can we get back to my happiness?" Grace tried to sound exasperated but knew she fell short.

"Sex isn't fun? Oh no. We've got bigger problems than I thought. I'll get on a plane. I'm not offering my services, but I'm a damn good wingman. We can get you hooked up, literally, in no time." Madison was actively laughing now.

Grace joined her. As was usually the case, she felt lighter and happier after talking with her best friend. "You're the worst. And the best."

"Don't ever forget it. But." Madison was suddenly serious. "I don't ever want to be farther from you than across the city, but if you're not happy here, Gracie, I want you to find somewhere you are."

"What if I don't know where that is?" Grace choked back a sob she didn't want escaping. How many times could she cry in a week? Surely she'd reached her quota.

"You're the smartest, most intuitive woman I've ever met. Even if you don't know where you're happy, I have a feeling you already know where you're not." Madison sounded sad. "Does that house of yours have an extra room? I don't know that I can live across the country from you."

Grace smiled at Madison's devotion. "You always have a home with me, but you do remember the village has a population of less than four hundred? Plus, there are no parties with celebrities any night of the week, and you could run naked down Main Street and no paparazzi in any part of the world would know about it or care."

"The paparazzi don't care about me now. I'm nobody to them unless I stumble into the background of a shot of someone they do care about. Then they get angry and shout at me for a while. I could totally do without that. The other two points you make are valid, especially the population size smaller than my high school graduating class. Let's keep in touch on relocation negotiation." Madison was back to goofy teasing, but Grace could still hear the sadness beneath the put on good cheer.

"I haven't made any decisions yet." Grace looked across the lake again and felt the weight of her father's letter. She shook it off. "Oh my God, did you make a deal with my landlord? Is my lease already terminated and you're moving into my apartment? What did you do with my stuff?"

"That's a good idea. I do love that apartment. What's your landlord's name again?" Madison sounded more like herself again. "I'm serious though, Gracie. I want you to be happy and if that's not here, then go where you are. You and I aren't going to change no matter how far apart we are. You hear me?"

"I hear you." How did she get so lucky finding Madison? "I'm sitting on a bench by a lake ready to do some life planning. I'll get back to you."

"I threw up a little in my mouth. I can picture it. You're like a greeting card, inspirational poster, and Hallmark movie all rolled into one. Enjoy your soul-searching at the lake. I'm going to trampoline fitness. After I take a nap." Madison made a kissing sound into the phone.

"It's not my fault I find the lake relaxing and a good place to think." Grace tried to argue but Madison was already gone. "I'm not a greeting card or a Hallmark movie." She wasn't opposed to the inspirational poster idea.

As it turned out, she didn't need the bench of contemplation or the serenity of the lake. She knew what she wanted before Madison called but needed her best friend to give voice and permission to her giant leap.

She didn't want to call her boss and ask for a leave of absence sitting on the park bench. No reason to cloud such a beautiful view with her indecision and angst. She let her nerves drive her around the three-mile loop circumnavigating the lake. After it was done, she had nearly two miles left to perseverate on the decision she'd made. The extra time would either provide more opportunity for her to endlessly evaluate her happiness in LA versus anywhere else, or it would give her the time she needed to settle her father's affairs and find what did make her happy in LA so she could chase that. When she returned to her car, she was winded and her heart was pounding loudly in her ears even though the walk wasn't strenuous. There was only so much more upheaval and stress she felt like she could take.

Garrison looked different to her when she returned to the village limits. It might not be home, but she no longer had a reason to rush back to LA. When she stopped considering Garrison a short-term destination, the flaws and beauty of the place were easier to see clearly. But was she seeing clearly or was her view clouded by her experiences fifteen years ago? She'd had her eyes opened during her rounds with Bonnie. What more was there to learn? Branch had been a pleasant surprise, but surely there were some discoveries waiting to be uncovered that should stay hidden under the rocks beneath which they dwelled. What if those outweighed all others? There were reasons aside from Bonnie she'd not returned to Garrison, right? There had to be.

By the time Grace pulled into the driveway at Ms. Babs' she was in need of a glass of wine and a long soak in the tub. She'd done enough fretting for the day. There was plenty of time for more tomorrow. Tonight, she had other things to do, like get lost in the latest romance novel she'd purchased.

Once upstairs, she started the tub and slipped out of her clothes. While she waited for the bath to fill, thoughts of the day flitted back into her mind. She had plenty of money in savings to live a few months without income, since her leave wouldn't be covered. Bereavement leave at her company was a pitiful three days. Not to mention she was now committing to live for an as yet undetermined time nearly three thousand miles away from her possessions, her friends, and her life in LA. At the very least she'd need a few more pair of underwear.

As she sank into the warm water and consciously chased away stressful thoughts again, one lingered in the back of her mind. It was like a low drumbeat pounding out the refrain "have I made a terrible mistake?" over and over. She ducked beneath the water and when she resurfaced, took a few deep, calming breaths. The answer to that question didn't matter tonight but deep down she knew whether LA was home or not didn't matter. She wasn't ready to say goodbye to Garrison because leaving felt like a final goodbye to her dad. She could say without hesitation she wasn't ready yet for that moment. As for all the rest, she'd worry if and when there was something to worry about. She could do that. Absolutely. Probably. Maybe. The feel of Bonnie's hand in hers and Bonnie holding her while she cried sprang to mind. Ah, crud.

CHAPTER TEN

Bonnie waved to Jimmy, one of her longstanding employees, and pulled the door of her shop closed behind her as she left. One of the perks of being the boss was finally being able to pay someone else to do the thankless work after store hours to get ready to open for the next day. Jimmy seemed to like the quiet and she was happy to leave him to his work.

As was their routine, Duck, Carl, and Stumpy were waiting for her when she exited. Family, work, and adult responsibilities had cut down their everyday routine to a few times a week, but they still met up for a quick drink, bite to eat, or fifteen minutes to catch each other up on the latest.

"What took you so long? You said you have a curfew, but you wasted three whole minutes in with Jimmy. Wait, did you hire a Jimena that we don't know about?" Duck batted his eyelashes at Bonnie.

"Yes, Duck. That's exactly what happened. It's like we're back in high school and it's my first time. Three minutes and I'm done. There are about four lesbians within twenty-five miles of here. What do you think if one of them starts telling people I'm lousy in bed?" Bonnie slung her backpack over her shoulder and started walking toward the center of the village.

"Are you? Lousy in bed?" Carl poked Bonnie in the shoulder.

"Ow. What kind of dumb question is that? No, I'm not lousy in bed." Bonnie gave Carl a playful shove.

"Convenient that we don't have a witness willing to back up your claims." Stumpy raised an eyebrow.

"Why's it three versus one here? I'm not calling Candace to ask for a full report." Bonnie pointed at Duck. She moved slowly to point at the other two in a semiserious threatening way. "Don't make me look up your last partners."

"Candace would take your side over me in almost anything. She loves me, but she's got something different for you." Duck didn't look at all concerned.

Bonnie laughed. "Proof positive. The ladies love me." Bonnie had no romantic interest in Candace and never had. She knew she'd never turn Candace's head either. They were good friends and that's where it ended. Duck knew it too. Candace loved to tease both Duck and Bonnie, but there was nothing beneath the flirting.

"You know who we could ask?" Duck had a wicked look on his face.

Bonnie's heart thumped in her chest. Her hands felt clammy. "Don't say her name. Not when you're talking about this."

Duck started to say Grace's name but both Carl and Stumpy slapped their hands over his mouth. Maybe they saw the look on Bonnie's face or maybe they too thought it was a bridge too far. Either way, Duck seemed to get the message. He licked both their hands.

"Gross, man. Now I've got Duck slime all over me." Stumpy looked at his hand as if it were radioactive.

Carl shook his hand, looked at it carefully, then shook again. "Everyone knows Duck slime is the stickiest of all the fowl. Low blow."

Duck waggled his tongue at both of them and all four of them cracked up. Stumpy and Carl each wiped their hand on Duck's shirt.

They got in line at the takeout window of one of the restaurants in the middle of the village. The restaurant itself was fancy enough that you couldn't go in with mud on your boots or jeans, but the takeout window was altogether different. They served fancy hot dogs, sausages on buns with unique toppings, local soda, and chips. The offerings changed regularly so there was almost always something new to try.

"What's up with the curfew tonight, Runt?" Stumpy looked curious.

Bonnie shifted from foot to foot, uncomfortable with the question. "I'm meeting Grace at the house. We're going through some of the stuff up in the attic."

"Jesus, Runt, you look like you swallowed a handful of ghost peppers. What's got you discombobulated like this?" Carl waved his hand up and down in front of Bonnie indicating her current state.

Bonnie sighed. She looked skyward. "I've got a little bit of a Grace problem at the moment. You three can't tell anyone, understand?" She looked at each of them, waiting until they nodded before she moved on to the next. "When the Realtor came, Grace was upset. It was hard to think about selling. Neither one of us thought about it, it just happened. She was going to cry so I held out my arms and she ended up crying on my shoulder. I sort of, held her."

All four of them were so wrapped up in the retelling of the events of the Realtor's visit they didn't realize it was their turn to order. Bonnie paused the story until after they got their food and found a quiet place to sit.

"You're telling us that you were all wrapped up with your ex-girlfriend? *The* ex-girlfriend?" Carl's mouth was hanging open. "Any other news you want to share?"

"We weren't all wrapped up. We were standing in the entryway and I was sort of hugging her while she cried. Like a friend would." Bonnie replayed the moment and how it felt to have Grace in her arms. She liked to think she would have done that for any of her friends in distress, but she knew she wouldn't still be thinking about how many superlatives fit the way it felt to have them in her arms.

"Were you having friendly thoughts while you were holding her?" Duck quirked an eyebrow. "I have very different thoughts when I hug Candace than when I hug anyone else."

Bonnie didn't want to answer that question. "Later, she looked unsure of herself so I took her hand. It was a mistake. She pulled away and I regretted it immediately."

"Spit it out, Runt. Whatever you're dancing around, let's hear it." Stumpy eyed her intently.

"Fine. Whatever I was feeling at the time, my feelings are a bit more than friendly now and I don't regret taking Grace's hand because I liked the way it felt in mine. But I can't." Bonnie hung her head heavily.

All three of the boys laughed. Bonnie looked up and scowled.

"You've loved her since you were old enough to know what love was. What makes you think she wouldn't still be able to twist you up inside?" Duck was smiling, but his eyes were sympathetic and kind.

"It's been fifteen years. We're different people now and I can't. You have to help me stop feeling anything for her. It can't happen." Bonnie wrung her hands. She wanted to fling her food container and her drink as far as she could to release some of the frustration that was threatening to bubble over, but only toddlers were allowed to throw their food when angry.

"Why can't it happen?" Stumpy was giving Bonnie his full attention.

Bonnie sputtered. How was it not obvious? "Well, until very recently she wasn't speaking to me, we haven't sorted out any of those feelings. We own a house together, left to us by her father who just died. No one is supposed to make big life decisions in the throes of grief, which we both are. We don't know each other. She lives in California. To name a few reasons."

"Why don't you think about all the reasons you broke up with her in the first place. That should help, right?" Carl's face lit up like he'd come up with the perfect solution.

Bonnie caught Stumpy's eye. He smiled a tight smile. He knew exactly why that wouldn't help her now.

"Maybe don't freak out," Duck said timidly. "This is the first time you've seen her in years and the last time you spent time together you were a couple. Like you said, you don't know her and emotions are high right now, so it's hard to say whether all this will go away in a few days. But look, if it gets stronger and you think it's not some weird time warp, don't dismiss it. Meant to be is meant to be, timing be damned." Duck looked like his mind was far away. He had a smile on his face that clearly wasn't intended for anyone at the table.

"I thought you were the knucklehead smart-ass of the group. When did you get romantic and wise?" Carl stared at Duck suspiciously.

"I'm romantic as hell. And I'm the only one of the four of us married. I know what it means to hand your heart over to someone else and risk them squashing it to a pulp and handing it back to you." Duck pointed at Carl and Stumpy. "Don't you dare make fun of me either. Not until you've got someone in your life who could really hurt you because you've let them all the way in."

"Candace is too nice to squash your heart. She'd probably take it to the post office in a neat package addressed 'return to sender.'"

Bonnie nodded her thanks to Duck. He nodded subtly back. She hadn't thought about his being married and how that set him apart from the rest of them.

He was right, putting your heart on the line was risky, but the risk never outweighed the benefit if you went all in on the right person.

"To romance and married men." Stumpy raised his glass.

The four clinked glasses and continued their meal in silence. When it was time to leave, Stumpy offered to walk with her back to the shop and her truck.

"Is there really something still there with her?" Stumpy had his hands in his pockets as they walked.

"I'll answer your question if you promise to stop with that tone of voice. What is that? Are you trying to pretend we didn't just talk about almost nothing else all of dinner? I know you've been dying to ask me without the others so knock it off acting like the question sprang to mind thirty seconds ago." Bonnie joined Stumpy when he started laughing.

"Guilty." Stumpy held out his hands and shrugged. "What was I supposed to say, I know you broke up with her fifteen years ago out of misguided nobility, but now that it's come back to bite you in the ass, how do you feel?"

Bonnie stared at Stumpy. "Yes."

Stumpy straightened his shirt sleeves, ran his hands through his hair, put his hands in his pockets, and then pulled them back out again. He was clearly flustered. "Okay, well, how are you feeling?"

They stopped in front of Bonnie's truck. She let down the tailgate and they both hopped up, letting their legs dangle over the edge. "I suspect I'm feeling about how you'd expect me to be feeling. Exactly how you said I'd be feeling in this position when I first broke up with her."

Stumpy shook his head. "I'm not playing 'I told you so.' I only care about you here and now."

Bonnie sighed and didn't answer right away. Finally, she looked at Stumpy, desperate to see an answer clearly in his eyes. "I don't care what Duck says, I can't entertain feelings for her. She's the most interesting thing that's rolled into the village in a long time. And I wasn't kidding about there not being much variety in the dating pool around here. I'm probably reacting to those things, right?" Bonnie's tension eased slightly. What else could it be?

Stumpy frowned. "It could be either of those, sure. But I don't think it is. If it were some random lady in from out of town, sure, but this is Grace. She's not some woman, she's *your* woman."

"She's not mine anymore." Bonnie looked at the ground. She swung her leg as if it had grown long enough to kick the rock directly beneath her. It had not.

Stumpy looked contemplative. "Well, I think the answer to my question won't come until you decide what you're going to do about that." Stumpy slid off the tailgate. "You're going to be late." He pulled Bonnie to standing and closed up the truck bed. "You're going to be all right."

"You can't promise me that." Bonnie did kick the stone she'd been staring at. "I'll let you know how tonight goes."

Bonnie took her time driving to meet Grace. Would she ever stop thinking of the house she co-owned as Lionel's house? The closer she got to the house, the more her stomach knotted and her eyes stung. Her life had been neat and orderly and comfortable before Lionel had up and died on her and Grace had reentered her life. Now everything was topsy-turvy and a good old-fashioned temper tantrum didn't seem out of turn.

The surprise of the house, seeing Grace again, leading her around town, all of that had been a shock, but she'd adjusted. It was the flicker of feelings that had her worried. Watching Grace walk away had almost destroyed her once. Her heart hadn't healed despite the years. Some wounds never fully closed. If Grace found her way back in, would anything remain if she had to watch Grace leave again? And wouldn't it be her fault again this time too since she knew Grace *was* going to leave?

She slammed her hand on the steering wheel as she parked in Lionel's driveway. She had to pull it together. There was no other choice. The well-being of her heart depended on it.

CHAPTER ELEVEN

Grace climbed the comically small staircase to her father's attic and opened the door. She'd been scared of the attic as a child even though it was a perfect place to hole up during hide-and-seek or snoop on forgotten items her parents hadn't been able to part with.

It still felt like snooping to be in the attic now, but she needed to go through what was up there. She and Bonnie had agreed not to sell the house, but whether one of them moved in, they rented it, or they eventually sold, her parents' attic collection had to go.

Luckily, the roof had a steep pitch and the attic had plenty of space to stand as long as you stayed close to the middle of the room. Grace spun slowly, taking in the neatly labeled boxes, random pieces of furniture, and scattered artwork. Not sure where to begin, she opened the closest box on her right. She had to stoop to peer inside. It had children's stuffed animals. She recognized a few from her younger years. Why had these been saved?

"There you are."

Grace startled at the unexpected voice and stood, banging her head on the sloped ceiling in this part of the attic. "Bonnie, you scared me."

"Are you okay?" Bonnie climbed fully into the attic. "I rang the bell, but now I see why you didn't answer."

"I'm fine. I have a hard head." Grace rubbed her head anyway. "Are you sure you want to help with this? I don't think cleaning out my dad's stuff is part of the co-ownership agreement. You're officially off the hook."

Bonnie shook her head. "I'm in it to win it. Embarrassing family photos, your great-great-great-grandparents' fine china, the Picasso knockoff from a yard sale that your mom insisted was real, I want it all."

Had Bonnie hesitated? Grace gave herself a mental head slap. She needed to stop analyzing every move Bonnie made. While she was at it, she should probably stop looking at her so much too.

"I haven't stumbled across any of those items yet, but I did find an entire box of my childhood stuffed animals." Grace pulled out a seated Dalmatian with a red fireman helmet. "Meet Spot."

"Nice to meet you, Spot." Bonnie shook Spot's small stuffed front paw. Bonnie held out her hand until Grace handed over Spot. Bonnie set him atop a pile of dining chairs overlooking most of the attic. "You're in charge, Spot. Keep us on track."

Why did Bonnie have to do things like that? Why did she have to remind Grace so much of the goofy, sweet young woman she'd fallen in love with in high school?

"Where do you want to start?" Grace looked around the room, overwhelmed.

Bonnie surveyed carefully. She pointed to a box obscured behind Spot's chairs. "That one looks interesting."

Grace helped Bonnie excavate the box. Her stomach pinched when she saw the label on the back. "G + B." Gardens and books? Greens and beans? Goblins and broomsticks? She sighed. "I'm scared to look."

"I know how to get us started, right? He already left us a house. How bad can it be?" Bonnie didn't look as confident as she sounded.

They sat on either side of the box and pulled off the tape. Grace pulled up the flaps and they both peeked in. "No way." Grace laughed.

"I figured you burned all this. After, you know." Bonnie was smiling too.

Grace pulled out stacks of letters, cards, notes, and drawings Bonnie had given her first as friends and then as much more. There were even some of her journals and scrapbooks from those high school days. She pulled one of the cards from the pile. It was full of the overly saccharine declarations of love only to be found in young love, but Grace was easily transported back.

Bonnie was reading another note. She was smiling wistfully, her eyes distant as if she too were looking back, well into the past. She snapped back to the present and caught Grace's eye. "We were quite something, weren't we? What does yours say?"

"It's a card you gave me for our two-week anniversary. I remember how much those time points meant back then." Grace mindlessly reached over and put her hand on Bonnie's knee. The contact was fleeting but still sent a shiver through Grace. "What about yours?"

"We were writing back and forth to each other in English class. We were reading *Romeo and Juliet*." Bonnie scanned the lined binder paper again. She inched closer to Grace.

"I remember writing that." Grace grabbed the paper and read it herself. "Mr. Zhang almost got his hands on this, but I handed him my page of doodles instead."

Bonnie fidgeted and nodded. "He scolded you. Said he was disappointed his best student was wasting time doodling instead of paying attention in class."

Grace didn't want to think about that part of high school. She didn't like thinking about any of high school given how things had turned out with Bonnie.

"You were under so much pressure, academically junior and senior year." Bonnie didn't finish her thought. She didn't need to.

"I don't think I would have gotten through it if I didn't have…" Grace indicated the notes and letters in front of them. Grace picked up another. "Let's see what other treasures we uncover."

Bonnie looked unsure if she should respond to Grace's admission but ultimately didn't say anything. She got on her knees to circle around the pile. That brought her closer to Grace once again. Bonnie finally selected new reading material and sat down. Almost immediately, she guffawed. "I wrote you a poem. Safe to say it's a good thing I went in another career direction."

Grace scooted closer so she could see what Bonnie had written. They were now shoulder to shoulder and, if they turned, face to face. She felt the pull to do just that. It was unnerving and natural to feel drawn to Bonnie.

I love you in the morning.
I love you when you're snoring.
I love you when you're awake.
I love you when you bake.
I love you every day.
I love that you're gay.
I think that you're divine.
I love that you're mine.

"That is really bad. But it's sweet that you tried. I'm sure I appreciated it at the time." Grace, without thinking, placed a quick, chaste kiss on Bonnie's cheek. It was the kind of thing Grace did all the time with her friends in LA, but as soon as she did it the air in the attic changed. Why was it so hard to breathe? Her stomach felt wobbly, as did her legs. It was a good thing she was sitting. She hoped no noticeable sweat would trickle down her forehead.

Grace reached for another note from the pile to ease some of the tension. Maybe there would be another poem for a laugh. Unfortunately, Bonnie must have had the same idea because she reached out at the same time. Their hands brushed. They both froze like that for a millisecond before yanking their hands back. Grace muttered an apology. Bonnie might have too, but Grace was too distracted by the way her hand was tingling, betraying her and her rules about being completely over Bonnie.

"What else is in the box?" Bonnie pointed, with the hand farther from Grace this time.

Grace got up and took a look. There was a glass jar with marbles inside and a small wooden mailbox. She picked up both and returned to the seat right next to Bonnie. There was a whole attic and somehow she ended up practically sitting on Bonnie's lap. What was she doing?

"Uh-oh. I remember those." Bonnie flopped backward, her hands over her face. "Maybe we shouldn't look. They're a little different than the letters."

When she lay back, Bonnie's shirt rode up revealing enough of her stomach to get Grace's attention. There were muscles clearly defined that Grace had heard rumors existed on the human body but was pretty sure she herself did not possess. Her stomach fluttered at the sight. *Traitor.*

"With a tease like that, you better follow through." Grace wasn't talking about what Bonnie was, but Bonnie didn't need to know that. Besides, Grace didn't really mean it. She couldn't mean it.

"Okay, but remember, this was my high school self. Don't tear apart the much older messenger." Bonnie looked nervous as she opened the door of the little mailbox. "Do you remember my giving this to you on our one-year anniversary?"

Suddenly, Grace did remember. She knew what was inside and why Bonnie had hesitated. This was her chance to stop Bonnie from pulling any of the envelopes out. Grace nodded but said nothing.

"I wrote twelve letters, one for each month. Each letter had something I loved about you." She pulled the envelopes out. Her hands were shaking. "This first one." Bonnie opened the envelope labeled with a one. "Says 'I love the way you tuck your hair behind your ear when you're nervous.' You still do that you know." Bonnie reached toward Grace tentatively. She carefully tucked the hair on one side behind her ear.

Grace put her hand over Bonnie's. Clearly, Bonnie thought Grace was upset by her forwardness because she started to pull away. Grace held her hand tighter and leaned into the touch. She repositioned so she was facing Bonnie. "Read month twelve."

Bonnie's eyes widened. She moved her hand from Grace's face and fumbled with the envelope. She removed the card and read "I love the way we kiss. It's magic." Bonnie licked her lips.

"Do you think it still would be?" Grace quirked an eyebrow, but her voice was shaking. What was she doing? Desire and terror fought a fierce emotional battle.

"Is finding out a good idea?" Bonnie moved closer. She tangled her hand in Grace's hair at the base of her neck.

"Probably not." Grace closed the distance between them and kissed Bonnie for the first time in fifteen years.

It was a cautious kiss, exploratory and gentle, but it set Grace alight. Her heart felt full and whole in a way it hadn't in years. Bonnie pulled her closer and deepened the kiss. Grace felt at home.

As soon as she let herself feel the wonder of the kiss, memories of her heart shattering from Bonnie's rejection flooded her brain. She broke the kiss and scrambled back. She needed distance. "I'm sorry. I know I started it, but I can't."

Bonnie was breathing heavily and looked like she was wrestling with warring emotions as well. "Don't apologize."

"Kissing you has always been magic. It still is by the way, but I can't forget how I felt when you shoved me aside. My heart can't recover from that kind of pain again. I thought we were happy." Grace bent her legs and rested her cheek on her knees.

Bonnie's eyes were glimmering with unshed tears, much to Grace's surprise. Why was Bonnie crying?

"Can we go downstairs? Seems like we've done plenty up here for now." Bonnie half smiled and helped Grace to her feet. Bonnie grabbed Spot before leading the way down the stairs and to the front porch swing.

Grace sat at one end. She bent her knees and pulled them close again. She needed distance while Bonnie spoke her piece.

"I never wanted to break up with you. That's the first thing you need to know." Bonnie was bouncing her foot on the worn porch floor so rapidly the swing started to jostle erratically.

"Why did you?" Grace put her foot down to stop the swing's motion.

Bonnie looked at Grace. Her eyes were pleading, but what they were seeking, Grace couldn't decipher.

Finally, Bonnie looked away and sighed. "You know what Garrison was like in high school. It was the homophobic place you were expecting when you got back here. Well, way back then you were the closeted pride and joy of the village, rightly so, and I was the kid everyone suspected was as gay as I actually am."

"Wait, what do you mean they suspected? How did you know?" Grace turned quickly to fully face Bonnie.

"That's not the most important part of the story." Bonnie looked uncomfortable.

"It's important to me." Grace started the swing rocking gently. Maybe the movement would lessen some of the pressure of the past building inside her. Had she missed something happening to Bonnie right under her nose?

"Normal dumb stuff. I got called names, shoved around a little, occasionally something tossed my way. We've all grown up a lot since then. Minds and hearts change." Bonnie looked out across the lawn at some spot far in the distance. Grace started to respond, but Bonnie stopped her. "I didn't want you to see it happening. I didn't want you anywhere near it."

Grace stopped the swing again and stared at Bonnie. She'd heard her but couldn't find a sensical reasoning. "Why on earth not? You were my girlfriend. I would have done anything for you. I would have dropped fire ants into pants, marched down Main Street, toilet-papered houses. You should have let me help."

Bonnie laughed. "See, that's why I didn't tell you. We were keeping our relationship a secret for a reason. The whole village was raising money to send you to college. They were more excited when you got into Stanford than when their own kids got their acceptance letters."

Grace was confused. "What does that have to do with you and me?"

"We spent a lot of time together." Bonnie looked at Grace as if that was enough for her to understand.

"So what?" Grace didn't want to believe what Bonnie was implying.

"We spent almost all of our time together. People started talking. It started as a way to get to me, but then people like Branch began asking questions our senior year. Do you think that scholarship money was going to be there for you if you were outed as my girlfriend?" Bonnie's face was the picture of pain.

"You broke up with me over rumors and scholarship money?" Grace tried not to raise her voice, with partial success.

Bonnie looked confused. "No. I wanted you to have the future you always talked about wanting and the one you deserved."

"I wanted a future with you." Grace wasn't successful in keeping her voice level and calm this time. "It wasn't your decision to make. It didn't have to be college or you. You should have been honest with me instead of making the choice for me." Grace got up from the swing and moved to lean against a porch rail, crossing her arms. "All these years I've been so confused about the end of our relationship. I don't know if this is better or worse than if you'd stopped loving me and moved on."

Bonnie took her time inspecting her shoes before finally looking at Grace. "Your father told me more than once that distance provides clarity and age bestows wisdom. Obviously, I could have handled everything better back then, but at least now you know the truth."

Grace was in turmoil. What was she supposed to do with this new information? Before thinking too much about it, she grabbed Bonnie by the shirt front and pulled her to her feet. They looked at each other, deeply. Grace held on, her fists balled in Bonnie's shirt a long time. Bonnie didn't move. It seemed she was waiting for Grace to make the next move.

Without thinking, Grace pulled Bonnie forward. She wanted to feel Bonnie's lips against hers. She hadn't been kidding about the magic. As their mouths were about to meet, the fear and hurt that had always been present when she thought about Bonnie crashed to the surface. She let go of Bonnie's shirt and jumped away.

"Bonnie, I'm so sorry. I can't." Grace turned and rushed to the house.

"If you still want my help with the house, let me know." Bonnie called after her and strode slowly down the stairs.

She looked back once before climbing into the truck and driving away.

Grace watched her depart from the living room window, her emotions sparring violently. As Bonnie's truck disappeared, Grace finally managed "of course I want to see you again." She returned to the swing and put her head in her hands. She was furious at her father for dying and angry at him for leaving her such a complicated inheritance. She was mad at Bonnie for her disclosure, her misguided protection, and robbing her of what her future might have been, and perhaps most of all, angry at herself for not seeing what must have been under her nose all those years ago.

After she'd had her fill of the emotional destruction derby ride, she slowly rocked in the fading light of the evening. What good did it do to dwell on things outside of her control? Rage wouldn't bring her father back or change the distant past. She evaluated what was true in the here and now. First, she did have joint custody of a house, and second, the Bonnie of today seemed like someone she'd like to call a friend, as long as there was no repeat kissing.

After her moment of evaluation, Grace stopped to consider how hard it must have been for Bonnie to walk away if, as she said, the breakup wasn't about their feelings for each other. Bonnie must have hurt too. Another thing they shared now, along with the house, was mutual heartbreak. And the attic kiss. Grace blushed even though she was alone. The magical attic kiss that led to confessions and nearly a second kiss. If they ever did that again they needed to stick the landing a little better.

Grace pulled out her phone to text Bonnie, first an apology for not asking about her feelings, then not stopping her when she walked away, and finally an invitation to get coffee or a meal. Their shared experiences were painful; maybe they should make some happy ones as well. Before she could think too hard she sent the text. As soon as she did she wanted to undo it. What was she thinking? Even with an explanation for her actions, Bonnie had still broken her heart. But, she reminded herself, it was just a meal, no reason to blow it out of proportion. They were business partners after all. It was perfectly reasonable to talk shop over dinner. If only Grace could slow down her heart. Damnit, it was only a meal. Surely they could handle just one meal, right?

CHAPTER TWELVE

Bonnie hadn't ever been nervous knocking on Duck's door. Hell, she rarely knocked at all, but here she was, racing heart, rapping on the door, unannounced, in the middle of the day. She felt like a traveling salesman hawking bullshit and self-pity.

"Bonnie, you know Roy's at work, right?" Candace looked surprised to see her and a bit worried. "Is everything all right?"

Bonnie shifted from one foot to the other. "You're a woman." Before Bonnie could continue Candace nodded knowingly and made an "ah" sound. The "ah" almost drove Bonnie from the porch at a dead sprint.

"Don't spook on me." Candace wrapped Bonnie by the shoulder of her shirt and dragged her inside. "I am a woman. Thank you for noticing. Leave your boots by the door, go wash your hands, and don't make a lot of noise doing it. Avery's asleep. I love every minute with her on my day home during the week, but those minutes are much better with a well-rested baby."

Bonnie figured a mime couldn't have made less noise removing their boots and she was quick and quiet at the sink. Candace was waiting for her in the living room.

"So if you're asking me if I'm a woman, it means you're in need of a woman's opinion." Candace had her feet on the coffee table and an iced coffee in her hand. She also looked subtly amused.

"Shh." Bonnie put her finger over her mouth. "What about Avery?"

Candace raised an eyebrow. "I talk to myself all day on my day off. She's used to hearing my voice. If she hears Auntie Bunt though, let the rumpus begin." Candace shook a finger in Bonnie's direction. Bonnie smiled at the nickname. Candace had insisted on calling her Auntie Bonnie, Duck was equally set on Auntie Runt. When Avery first started talking, she shrieked with joy and yelled "Bunt" every time she saw Bonnie. The name stuck. She was now Auntie Bunt.

"Can we get back to why you're here? You need a woman's opinion but don't trust your own so it's not about the right size hammer for a petite gentlewoman or something else in your wheelhouse. Age-old cliché? Lady trouble?" Candace's eyes were sparkling with excitement more than Bonnie would have liked.

"We kissed and it was great and then I told her some things and then it was awful and I left and then she texted me to apologize and asked me to dinner." Bonnie finally took a breath.

"Hold on." Candace put her coffee down and sat up straighter on the couch. "I'm going to need more details. That was half a romance novel in one giant breath."

Bonnie replayed what she'd said, then groaned. "You're right, I'm a walking cliché. I kissed Grace. Actually, I think she kissed me. I guess that's not the important part. It got complicated after that and I left, even though I didn't want to."

"Seems to be a bit of a pattern with you." Candace quirked an eyebrow.

Bonnie felt like her stomach took off on a roller coaster drop-off. "What do you know about that? Did Stumpy tell you anything?"

Candace looked sternly at Bonnie. "I was young and stupid, like everyone else at the end of high school, but wasn't so blinded by teenage idiocy to see you were as hurt by the breakup as she was. You'd be hard-pressed to convince me you were right in whatever justification you came up with, but I know you didn't want to leave her."

"That was a long time ago. What do I do now?" Bonnie picked nonexistent fuzz off her well-worn work pants.

Candace's phone pinged and she picked it up to check the alert. "Do you care about her as a friend, co-homeowner, neighbor, acquaintance, or future something?"

"Of course." Bonnie answered quickly and easily. One of those had to fit, right?

"Then you're going to get your tools and the list of things that need fixing at Lionel's house out of your truck, you're going to walk across the yard, and you're going to start fixing some of the things on your list." Candace pointed to the door. "You think best when you're busy, not fidgeting on my couch. You and Roy are the same. Figure out if you want to go to dinner and why. Then decide if it's a good idea. Don't give her an answer until you know."

Bonnie got up and hugged Candace. She could have asked any of the boys for their advice, but she'd come to the right place. She put her boots on as silently as she'd taken them off and snuck out the door. As instructed, she got her tools and the list she'd begun compiling of projects that needed doing at the house.

She was halfway across Candace and Duck's yard when she saw Grace leave their house and turn her way. Bonnie's tools were slippery in her now damp palms. She didn't know what to say as Grace approached. What was happening to her? Had she forgotten how to pronounce "hello"?

They met at the property line between the two houses. Grace looked at her suspiciously. "Were you borrowing tools from Candace?"

Bonnie looked at the tools in her hand as if she'd not realized she was holding them. "No, I stopped in to chat for a few, but Candace thought my time was better spent doing actual work. She sent me over to work on my list." Bonnie tried to hold up her list which was tucked under her right hand pinky. Her hands were too full to have much success.

"The door's unlocked. I brought some things down from the attic so the dining room's a little messy." Grace looked self-conscious.

Why couldn't they rewind time and erase this awkwardness? Bonnie considered. Would she really give up that kiss?

"I shouldn't need the dining room. Plumbing's my first stop today."

Grace shuddered. "Better you than me." She smiled. "Good luck."

Bonnie smiled reflectively. It reached her restless nerves and eased them. "I'll probably be a few hours. Will I see you before I go?"

"I'll check back in on you, make sure there isn't water spouting from every faucet and pipe in the house." Grace started walking again.

"So little faith. I'm hurt, Ms. Cook." Bonnie walked backward toward the house, watching Grace. She tried not to notice how nice Grace looked in her jeans, but she was only human.

"Off you go, Bonnie. Our house isn't going to fix up itself." Grace turned back and gave Bonnie a small wave and another smile.

Bonnie strode toward the house feeling lighter. She and Grace had plenty they needed to talk about, but at least Grace didn't appear to be holding a grudge. Her invitation to dinner or coffee should have been enough of a clue, but Bonnie needed to see the proof in person.

She let herself in the house, set down her tools, and took her time walking through the first floor. She hadn't been alone in the house since Lionel died. Although Grace had a childhood of memories here, she'd built up a heartful of her own here in the recent past. Some of her experiences had been bittersweet, but none were things she would trade.

When she came to the living room, the visage of Lionel's hospital bed, her chair at his bedside, and the table next to both of them holding medications, water cups, and stacks of books bombarded her. She returned to the place in the room where she'd sat and read to him, holding his hand, as he took his last breaths. She'd told him how much she loved him and he'd returned the sentiment. He didn't know how much of a gift those words were to her, or perhaps he did.

Bonnie pulled herself out of her memories and focused on the reason she was there. She looked around the room once more, retrieved her tools, and set her sights on the first floor half bath. The sink was leaking. Lionel had put a pan under the P-trap to catch the drips, but Bonnie needed to solve the problem. Grace had also mentioned the toilet running on and off.

After some detective work, Bonnie determined the sink leak was a result of a worn rubber gasket between the strainer body and the tailpiece. She didn't have a rubber gasket she was confident would fit this sink so she'd have to revisit this problem another day.

Disappointed to not have solved the first problem, she turned her attention to the toilet. She flushed it, and as Grace reported, it continued to run after the tank should have filled. She jiggled the handle and although momentarily it seemed to stop the fill, it soon continued to run.

Bonnie removed the tank top and laughed. Undoubtedly this would be the easiest fix of anything she encountered in the house. The chain connecting the handle to the flapper had detached and was lodged under the flapper. Water was continuing to flow out so the float never reached its position to stop the tank fill.

She reached into the tank, reattached the chain, and let the tank fill completely. She flushed twice to ensure the chain remained in place and then replaced the tank lid. She washed her hands and went to return her tools and check the next item on her list.

As she passed through the dining room, the wooden mailbox from the attic caught her eye. Why was that on the dining room table? She put her tools down in the hall and returned to the dining table. Spread from one side of the table to the other were the letters, notes, and gifts she and Grace had begun sorting through in the attic.

It looked as though Grace had begun organizing them into piles, although Bonnie couldn't decipher her strategy or intention. A note on the top of one pile caught her eye.

Dear Grace,

I read the book you gave me. You're right, reading about a love like ours was very cool. I was confused though. It seemed hard for them to love each other. They fought it and found a million ways to not be together. Who does that? It made me wonder if they really loved each other. Maybe they never felt what I feel for you. If not, I feel bad for them. The author should totally write a sequel so everyone gets to see if they're as happy as we are.

I'll always fight for you. I love you,

Bonnie

"We really did love each other, didn't we?"

Bonnie snapped around. Grace was standing in the doorway between the dining room and the front hall, leaning on the doorframe, her arms crossed, her head against the crisp white frame.

"I can't speak for you, but I did." Bonnie put the note back down carefully. "Although I guess I lied about fighting for you."

"You were right about the book though." Grace moved into the room. She picked up the note and looked at it thoughtfully. "I remember that one."

Bonnie moved away from the table. Being that close to the letters and that part of her past was like getting sucked into a black hole. "Isn't it funny how pure young love is? It was so easy to judge the fictional adult relationship because we'd never experienced any of what those two characters had. I wonder how I'd feel if I read it now."

Grace returned the note to the stack and she too moved away from the table. She stepped into the kitchen and Bonnie followed. "I think I still have it somewhere if you want to find out." She called out from the refrigerator where she was riffling through the second shelf looking quite on a mission.

"Don't trouble yourself. I have plenty of reading material." Bonnie watched Grace with amusement. What was she looking for?

Grace pulled a wedge of brie out of the fridge triumphantly. "I knew this was in here. You'd think it would be easy to find one wedge of cheese in an empty fridge." She held the cheese up toward Bonnie. "Hungry?"

Bonnie hesitated.

"I'm trying to figure out that look. Do you think my plan is for the two of us to trade bites of this like we're sharing a lobster roll?" Before Bonnie could answer, Grace turned to the cabinets, pulled out a plate, a box of crackers, and two knives. She returned to the fridge and deposited the cheese, crackers, and a box of grapes on the kitchen island. "Snack?"

Bonnie joined Grace at the island. "I always pictured that someday I'd spend the day at the shop or doing home repairs and come home after work to share a quick snack or a drink on the porch before dinner."

"Bet you didn't imagine the house being co-owned with someone you weren't committed to and your snacking partner being your ex-girlfriend who you recently kissed in an attic." Grace handed Bonnie a cracker with brie.

"My daydream wasn't that specific. I guess I should have been a little more detail-oriented. Are we going to talk about the kiss and the porch and the rest?" Bonnie shuffled her feet under the cover of the island. She was in socks so her nerves made no sound.

Grace looked at Bonnie, her eyes intense, her face serious. "I meant what I said when I texted you that night. I am sorry for how I reacted. I went back in time to defend the heart of eighteen-year-old me, but you must have been hurting too. I don't think I'll ever agree with what you did, but thank you for telling me."

"You're welcome." Bonnie found it hard to make eye contact. "I was miserable back then too. After I mean. Not that that means it's all okay, but I was."

"Would you like to talk about it?" Grace reached across the island and put her hand on Bonnie's.

Bonnie gave Grace's hand a quick squeeze and looked her in the eye. "Not particularly." A smile crooked the corners of her mouth. "How about something, anything, else. I fixed our toilet today. Leaky sink is next on my list. Your dad usually kept me busy with fixing problems as they popped up, but there at the end, he wasn't up and about much to take stock. How was your day?"

Grace wiped her fingers slowly on a napkin, then returned to the refrigerator and pulled out two seltzers. She handed one to Bonnie before opening her own. "My day was fantastic. I spent the last two hours with Candace talking about you."

"You what?" The seltzer fizz threatened to go up Bonnie's nose as she choked on her first sip.

Grace gave her a good hard whack on the back as she picked up her seltzer and sashayed into the dining room. "Was it something I said?"

Bonnie could hear the laugh in Grace's voice. Although they were fifteen years older and memories and distance and mistakes apart, this playful side of Grace was as familiar to Bonnie as her favorite book.

Although it was getting close to the end of the day and Bonnie needed to get home, she lingered at the house. Grace was at the dining room table continuing her work on sorting through their past. Bonnie trudged upstairs and reevaluated a few of the projects on her list. Her cover story was the need to pick up the new gasket. If any of the other projects required parts, it made sense to get it all in one trip.

It was plausible, but she couldn't fool herself. She was here because the daydream she'd told Grace about wasn't an idle fantasy, it was what she wanted for her life. This was not that, but it was the closest she'd ever experienced. If she closed her eyes and cleared her mind, all she experienced was the smell of a well-loved house, the soft humming of a woman downstairs, and gentle swishing of leaves outside.

Bonnie put her hand heavily against the wall. Her eyes flew open. What was she doing? This wasn't a picture-perfect fantasy. This was her life. The woman downstairs wasn't an abstract woman from her imaginings, it was Grace. Happy homemaking wasn't in their future. If Bonnie could have yanked the squeaky thought saying "but what if" and stomped it into the hardwood she happily would have. Feelings, magical kisses, and daydreams of domestic bliss be damned, Grace was off limits unless she wanted to end up as broken as she had all those years ago when Grace returned to her real life as far geographically and culturally as possible. Her head understood the mandate. Hopefully her heart didn't get any funny ideas.

CHAPTER THIRTEEN

The smell of Ms. Babs' blueberry muffins lured Grace downstairs. Since she had extended her time in Garrison Grace had begun rising with the first clattering in Ms. Babs' kitchen and descending when the smells were more inviting than her opposition to putting on pants.

As soon as she appeared, Ms. Babs magicked a cup of coffee into one of Grace's hands and a blueberry muffin into the other. She gave Grace a gentle push toward the long communal dining table and Grace dutifully sat with the rest of the guests.

"Good morning. My wife and I arrived last night. I'm Jeff and this is my wife, Gita." A young African American man and his wife, an Indian woman with a friendly face and intelligent eyes, smiled at her, radiating happily ever after and copious joy.

"Good morning." Grace liked meeting new people, but she much preferred doing it after a cup of coffee or two. "Do you live in Rhode Island or are you passing through?"

Jeff's face lit up. "We're on our honeymoon. We're touring small towns in the northeast. We live in Washington, DC."

"What about you?" Gita asked Grace.

Grace looked at her coffee. "A little of both I guess."

Neither Jeff nor Gita looked like they knew how to respond to her answer.

"What do you do for work?" Smiley Jeff was not easily deterred, apparently.

"I'm on a family leave of absence right now, but I'm usually in marketing." Grace chuckled. "I'm three thousand miles from home but once upon a time I used to be at home here too. Now, who knows?" Grace took her last sip of coffee and sighed. "I'm really sorry, guys. You picked a lousy breakfast companion this morning." What had gotten into her?

Ms. Babs appeared over Grace's shoulder and refilled her cup. "What she means by all that is her father recently passed and she's in town settling his affairs. We are lucky to have her around as long as she is willing to stay." Ms. Babs gave Grace a kiss on the head before moving off to other cups in need of a top off.

Gita took Grace's hand. "I lost my mother two years ago. It knocks your whole world askew, but there is fresh air and level ground on the other side, I promise. We're going somewhere called 'Lincoln Woods' for a hike if you're interested in joining us."

"You're on your honeymoon, you don't need me around. I do not have a history of being lucky in love. But Lincoln Woods is one of my favorite places in the state." Grace took a last gulp of her second cup of coffee. She was nearly functional again. She turned her attention to the blueberry muffin.

"I could not have been more unlucky in love before I met Gita." Jeff gazed at his wife with a look that should be reserved for Hallmark movies and descriptions in romance novels. "Your person's out there. You'll see."

They exchanged numbers on the off chance Grace was in the mood to hike with the most in love couple she'd ever met. No, strike that, the most in love couple since she'd been with Bonnie. Was that what turned her mood so dour at breakfast?

Grace lingered long after the last guest had left the table. She thought about calling Madison, but it was still early there and soon she'd be at the office anyway.

"Are you planning on sitting in my dining room all day?" Ms. Babs handed Grace a damp dishcloth. "If you are, tidy up the table for yourself."

Grace got up and started on the table. The dishes and extra food had been long cleared, but the table did need to be wiped off. "Do you think I should be staying at my dad's house instead of over here with you?"

Ms. Babs stopped what she was doing and looked at Grace seriously. "As I said earlier, you are welcome here as long as you like. My door, kitchen, and ears are always open to you. But I would ask one question. What *is* stopping you from staying there?"

Grace sat again. She propped her elbows on the still damp table. She studied the woodgrain as if an answer might be hidden in the winding paths and delicate swirls. When nothing appeared, she answered the only way she could. "I don't know."

"Might be worth giving some thought." Ms. Babs retrieved her dishcloth and returned to the kitchen.

Grace was tired of sitting in solo contemplation. It felt like that's all she'd been doing since she'd arrived back in Garrison. The image of her riding along with Bonnie on her rounds, then of them kissing in the attic popped into her head. Proof that not all of her time had been solo or well thought out.

Although she was tired of sitting alone with her thoughts, she didn't want to talk to anyone, Ms. Babs included, so she returned to her room. Why didn't she want to stay at her dad's house? Because it was her dad's house seemed like the most obvious answer. It was his house and he wasn't there anymore. She didn't believe in ghosts, but it was possible to be haunted by memories. She needed the house to not be quite so, itself. How could she live in a place that yanked her to the past the moment she was through the door or opened her eyes. If she wasn't going to sell and she was going to make it livable for herself, the house had to change. At least enough so she didn't get forced into the past every time she turned a corner or caught sight of a memory dancing in a hallway.

As soon as the realization hit, Grace grabbed her phone and called Bonnie. She justified it because change should be discussed between both owners. If she was honest with herself she needed Bonnie's help and she wanted to hear Bonnie's voice. And see her smile. In that order, or maybe the other way around. Sometimes it was hard to sort out and why did it matter anyway?

Bonnie answered quickly. "Grace, is everything okay?"

Grace looked at the time. Well before ten on a Tuesday morning. Of course Bonnie was concerned. "I'm sorry for calling during your workday. It can wait. Why don't you call me later, when you are free." Grace nearly hung up without waiting for Bonnie to respond.

"Hold on. I've got time now. I'm reconciling invoices and checking stock at the store. We don't open on Tuesdays until noon. What's up?"

Grace could hear the screech of metal on concrete, probably as Bonnie slid her chair back, and the rustling of papers. "I was calling about an idea I had for the house. I was hoping to run it by you and maybe get your help."

The line was silent long enough that Grace was worried they got disconnected.

Finally, Bonnie responded. "I'm trying to figure out if there is something I'm missing. Are you really calling me about the house? You know you don't need my permission for whatever it is you want to do."

Some of the tension Grace didn't know she'd been holding eased. "But I need your help with my plan, so I at least need you to show up and hear me out."

"I thought you called to tell me about your plan. Now I'm committed to a field trip? Is there a dress code or should I surprise you?"

The air in Grace's room felt a little warmer than usual. She licked her lips hoping to find some moisture to ease her dry mouth. "I've always liked surprises."

Bonnie let out a slow hum on the other end of the line. "I know. Meet me for lunch today and you can tell me whatever you like."

"That sounds like an innocent, perfectly safe thing to do with your ex who you recently shared a kiss with." Grace couldn't help it, she liked flirty Bonnie.

"A magical kiss if memory serves. Meet me at the shop at noon and we can eat nearby or I can meet you at the house." There was a hint of challenge to Bonnie's voice.

The next move was hers. She kept setting her line in the sand and then spending a moment with Bonnie and smudging the boundary.

The push-pull was exhausting for her; it must be infuriating and confusing as hell for Bonnie. "Doesn't the store open at noon?"

"Perk of being the boss."

"Why don't I meet you there?" Flirting over the phone felt innocuous. The prospect of continuing, just the two of them, in their house, was a bridge, three highways, and a border crossing too far for Grace. Right now.

"I look forward to hearing about your big plans." If Grace wasn't mistaken, Bonnie sounded relieved too.

After they hung up, Grace was left with an annoying amount of time before she met Bonnie. It was too early for Madison, she didn't have time to get anything meaningful done at the house, and she wasn't interested in racking up more billable hours getting an update on the probate proceedings of her father's will.

She considered a run, but running to keep up appearances, literally, was her least favorite part of her life in LA, which was saying something. Maybe it would be more fun in Garrison. She flopped on the bed and grabbed her computer instead. Running was out.

If she wanted to change the feel of at least one or two of the rooms at her dad's house, it would help to have a new target in mind. Before she knew it she was down the rabbit hole of interior decorating, signature colors, calming bedroom design, and selecting the right style for every personality.

She pulled herself out of the internet vortex in time to realize she was in danger of being late. Thankfully, she had little to do to get ready and was out the door quickly with a much better understanding of her decorating likes and dislikes.

By the time she found parking and walked the block to Bonnie's store, it was five minutes past noon. Bonnie was leaning casually against the brick wall, looking like a model for Butch New England if such a thing existed.

Her slim fit jeans hugged her hips and thighs, and she wore a crisp white button-up shirt with the sleeves rolled past her elbows. Her forearms were toned in a way only someone who wielded tools for a living would possess. A light breeze had rearranged Bonnie's short hair making it look like she'd been running her fingers through it all day, or inviting someone else to do so. Even Grace's sane, rational, risk-averse brain could admit Bonnie was hotter than the Devil eating a ghost pepper.

Bonnie saw her before she could embarrass herself further staring on the sidewalk. "I was starting to worry I'd been stood up." Bonnie's smile gave away she thought no such thing.

"Why would I give up lunch with so handsome a date?" Grace batted her eyes dramatically.

"A date you say? Well, then." Bonnie held out her arm dramatically. "Let's head off for the finest food we can find on our one Main Street."

Grace took her arm and they set off. "I didn't mean to imply this was a date." She stumbled over her words. Her nervous chuckle gave away the jolt of nerves her own words had caused.

Bonnie looked at Grace seriously. "Relax. It's just me. Flirting is fun, but I'm not sure either one of us thinks it's a good idea to move beyond that, right?"

Grace nodded. Bonnie was right, of course. She should be relieved, so why was there a pang of disappointment eating at her gut?

They settled on the diner. It was housed in an old commuter train car and served breakfast all day. As far as Grace was concerned that made it her favorite restaurant anywhere on earth. It was crowded and loud inside so they opted for a picnic table outside. Garrison was small, but it saw plenty of visitors passing through or visiting the local farms and scenery.

"So, tell me your plans for the house." Bonnie took a sip of her water, then put her hands on the table. She looked ready for anything.

"First, I was thinking about what you said, about my not having to run changes by you before I make them. I think we need some ground rules for our joint ownership. It's not any more my house than yours. I'd be pissed if you painted all the bathrooms pink and yellow stripes or put up ugly wallpaper in the kitchen without asking." Grace peeked over her menu to see Bonnie's reaction.

"Is that your plan? It is, isn't it? I fixed the toilet downstairs so now it's time to decorate? Does it have to be pink and yellow? I like green better with either of those colors." Bonnie winked.

"No, no stripes. No wallpaper. But I'm serious about the ground rules. I run big changes by you, you run them by me, got it?" Grace pointed at Bonnie and tried to look stern and serious.

Bonnie looked like she was contemplating a salute but restrained herself. "If we're on the topic, what about knocking? I never know what to do about that. I know you say we're equal owners, but I can't help but think it's your house. It should have been. I loved your dad, but what he did was bonkers."

"It was part of his charm." For the first time since he died, the first thing that popped into Grace's head was a happy memory and not a slideshow of his illness and funeral. "How about we both knock if the other's car is in the driveway."

"Should I leave a sock on the door or something if I get a ride over?" Bonnie grinned widely.

"Gross. If there's a sock on the doorknob I'm storming in and chasing your naked ass out of the house with a broom. The lady you're entertaining too. No sex in the house. At least not until we figure out who's going to live here." Grace cracked a smile too, but it felt more forced than it should have. Under the facade there was a heavy dose of jealousy. What would she do if she walked in on Bonnie having sex? Hopefully, she'd never have to find out.

Bonnie's expression changed. She was serious now. "What if you move in? I mean, while you're staying in town?" Bonnie looked at her hands and picked at something on one of her nails. "I don't know how to say this without making it weird. I don't know about you, but I'm not flexible enough for the car anymore, so if there was a time you needed privacy…"

Grace knew she was blushing. She wouldn't be surprised if she was as red as ketchup. "Let's revisit if that becomes an issue. Not something we need to solve today."

Now it was Bonnie's turn to redden. It was cute on her. "I'm sorry I embarrassed you. I'll leave it to you to tell me if you need me to stay away. You wanted to talk to me about an idea you had for the house?"

It seemed rude to be disappointed at Bonnie's chivalry, but Grace couldn't help but wish she were a little less concerned with providing Grace privacy for hookups and a little more bothered with the idea in the first place. But why would she be? Grace was the one who slammed on the brakes when they'd kissed and freaked out when Bonnie had been honest about their breakup. But now Grace was noticing how damn good-looking Bonnie was and daydreaming about what it felt like to kiss her, both of which were damn inconvenient.

"It's funny you mentioned moving back into the house." Grace cleared her throat and took a sip of water. "I don't know how long I'll be staying and my leave from work is unpaid. I have free housing available to me and I think I'm ready to take advantage, but not how it is now. I can't wake up every morning and have my room look exactly as my father had it. Does that make sense?" She needed Bonnie to understand.

"Of course. I'd need the same. We could start with paint. A lot can be done with furniture to give it a new feel. If you're thinking of tearing down walls, I'll need to call in some reinforcements, but I know a few contractors who could help us out." Bonnie looked like she was making mental notes or creating schedules and materials lists.

Grace reached across the table and put her hand on Bonnie's forearm. Her hand to her elbow felt alight from the contact. She would have pulled away, but it was too pleasant a feeling. Bonnie looked at the place where their bodies connected with a quizzical expression. Did she feel it too?

Finally, Grace pulled her hand back. She needed to focus. "Let's start with paint. Would you be able to build a small shelf or two for me if I get especially frisky in my design?"

Bonnie laughed. "I'd agree to build almost anything to see your frisky side." As soon as she said it, Bonnie seemed to realize the implication of her words. "I only meant—"

"Be careful what you wish for." Grace interrupted Bonnie's stumbling retreat.

Bonnie nodded with a smile. Their food arrived shortly after, and they turned the conversation to other topics. After lunch they went their separate ways for the rest of the day. Grace felt immeasurably better when she returned to Ms. Babs'. Her plan was to go to the house and continue sorting through some of her dad's things.

She wasn't sure when the shift started to happen, but the house was feeling less like his house and more like "the" house. Not quite hers, but somewhere in between. She was actually looking forward to making changes upstairs so it felt more comfortable for her. What role Bonnie was playing in healing some of the broken places her father's death had created she didn't know. All she knew was that the raw, screaming pain was fading to an ache. She'd finally stopped picking up her phone daily to text him something that happened she knew he'd love to hear about. That felt like a victory in and of itself. If Bonnie was facilitating the transition in any way, Grace was grateful. Her search for "home" had gotten easier and immeasurably more complicated since Bonnie had reentered her life. It had also gotten spicier and more exciting for parts of her body that hadn't been turned on like they were now in years.

Grace thought back to her boundaries conversation with Bonnie earlier. Even if she knew she'd never act on any spark that remained between the two of them, she knew without a doubt, Bonnie would be in big trouble if Grace ever found a sock on the front doorknob.

CHAPTER FOURTEEN

Bonnie lugged two cans of paint, rollers, drop cloths, brushes, and others supplies up the stairs of Lionel's house. Her house. Carl and Stumpy were waiting for her in what used to be Grace's childhood bedroom.

"Thanks for the help, boys." Bonnie dumped her load on their feet.

Carl jumped back and looked at his left foot. "You have to keep those muscles ripped. You have a lady to impress. And I can't shrink or grow my ass with that kind of workout. My computer chair and I have been working for years on the perfect imprint."

Bonnie shook her head and looked at Stumpy. "What's your excuse?"

"Why do I need one? I'm not punching a clock. My favor includes watching you carry all that stuff up here. You asked me to help you paint." He ruffled Bonnie's hair, something he knew drove her crazy.

"What are you waiting for, Runt? These walls aren't going to prime themselves." Carl was kneeling next to the can of primer, prying off the lid, stir stick at the ready.

Bonnie couldn't believe she'd begged these guys to come help her today. She had a busy week, but she wanted to get Grace's project done as soon as she could. With Carl and Stumpy painting, she could work on the shelves and built-in bookcase Grace had asked for.

Over the weekend they'd removed all the furniture and scrubbed the bedroom top to bottom. It already felt like an entirely new place.

They'd pulled all the furniture out of the master bedroom and cleaned that and the en suite too, in case Grace wanted to move in there instead, but she'd not been ready for that step.

"What's Grace's plan for the new furniture?" Carl was standing in the middle the room, dry roller in hand, surveying the space.

"I'm not sure. She wants the bookcase over there." Bonnie pointed to the far corner, next to one of the windows. "And two shelves there." She pointed to the opposite wall.

"What about there and there? Or maybe over there in a cluster." Carl started pointing to walls and tapping his chin. He put the roller down and scooted down the hall. He hollered back from the master bedroom. "She's sure she doesn't want to rework this room? There're so many things we could do in here."

Bonnie held up her hands. "Go talk to Grace. She's downstairs. I only work here."

Stumpy snorted but didn't say anything.

A few minutes later, Carl returned with Grace. They were excitedly discussing design possibilities.

"I had no idea you were an interior designer. Bonnie should have said something." Grace looked at Bonnie with a mock disapproving look.

"Oh, come on. He's a web designer. How am I supposed to know he's really good at moving shelves around in his head?" Bonnie crossed her arms. Grace and Carl tossed ideas back and forth for what felt like an eternity. Bonnie was left with nothing to do but sulk.

"You can't always be her hero, Runt." Stumpy patted her on the shoulder. "It's nice Carl gets a turn. He's a nocturnal web designer. When was the last time he got to impress a lady face to face?"

"It's not like he ever makes much effort when one's in front of him. Why start now?" Bonnie grumbled. Stumpy was right, but why'd it have to be Grace? Not that she was trying to impress her. Oh, who was she kidding, of course she was. What self-respecting, tool-wielding, truck driving, walking stereotype of a lesbian wouldn't try to impress a pretty lady if given the chance?

She and Grace were complicated, but so was this house, her relationship with Garrison, and her grief for Lionel. Why should flirting be any different?

"Are you two almost done? My paint's going to need another shake if you take much longer." Stumpy rolled his finger in the universal sign to speed it along, but his put-on annoyance fell apart once you saw the twinkle in his eyes.

"Sorry for the delay." Grace smiled at Bonnie. "Carl is a man of vision." She pointed out the new placement for the built-ins and her furniture in the room. "He's ready to move me down the hall and gut the bathroom, but since I'm not getting paid right now, I'm holding off on that project so I don't have to fly back to LA and start work again tomorrow."

Bonnie turned quickly from the paint tray she was about to dip a roller in, back toward Grace. "Please don't do that." Her stomach churned and her palms began to sweat at the thought of Grace disappearing from her life again so quickly. Even if it wasn't going to happen, the thought was enough to bring up emotions she'd never wanted to experience again.

"Bonnie's right, please don't go." Stumpy dipped his brush in the paint and gave Grace a serious nod and smile.

Carl put his hands under his chin and pouted. "Yes, we'd *all* miss you too much. I don't think we'd survive without you."

Bonnie threw a rag at Carl. "You just had a whole design moment and now you're making it seem like you wouldn't miss her. What the hell?"

Grace laughed. "I'm going to give all three of you a chance to miss me terribly by going back downstairs. Good luck up here. Thank you for your hard work." She blew them each a kiss before she disappeared out the door.

The sight of Grace's lips as she blew kisses was almost Bonnie's undoing. It was too easy to fall into the feeling of their attic kiss and how the feeling was unique to the two of them and unlike anything Bonnie had ever felt. Bonnie felt like someone was holding a torch to the tops of her ears, a surefire sign she was thinking thoughts she shouldn't be.

"Already looks better in here with the primer going up." Carl didn't appear to have any idea about Bonnie's fiery ears.

Carl was right. The room had been a dark blue which made it always feel like dusk. Daylight was seeping into the walls with each roller stroke. Grace had excellent instincts; new paint did breathe new life into the room.

"Here, Runt you can cut in for a while until you cool off." Stumpy tossed a brush Bonnie's way. Apparently he was a good judge of ears.

"Cool off? My balls are starting to sweat in here." Carl looked confused. "Why aren't you downstairs working on the building projects?"

"I don't want her getting hurt." Stumpy looked away from both of them and returned to his painting.

"She's been using power tools since she was about five. Am I missing something?" Carl leaned on the long handle of the roller and looked from Bonnie to Stumpy. "I feel like I missed something."

"I got myself a little in my head with Grace a minute ago. Stumpy's worried I'm going to get hurt, but I'll be okay." Bonnie started painting a little more aggressively than she meant and made a mess of the corner she was cutting in. She slowed down and cleaned it up.

"Oh, don't worry. You'll get used to it. Happens to me every time Stump Man walks into a room. Still perfectly capable of operating a table saw." Carl had a big goofy grin on his face.

Bonnie and Stumpy both stared at Carl. Was he being serious? His face was unreadable aside from his floppy, golden retriever-like grin. In their thirty-two years of friendship had she missed something that momentous about one of her closest friends? Stumpy looked like he was having similar thoughts.

Carl looked at both of them and laughed. "What's up with you two? So serious. Get back to work so we can finish up in time for Runt to buy us all the drinks she owes us. I plan on opening a tab."

Stumpy shook his head as if maybe he'd imagined what he'd just heard. "We always open a tab, Carl, and you never make it more than one drink before you start yawning."

Carl shrugged, undeterred. "Maybe tonight's the night."

After half an hour of painting and joking, Bonnie left the boys to finish the walls and she returned to her truck to unload tools and the lumber she'd purchased for the projects of the day.

She set up what she needed and was about to start measuring and cutting when the screen door banged. Grace was standing on the porch looking down at her when Bonnie squinted up against the midday sun. The sun wasn't bright enough to blind her to Grace's beauty.

"Come out to supervise?" Bonnie shielded her eyes to get a better look at Grace.

"I don't think I'd know if you were doing something wrong. I came out to say hi I guess. It sounds creepy if I say I wanted to watch you work." Grace came down into the driveway and perched on the bumper of Bonnie's truck.

"That's why you have to say you're supervising. You bring out some cider and you can watch anything you like." Bonnie's ears acted up again when she realized how that sounded.

"Is that right? Anything I like?" Grace swung her legs playfully. "I do like the sound of that."

Bonnie stood and ran her hand through her hair. "Now I'm a little flustered. Look what you've done to me. I think we're talking about bookcases and then you're flirting with me." She grinned at Grace. "We need a code word or something."

Grace smiled back and hopped off the tailgate. "A code word? Like if you say 'fiddlesticks' it means you're about to flirt with me?" Grace tilted her head, clearly considering.

"Sure, why not? No crossed wires that way." Bonnie tried to keep a straight face and failed.

"Now it seems like I'm doing more distracting than supervising and I'm motivated to have finished furniture." Grace moved closer to Bonnie and gave her chin a playful shake. "I'm heading back inside. We can both think about all the things I could have been out here watching."

Bonnie felt like she swallowed her tongue. "Was that a fiddlesticks?"

Grace pointed to herself and looked innocently at Bonnie. "From me? I meant building and sawing and nailing, of course." Grace winked and returned to the porch. Despite her promise, she didn't move back inside. Instead she brought a pile of papers out and sat in the porch swing and flipped through them.

Bonnie returned to her work, but her hands were slightly shaky. How was Grace still able to have this effect on her? Why was she letting her?

She worked the rest of the afternoon building the bookcase and shelves and sanding and painting them. While they dried, she helped Carl and Stumpy finish upstairs. They'd done a masterful job. It might not need a second coat, but she'd wait until the morning when everything was dry to make that call.

"Look at this room. It's a palace now. Time to pay up, Runt." Carl grabbed Bonnie around the shoulders and pulled her into a tight side hug.

"I never promised payment." Bonnie wriggled free.

"Neither did I, but I'm paying up anyway. Come on downstairs, fellas. I've got drinks and food with your name on it." Grace appeared in the doorway and waved them all toward the stairs.

"Make sure Runt's at the back of the line." Carl cut Stumpy off at the door and the two of them raced down the stairs like they'd been doing since they were old enough to be trusted on stairs.

"You didn't have to do that." Bonnie waited until the crashing footsteps made it to the first floor. "I was planning on buying them dinner."

"Now you don't have to and I get all of you longer. Besides, you were helping me. Of course I should buy." Grace started down the stairs before looking back. "You are going to join us, right?"

"Yes, of course." Bonnie hurried after her. What would it be like if this was her life? If she had a home and a partner and her friends came over for dinner? She'd never known how much she wanted it until she owned half a home. Why didn't seeing Duck and Candace living this life spark these feelings? Was it something about the house? About Grace? About her? The answers were unlikely to be found in the kitchen, but there was pizza and beer, which at the moment was more inviting than soul-searching.

"Beer seemed safe, but there's also wine, and maybe a bottle of scotch. You're welcome to my father's bottle of peppermint schnapps, vintage unknown, but if you try it, you're far braver than me." Grace handed out plates and set a couple of pizza boxes on the dining room table.

Bonnie, Carl, and Stumpy stood next to chairs but didn't sit. Grace looked at them, clearly confused.

"We're in paint clothes. No way I'm sitting on a real chair tonight unless I stripped to my underwear, and no offense, Grace, but I don't know you that well." Stumpy's ears turned pink.

"I like you a lot, Stumpy, but I'm not sure I ever want to know you that well." Grace and Stumpy shared a smile. "Only one thing to do." She scooped up the pizza boxes and handed a six-pack to Carl. "To the porch."

Grace took a seat on the swing, Carl sprawled on the lawn, Bonnie leaned against the house a few feet from the swing, and Stumpy took over the steps. They looked like exactly what they were, tired workers at the end of a long day.

"You know what you need out here?" Carl sat up enough to survey the grass around him. "You need a fire pit."

Stumpy perked up. "He's right. What's wrong with you, Runt? Why doesn't your house have a fire pit?" He threw a pizza crust at Bonnie.

She threw the crust back. "Tomorrow, I'll buy you a sandwich and you can build us one."

"Afraid I'll have to pass. I have clients the rest of the week." Stumpy closed his eyes and leaned his head against the porch rail. "But I'll enjoy the hell out of it once you finish it."

"Me too." Grace gave Bonnie's leg a gentle nudge with her toe on one of her upswings.

"What about you, Carl?" Bonnie looked his way, but Carl was snoring softly, starfished on the lawn.

Stumpy shook his head. "I told you, one beer and the guy's out." There was no annoyance in Stumpy's voice. In fact, he sounded like he thought Carl's lightweight tendencies were endearing.

"Should we bring him a blanket?" Grace shivered and rubbed her arms.

Bonnie rose and went inside quietly. She retrieved a light throw from the couch and brought it to the porch. Instead of draping it over Carl, she wrapped it around Grace.

Grace pulled the blanket tighter around her shoulders. "You were supposed to give this to him." She pointed at Carl.

Stumpy looked at Carl and shook his head with a smile. "He's fine. Good training for our camping trip. He ends up asleep outside the tent at least once while we're there."

Grace looked interested. "You have to train for a camping trip? Do you hike for miles and make your own site in the woods far from the beaten path?"

"Don't let him fool you." Bonnie shook her head, amused. "We rent a group site at one of the state parks and play Boy Scouts for a few days."

"You should come this year." Carl hollered from his position on the lawn and attempted to point toward Grace.

"Now you're awake?" Bonnie took a slow sip of her beer. But Carl didn't seem to be anymore.

"He's right." Stumpy turned to Grace. "You should come. How do you feel about camping?"

Grace looked taken aback. "Camping and I don't have any strong personal feelings for each other one way or another. I haven't been since I was a kid, and even then it was barely camping. The family I went with had a fancy RV. They brought an espresso machine and had a microwave."

"We don't camp like that." Carl chimed in again.

"Man, either wake up and join the conversation or go sleep in the flower bed over there and stop eavesdropping. You're freaking me out." Stumpy tried to shoo Carl farther away, but he was back to snoring.

"You should come with us. It's always fun." Bonnie looked at Grace seriously. She'd never invited anyone camping. It was her uninterrupted time with the guys. So why didn't she feel weird about the possibility of Grace coming along?

Bonnie looked up at Grace, framed against the setting sun, blanket wrapped snugly around her shoulders. The light made it look as if she were glowing. Bonnie's breath caught. In that moment, in that light, Grace was more beautiful than Bonnie could ever remember. That was saying something because in high school everything was the most, the best, and the greatest ever. But she was older now and wiser. She knew beauty when it was right in front of her.

Grace coming camping wasn't a problem. Bonnie welcomed it. More time with Grace and her three favorite guys sounded like paradise. The problem was the way her heart caught just now when she looked at Grace framed in the evening sun.

It suddenly felt like they were both playing a dangerous game full of flirting and potential heartbreak. How was she supposed to navigate her own feelings let alone decode Grace's? It felt impossible. Ah, fiddlesticks.

CHAPTER FIFTEEN

G race couldn't stand it anymore. Bonnie had been working upstairs for over an hour. She'd been a distraction since the moment she'd arrived. The stack of papers Grace had hoped to sort through were about as comprehensible as if they were a plate full of tie-dye lasagna noodles.

She gave up on the paperwork and went to check on Bonnie. Surely Bonnie was in need of a glass of water or someone to dab the sweat off her forehead. When Grace got to the top of the stairs she heard Bonnie cursing colorfully from the bedroom.

"Are you okay?" Grace sped up.

"I could actually use a little help." Bonnie sounded out of breath.

When Grace entered the room, Bonnie was wedged on her back under the nearly fully assembled bed frame. "You might need a refresher on how a bed works."

Bonnie grunted. "I'd love to make a sassy comment about you giving me some hands-on training, but I'm too uncomfortable under here. If I point to them, can you pick up the two screws I dropped?"

"Yes, ma'am, I'm here to rescue you. At your service for all your screw-related needs." Grace realized what she'd said and wanted to flee from the room.

"Is that so? I might have to find excuses to need rescue if those are the sort of services you're willing to provide. But I thought we'd decided not to stray down that path of lust and historically poor decisions." Bonnie's voice was lower and huskier than usual.

Grace pulled out her phone and took a few pictures before retrieving the screws. Maybe it would take her mind off the thought of Bonnie on the bed instead of under it, doing a very different kind of screwing. "Shh, I need to focus, I'm mid rescue. How did you end up under there anyway? Why didn't you do what I just did?" Grace stretched across the slats and reached down to get the wayward hardware.

Due to their positions, Grace was lying nearly on top of Bonnie, with only the bed holding her above. If it disappeared beneath her, her breasts would land within tongue's reach of Bonnie's mouth and Grace would be able to wrap her legs around her waist. She silently scolded her nervous system for ignoring the rules about Bonnie. She was wet and her heart was doing a solo tango looking for a partner. She quickly stood, avoiding eye contact with Bonnie below her.

"Did you take a picture before helping me?" Bonnie's attempt at a stern voice was undercut by the hint of amusement laced through. "That's cold." Bonnie wiggled and squirmed, slowly inching out from under the bed. "To answer your question, I couldn't find the screws after I dropped them. I shimmied under the bed to get a floor eye view, but my butt is too big to fit under beds."

As soon as Bonnie was out from under the bed and back on her feet, Grace made a show of looking at Bonnie's ass, which was a bad idea given the state she was in from lying on the bed. "It looks pretty damn good to me, under bed size or not." Why couldn't she keep her mouth shut around Bonnie?

Bonnie wagged a finger Grace's way. "You can't flirt with me when I'm working. I'll never finish."

Grace held up her hands innocently and started to back out of the room. "I'll leave you to it. No more flirting."

"Oh no you don't. You have the screws I need and now that you're here, I'm going to put you to work." Bonnie crooked a finger and beckoned Grace closer.

It shouldn't have turned her on, but something about Bonnie in work mode, taking charge and so confident really hit all the right notes for Grace in that moment. Being summoned as she was had her on the edge of breaking Bonnie's no flirting rule and a few others they'd agreed to as well. From the look on Bonnie's face, she knew what she'd done and it might have been on purpose.

"How may I be of service?" Grace thrilled at the slight fault in Bonnie's confident grin. Two could play the not flirting, flirty game.

Bonnie recovered quickly and instructed Grace on lining up the bed slats and screwing them in place. With two of them working it was done quickly. Bonnie wrestled the mattress onto the frame and they both got it oriented correctly and centered on the slats.

Once that was done, Grace sat on the bed and looked around the room, taking in the work Bonnie had done. "It looks amazing in here. Thank you."

Bonnie picked up stray tools and packed them in her toolbox. "I was happy to do it. I want you to feel comfortable here." She stopped her cleanup and looked at Grace, the sincerity written clearly across her face. Then her expression shuttered closed. "For as long as you're staying."

Grace nodded. "I want you to feel that way too. This isn't only my house."

"Are you suggesting I makeover the guest room down the hall and move in too?" Bonnie laughed.

"I wasn't, but maybe it's not such a bad idea." Grace considered. "You'd save money and it would make coordinating all of this"— Grace waved around them—"much easier." Grace didn't mention how much she'd enjoy having Bonnie down the hall.

"You went from hating me to asking me to move in, like that." Bonnie snapped her fingers. "That's impressive, even by lesbian standards." She offered her hand to give Grace a high five.

Grace crossed her arms, annoyed. "I'm not asking you to move in *with* me. I'm saying you should move into the house you own. You rent now, right? Think about not having to make that payment every month if nothing else. This house is paid off."

Bonnie shuffled her feet. "I don't think it's a good idea." Bonnie wrung her hands, without looking at Grace.

Embarrassment erupted from every cell in Grace's body. Of course it wasn't a good idea, what had she been thinking? She wanted to run from the room, from the house.

"Grace, wait." Bonnie was looking at her now. She stepped forward and put her hand tentatively on Grace's arm. "When I saw you again for the first time it took my breath away. It was like I was transported back in time and we were kids again, carefree and in love. But right on the heels of that feeling was what it felt like when I broke both of our hearts."

Grace nodded and sighed. "The same thing happened to me. I was as mad at you as I was fifteen years ago, for what you did and I reacted to you nearly as strongly as I had back then."

"Then you understand." Bonnie looked at her earnestly. "We foolishly kissed, which I absolutely do not regret, but you were right to stop us from continuing. Do I know that we'd end up in bed together if I moved in? No idea. Our flirting is fun, but it's easy for me because I know we won't go further."

"Me too. I never thought I'd have you back in my life, even as a friend. With our history and this new friendship we're building, it would feel weird not to flirt." Grace attempted a smile, but wasn't sure how convincing it was. Was Bonnie really as unaffected by their teasing as she let on?

"Maybe I'd feel different if you didn't live across the country or if we didn't have so much history complicating things. Or so much future together complicating things." Bonnie indicated the house around them. "But if I risk my feelings getting involved again, I don't know what it would do to me to watch you get on a plane and fly back home without me."

"Thank goodness the only time we can feel anything is within the walls of this house. We don't have to live with each other to risk hurting each other. But you're probably right. How about we make a rule just to be safe. No sex except in the master bedroom." Grace raised an eyebrow and looked at Bonnie.

"The master bedroom still looks like your dad's room and doesn't have any furniture in it." Bonnie shivered as she said it.

"Better than a cold shower." Grace stood from the bed and pulled Bonnie toward the door. "Enough of this, we have other things to do tonight."

Bonnie seemed reluctant to let go of Grace's hands. Grace took time letting go as well. They were face to face and close enough it wouldn't have taken much to lean forward and kiss her. Bonnie's lips were wet and inviting and right there.

Grace stepped back and broke the spell. That was what Bonnie meant by the danger of living down the hall from one another. Maybe seeing Bonnie in her pajamas and ugly seasonal underwear would quash the inappropriate feelings.

Hot on the heels of that thought was another complete with the mental image of Bonnie in a high fashion underwear modeling campaign. That was not helpful. Not at all.

"What are we doing tonight?"

Bonnie's look of confusion made Grace think Bonnie had had to ask more than once. She must have been daydreaming about underwear longer than she thought.

"What do you mean?" Was Bonnie volunteering to stick around to hang out?

"I don't know, there's still plenty to do around here. I don't have anywhere to be. We have to eat. It's a nice night." Bonnie looked like something dawned on her. "Unless you have plans. Sorry, I shouldn't have assumed."

"That I'm new in town without much of a social life?" Grace was teasing, but if she was going to stick around a bit longer she should probably address that issue.

"I didn't mean that." Bonnie was backpedaling so quickly Grace was worried she'd trip over her tongue.

"Relax, Bonnie. I was teasing you, but you're also not wrong. Let's see." Grace chewed on her lip while she thought. "Ah. I've got it." She waved Bonnie to follow her and shot down the stairs, into the kitchen to the fridge. She surveyed the contents, which were rather pathetic, and closed it empty-handed. "We need to make a stop at the store. Tonight, I want you to take me to a place you love but don't think I'll know about."

"That's tricky since you grew up here." Bonnie thought for a moment.

"It's been fifteen years. Surely there are some places left unexplored for us."

"I know just the place, but it's going to take a little while to get there. Do you want to wait until another day?" Bonnie's voice was soft.

"Of course not. You asked what we're doing tonight, not next week. I like surprises and I don't like to wait. You're driving." Grace grabbed her pocketbook and the keys.

"I'm still in my work clothes." Bonnie looked down at herself, then to Grace.

"Does it matter where we're going? You look more than acceptable to me." Grace laughed when Bonnie scrunched up her face.

"Ringing endorsement, thanks. Let's go."

As Bonnie had promised, the drive was long, especially by Rhode Island standards. In a state so tiny, anything over twenty minutes was nearly cause for an overnight bag. This jaunt took over an hour when the stop at the grocery store was factored in.

When Bonnie finally pulled over, it was into a parking lot that was barely more than a large gravel cutout on the side of the road. Technically, Grace could see large rocks spaced evenly along the ground that could pass as parking spot markers.

They parked in front of a particularly huge rock. Behind it was a wall of trees, thickly packed and impossible to see through. They stretched along the parking lot all the way to the street on either side.

"Where are you taking me?"

"Through there." Bonnie pointed to a barely visible break in the trees. A small sign was placed nearby.

"Should I trust you enough to let you lead me into the woods to parts unknown?" Grace winked so Bonnie didn't think she was serious about her insinuation that Bonnie had nefarious intentions.

"You coming?" Bonnie came around to the passenger's side and opened Grace's door.

"Of course. I'm hungry and you promised me something spectacular." Grace let Bonnie help her down from the truck, then reached back into the cab to retrieve their groceries.

Even though the path looked like something out of a horror movie from the parking lot, it was beautiful once you stepped inside. The trees were aglow in the evening light and a cacophony of bird calls filled the air. The way they were safely enclosed in the tunnel of nature felt like being in a temple.

Grace spun a full three hundred sixty degrees. "I can see why you love it here." She whispered as if speaking aloud might disturb the serenity of the place.

"But this isn't where I'm bringing you." Bonnie nodded up ahead. "This is only the pathway to get there."

It was hard to believe there was anything better at the end of this path, but she took Bonnie's word for it. She grabbed her hand and pulled her along. "If there is anything better than this, I want to see it now."

Bonnie laughed and followed her. They were both at a slow jog now. "Just around this bend and we're there." As they reached the curve in the path, Bonnie pulled Grace to a stop. "Take your time, no need to rush in at a full sprint."

Grace slowed her pace but didn't let go of Bonnie's hand. Was the anticipation she was feeling causing her chest to feel electrified and full or was it the direct current that seemed to be sparking between their joined hands? Either way, Grace wanted more, even if Bonnie was the cause.

They rounded the bend, and abruptly, the trees fell away. Grace caught her breath. She stopped to take in the view and Bonnie bumped into her.

"Was it worth the wait and the walk?" Bonnie was so close she was almost whispering in Grace's ear.

Grace shivered and fought her instinct to lean back into Bonnie's embrace. Instead she squeezed Bonnie's hand, which she still held, tightly and then let go so she could explore. Every one of Grace's footfalls made an audible "crunch." She stopped and took in the view once again. The bay stretched as far as she could see. It was calm now, so the water was relatively flat. The Newport Bridge was close enough she felt as though she could reach out and touch it. The houses visible across the water looked small enough to fit in her hand.

"Bonnie, this is gorgeous." Grace turned and hugged Bonnie. It was a hug of pure happiness with no underlying motivation or innuendo.

"Beautiful water views aren't hard to find in the Ocean State, but look at your feet. That's what I really love about this beach." Bonnie set the picnic down and squatted. She scooped up a handful of shells and held them up to Grace.

Grace reached out and plucked two shells from Bonnie's hands. They were exquisite. She looked down and then around. Instead of sand, dirt, or grass, the entirety of the area along the waterline was covered in shells. Most of them were slipper and moon snail shells, but she saw oyster and clam shells mixed in too. And that was at first glance.

"I'm going to be here all night looking for shells, you know that, right?" Grace felt like a giddy child.

"I told you, there's nowhere I'd rather be." Bonnie laid out a large blanket she'd insisted on bringing, sat down, and unpacked the groceries. "You should eat first though. Shelling is hard, focused work. You need your strength." She patted a corner of the blanket.

Grace obliged and dished herself some food. "Do you think this is what my dad had in mind when he left us the house?"

"Us picnicking on the beach just before the sun sets?" Bonnie looked around. She appeared content.

"Yes. No. All of it, I guess. The kiss, the freakout, whatever that back at the house was, whatever this is." Grace shrugged and sighed dramatically. "All of it."

Bonnie looked skyward as if the answers might be written in the clouds slowly turning pink in the light of the setting sun. "I loved your father more than almost anyone else in my life. You know my parents weren't the kind you put up for mother and father of the year, but your dad, he pulled me close when a lot of the town pushed me away because of where I came from and who I was."

Grace started to ask about Bonnie's relationship with the townsfolk now, but Bonnie interrupted her.

"I don't have the answer to the question you were about to ask. People grow and change, myself included. This is where I live and I wasn't interested in leaving, so I had to make it work for me, same as everyone here. We've more than made it work. This is my home. Part of that had to do with your dad." Bonnie looked at Grace. Her eyes were shimmery, but no tears fell.

"Sometimes I think you knew him better than I did these last few years. I shouldn't have stayed away so long." Grace leaned back on her hands and looked skyward herself. "I missed out on time with him because I was too scared I might run into you. I'm such a coward."

"Hey, no you're not." Bonnie slid closer. "You had a job and a life across the country. You shouldn't give me all the credit. It will make my head too big to fit through the door of our house. I'll never be able to move in with you then."

Grace tossed a napkin at Bonnie. "I didn't ask you to move in with me. You'd be lucky if I did, but don't go starting rumors you can't back up."

Bonnie leaned close. "But I can back it up. All I have to do is move in." She moved away again and smiled wickedly.

"Ugh. You're the worst." Grace flopped on her back and looked at the clouds passing overhead in the darkening sky. Was her dad looking down on them now? "Were you there with him? At the end?"

Bonnie lay down next to Grace so their heads were mere inches apart. "Yes." Bonnie sounded far away. "I held his hand as he passed."

"I should have been here with him. I don't know why I wasn't. I thought I had more time." Grace wiped a tear that escaped and began rolling down her cheek.

Bonnie rolled on her side and propped her head on her hand. "I don't know if this will help, but he told me on that last day that he wanted to go before you got to town. He said you two had so many good memories he didn't want the last one you shared to be him dying."

"I don't know if that makes me feel better or not. Is it a bad memory for you?" Grace turned so she was facing Bonnie, mirroring her position.

"No, it was an honor. I'd never tell you how to feel, but he loved you so much. Not asking you to be there wasn't a reflection of how he felt about you. You're all he talked about." Bonnie tucked a loose strand of hair behind Grace's ear.

There was still enough sun reflecting off the water that Grace put her hand up to shield her eyes. When she did, she saw a look cross Bonnie's face she couldn't name but made her insides somersault so wildly she was worried they might take the rest of her with them. Grace felt a greater pull to Bonnie than she had since high school. Maybe it was the intimacy of the conversation they'd shared. Wherever it was coming from, it felt more dangerous than any of the flirtatious banter they'd engaged in and desirous thoughts she'd allowed herself.

Bonnie got to her knees and leaned forward. Grace was terrified she might lean down and kiss her. She was equally worried she might not.

"Come on." Bonnie reached out and pulled Grace upright. "Let's walk so you can collect some shells. I think we could both use some space from the blanket. No one will steal our empty takeout containers. Let's walk and talk."

Why, oh, why did Bonnie have to be kind and considerate? It made her sexier and more unnerving. It was getting easier and easier for Grace to forget why she and Bonnie had missed their chance at happily ever after. Or why she'd stayed away so long.

But the past, how beautiful Bonnie looked framed against the sunset, how thoughtful and caring and kind she was, none of that mattered. Grace might not be sure LA was her home, but she hadn't felt at home in Garrison in years. The problem was her brain was losing its iron grip over her heart and body. Both were unruly and chaotic without a firm, logical hand. Where that led Grace only time would tell.

CHAPTER SIXTEEN

Bonnie angled her truck into Branch Tucker's driveway. Before she came to a stop she saw him using his cane to whack at one of his motion sensor lights mounted high on his garage. She slammed her truck into park and ran to Branch.

"What are you doing? That cane doesn't do you any good waving around in the air." Bonnie removed it from his hand, put it back in its proper orientation, and returned it to him.

"Bah." Branch waved his hand at her dismissively. "I was tap dancing before your grandfather was out of diapers."

Bonnie laughed. "I don't know how old you think I am. Or you are for that matter. What were you trying to do, aside from get an expensive ride to the hospital in an ambulance?"

"Don't start on me, youngster. If I want to wave my cane around and get that motion sensor facing the right direction again, I'll do as I please. Besides, it's your fault. You were late." Branch was scowling and shaking his cane in her direction, but his eyes were crinkled in the way they did when he laughed heartily.

"You can take it out of my tip." Bonnie clapped him lightly on the shoulder. "Do you have my list so I can get started?"

Branch looked nervous. He spun his cane in his hands and didn't look Bonnie in the eye.

"Everything okay, Branch?" Bonnie tried to make eye contact, but Branch looked away.

"Things are fine. I was wondering if you, well, you see I wanted you to do something different for me today. It's going to sound silly to a young buck like yourself, but I had friends that would come over and we'd play board games. I don't enjoy them much anymore. Most of those friends are gone now, but I do still enjoy puzzles." Branch leaned on his cane and furrowed his brow. He looked lost in the past.

"What can I do to help?" Bonnie tried again to catch Branch's eye.

This time he looked at her. "I'm almost done with my latest and I was hoping you'd be able to spare a bit of your time to help me finish up. I've saved the hardest part for the end and my eyesight isn't what it used to be. Besides, those last few pieces are the most enjoyable and it's never as much fun doing them by yourself." The hope in Branch's eyes gave away how much the request meant to him even though he was doing a good job of keeping his tone neutral. "If you have the time of course."

Bonnie mentally ran through her schedule for the day. She didn't have much planned out. She'd taken care of the shingles on Nadine's shed already, and she was waiting on supplies for a couple of other projects. She usually blocked off large chunks of time when she visited Branch since she never knew how extensive the work he needed was going to be. "I'd be happy to stay and work on your puzzle. I have to warn you, I haven't done a puzzle in years."

"Oh, that's okay, it's like riding a bike." Branch practically skipped to the door and held it for Bonnie.

"Do you need me to fix the light out here first?" Bonnie pointed to the motion sensor Branch had been brutalizing with his cane.

"I think I took care of it. You can take a look on your way out if you like, but we have a puzzle to conquer inside first."

Branch shuffled to the fridge and got out a plate full of vegetables and dip and a plate of cheese and crackers. Bonnie couldn't decide if she was predictable and easy or Branch was desperately in need of the company. Either way, the cheese platter was the deciding factor, Bonnie wasn't leaving until they finished the puzzle.

Little did Bonnie know what she was getting herself into. Branch was technically right that he was near the end of the puzzle, but when the puzzle was a two thousand piecer and had large monochromatic swaths, "near" was a subjective term.

An hour in, Bonnie had successfully placed three pieces. That felt like a triumph given that the stack of pieces Branch had handed her were blue. Not shades of blue or variations on a theme. They were all blue, same shade, same tone, blue.

"Why do you torture yourself with these things?" Bonnie groaned when she realized she was trying a piece in the same spot for what felt like the hundredth time. At least she thought it was the same piece, but it really was impossible to tell.

"I do my best thinking while I'm puzzling. It's not torture unless I'm thinking on something I find unpleasant. Don't wrap your brain so tightly around the pieces you don't think will fit together. Sometimes you have to get your head out of the way and see what happens." Branch wagged his finger at her and returned to his puzzle work. Luckily for both of them, he'd been steadily fitting pieces and had completed a large section.

"I don't know how to do that." Bonnie's hands were shaking slightly.

Branch looked confused. "Are we still talking about puzzles?" Then a huge smile lit his face. "Wait, this is about a lady, isn't it? I'm no help there I'm afraid, but I'm a good listener."

Bonnie smiled. Branch had always famously been a bachelor. There'd always been talk of who would finally tie him down, but it'd never happened. Now here he was, doing puzzles with her. Bonnie might be the steadiest relationship in his life right now.

"When did our relationship change, Branch?" Bonnie rubbed the back of her head. "You didn't seem to like folks like me much for a while and now we're eating cheese and crackers and doing a puzzle together."

Branch put his pieces down and looked at her thoughtfully. He had perpetual bags under his eyes and now, coupled with a look of regret, he looked sad enough that Bonnie wished she could un-ask the question.

"I'm old enough that you should cut to the chase, you hear me? All this beating around the bush and I might be dead before you get to the point. What you meant to say was I didn't like gay people and was loud about it, right?"

Bonnie squirmed in her chair. "I guess that about sums it up, yes."

Branch stared down at his puzzle pieces for a long while. He put two in place before he looked up at Bonnie again. "I wasn't a young man when I changed my thinking, you know. Before I opened my eyes I would have said there wasn't a prejudiced bone in my body. Can you believe that? It's what I thought about myself, it really was."

"So what happened?" Bonnie leaned forward, her elbows on the table.

Branch distractedly added another three pieces to the puzzle. "It was two things and they happened almost at the same time. The first was the birth of my good friend's great-grandson. That child came into this world a fire-breathing dragon and hasn't put out the flame since. Everyone who met him has said 'kids are born who they are.' Who am I to argue?"

Branch raised his eyebrows as if challenging Bonnie to disagree. She had no desire or basis to do so.

"So what's the second reason?" Branch was turning out to be an onion and Bonnie was enjoying this layer.

Branch winked with a smile dancing in his eyes. "You."

Bonnie pointed at herself. "Me? You're going to have to explain."

"I heard the rumors about you and Grace Cook when you were in high school, but I never believed them. Don't be offended, but I didn't think you were in her league, or that she would be stupid enough to throw everything away on a flight of fancy, an experiment, a passing phase. I'm not proud of those thoughts or the man I was then. I'm sorry." Branch stood, leaning heavily on his cane, and shuffled to the sink to get a glass of water.

Anger bubbled in Bonnie's veins. "I broke up with her because of the people in the village who thought like you. I didn't want her to lose out on her dreams because all the support she had would have evaporated if anyone found out about the two of us. So she could afford to go to college we both ended up heartbroken and she's spent fifteen years hating me for what I did."

Branch's shoulders sagged. "There's no excuse. I have nothing to offer you but an apology. After Grace left, I saw what her absence did to you. I wasn't so blinded by prejudice that I couldn't see the true love and heartache right in front of me." Branch returned to the table. On the way past he put his hand on Bonnie's shoulder. He left it there a few seconds and then squeezed before returning to his seat. "I might not have settled down and gotten married, but I can recognize true, pure love when I see it. Your love, even though you were so young, was beautiful. How could something so gorgeous be as wrong as I was preaching?"

Bonnie was pulled back into memories. Most were filled with Grace and her, happy and in love. High school problems felt life or death at the time, but looking back, Bonnie appreciated how carefree she'd been. Except when it came to her relationship with Grace. That had been stressful. Because of people like Branch. She knew everything Branch was telling her, but somehow hearing him say it aloud made it sink in in a way it hadn't before. Her client, her friend, had actively worked to make her life miserable. In the end he had succeeded because he'd cost her the one thing she cared about above all others. Were atonement and forgiveness possible for that? The anger churned in her belly again.

She took a deep breath, then another. Nothing would be gained from her losing her temper. She and Branch had a different relationship now and he wasn't ultimately responsible for the choice she'd made to break up with Grace. He certainly played no part in how she went about it.

"I'm glad you were able to take something good from that time in my life. I'm also glad we're friends." She reached to take Branch's hand but stopped midway. Another puzzle piece to fit in. It was lying there waiting for her to place. "You're right, Branch. Thinking of something else did help. Maybe next time a conversation that's a little less supercharged. What do you think?"

Branch nodded enthusiastically. Then his face turned serious. "Bonnie, I know you're friendly with almost everyone here. I'm glad you're comfortable in Garrison. When I asked questions of myself it led to more questions. I wanted to know the answer to all of them so I kept digging and putting in the work. Not everyone in the village was interested in coming along with me."

"Are you worried about me?" Bonnie resumed work on the puzzle but snuck a peek at Branch.

"Of course not. You can take care of yourself and anyone else you come across that might need protecting." He picked up a puzzle piece, handed it to her, and pointed toward a section close to her. "But if I were, I'd tell you to be careful is all. Same as I'll tell you about driving home in all the wind I keep hearing about coming later this afternoon."

Bonnie nodded. She could do that, at least in the area Branch was cautioning her about, although she hadn't heard anything about the wind. Grace still felt like jumping from an airplane without a parachute. The falling might be magical, but she couldn't see a parachute in their future. Without that, the abrupt end to the magic might destroy her.

She stayed with Branch another hour. They didn't quite finish the puzzle, but Bonnie promised to return the following week. She made Branch pinkie swear he wouldn't set even a single piece without her.

It wasn't late, but Bonnie didn't have anything on her schedule and was out of sorts after talking with Branch. It didn't seem fair that he got praised for the work he did becoming a better man. Meanwhile she and Grace were still reconciling the fallout from that time in their lives.

Bonnie turned into the driveway of the small house she'd been renting for a couple of years. The first time she saw it, it had reminded her of a box with a roof. There was nothing imaginative or charming about the design. It had four walls, doors, windows, and a roof. That hadn't ever been a problem, but today it felt jarring.

She unlocked the door and hung her keys on the hook. She had to step into the living room to close the door. There wasn't room in the entry alcove for a closing door and her. How many times had she done that in the time she'd lived there, but somehow it annoyed her today.

In the living room she kicked off her boots and tossed them harder than she meant into the corner where she left her shoes. Dried dirt flew from the bottom and scattered on the manufactured flooring. She grumbled but had no one to blame but herself.

On the way to retrieve a dustpan and broom, Bonnie was distracted by the austere feel to her home. She walked from room to room looking for some part of the house that felt like a warm, inviting space. She came up empty. How had she been living here, like this for so long? There were no pictures on the walls, no personal touches or attempts at decorations. Her college dorm had had more personality and sense of style.

Perhaps the biggest questions were how she'd not noticed the sterile feel to the place and why she was noticing now? Bonnie didn't need to stop and think long to answer the latter. Grace was the reason. Grace and the house they owned. There was nothing sterile or austere or uninviting about their house. It was the opposite of this place, full of memories and possibilities and color.

Their house also had Grace who increased the vibrancy and beauty of anywhere she was by tenfold. Even Bonnie's current place would probably look incredible the moment Grace walked through the door.

Bonnie sat heavily on the couch. She didn't want to live here anymore. She didn't want to live anywhere that had the feel of this place. Why hadn't any of her friends told her?

She grabbed her phone and dialed Stumpy. She went to retrieve her tablet and some notes from her truck while she did so. He answered on the first ring. "What's wrong? Did you cut off a finger? Do I need to come pack it in ice and take you to the hospital?"

Bonnie pulled the phone away from her ear and looked at it for a beat. What the hell? She returned the phone to her ear. "Nothing like that. Have you been waiting for the day I call you with that particular emergency?"

"Of course not." Stumpy sounded like he was trying too hard to sound believable. "But if you had been calling about that, then I'd have won a bet with the boys. Your fingers where they belong is obviously more important."

"You're really convincing me." Bonnie wished they were kids again and she could do the nut sack double tap as she'd called it. He deserved it for hoping she'd chopped off a finger. "Do I want to know about the bet?"

"We had a bet going to see who you would call first if you ever cut your finger off. That was a hypothetical. It could be any emergency, physical or otherwise."

Bonnie knew Stumpy well enough to know he was probably shuffling his feet double time to keep up with his nerves, and if he was really worked up, he'd have started to sweat.

"Don't tell the others, but it'd always be you." Bonnie smiled when she heard Stumpy's sharp, happy intake of breath through the phone. "My injury eventualities aren't why I called. I wanted to talk about my rented house."

"Okay." Stumpy dragged out the last part of the word in a way that let Bonnie know he'd rather not talk about it. She didn't care, she needed his opinion.

"What do you think of it?" Bonnie climbed into the cab of the truck while she waited. Turned out Branch was right. It was windy.

Stumpy didn't seem to be in a chatty mood. Finally, he began diplomatically. After he got that out of the way, he was less guarded. "I've never been there and seen any part of your personality coming through. Do you have a single piece of art hung anywhere?"

Bonnie pictured the rooms in her house. "I do not. I came to this conclusion late in life, but I'm here now. I need to live somewhere different."

"You need to live somewhere different or you need someone in your life to make you care enough that your house looks like a stripped naked Ikea?" There was laughter in Stumpy's voice.

Even though she knew he wasn't laughing at her, Bonnie couldn't help the annoyance that stormed to the surface.

"Before you get grumpy and hang up on me, you should think about it. This isn't me shrinking you, this is me being your friend. If you don't have any art to hang on the wall, that's going to be a problem at a new place too." The laughter was gone from Stumpy's voice. He was serious and sounded concerned.

"I can buy art." Bonnie knew she sounded defensive. She was working double-time to keep images of her house, the house she shared with Grace, out of her mind.

Before her mind could venture down a path to nowhere good, her thoughts were interrupted by a loud "crack".

"Holy fuck."

"Runt, you okay? What was that?" Stumpy sounded four levels past concerned now.

Bonnie started her truck, jammed it into reverse, and hit the gas hard. The phone connected via bluetooth so in addition to her thudding heart, she was treated to Stumpy's increasingly frantic hollering.

"I'm okay, Stumpy, by about three feet. You know that oak out front of my place that we always say is one wind gust away from coming down? Well, if I were a betting man, I'd push all my chips in right now. A big ass branch almost took out my truck." Bonnie was gulping air as she talked, trying to find a way to slow her heart and stop the shaking of her hands. She'd watched the branch start to fall as if in slow motion, convinced it was about to land in her lap.

She pulled over just outside the driveway, out of the range of the tree. She watched it swaying wildly, whipping back and forth far more than it should if it was solidly rooted.

"It's not that windy is it? You sure you're okay?" Stumpy sounded shaken up himself.

There was another deafening "crack" and the tree, slowly at first and then all at once, tumbled to the ground. Normally, Bonnie would have appreciated that the tree would now have a new life as a home to animals, bugs, and bacteria, and continue to nurture the soil and animals nearby.

"The universe has a sick sense of humor, Stump. I think you win the emergency phone call bet even if I technically called you before a tree landed on my house." Bonnie stared at her house hoping if she looked long enough the tree crashed through half the roof would magically disappear.

"Did you say the tree landed on your house?"

Bonnie took a picture and sent it to Stumpy. She added Carl and Duck as well. She knew they'd drop everything and rush over, so she sat in her truck and waited.

Fifteen minutes later, her friends were all standing with her, surveying the damage. Most of the first responders in town had shown up too. It was clearly a slow night in Garrison. Before she'd had a chance, someone had called Bonnie's landlord, so he was there too. She'd known him for years and they had a good relationship.

"Ah shit, Bonnie. I should have cut that tree down years ago. I'll get on the phone with my insurance and see if I can get you put up somewhere while we figure this out." He shook his phone as he trundled off to make some calls.

"You're not staying at a junker motel while they yank branches and squirrels out of your underwear drawer. Come stay with us."

Duck slung his arm over Bonnie's shoulder. "Fewer diapers for me to change."

"Speaking of underwear, what do you need us to get out of there for you?" Carl pointed to the house.

"I'm not letting you go in there." The adrenaline was wearing off. All Bonnie really wanted was her bed and pillow.

"Don't get me wrong, Runt, but you don't look like you could stop me if I had both hands tied behind my back. If you don't tell me what you want, I'm bringing back your toilet bowl cleaning brush, two left shoes, your ugly Christmas sweater, and one grape." Carl was scowling with his hands on his hips.

"I appreciate your willingness to risk your life for my toilet brush." Bonnie hugged him.

She didn't pull away immediately. Carl held on tightly and Duck and Stumpy surrounded her on either side.

"Alright, let me go before your man stink gets all over me." Bonnie wiggled free.

She settled on the tailgate of her truck while Carl and Duck wandered toward the group of firefighters staring at her house. She hadn't been specific about what they should grab if they made their way inside, she'd probably care more in the next couple days, but right now, it was too overwhelming.

Stumpy hopped up beside her. "You're welcome to stay with me too, you know. I'm sure Carl would say the same."

"I know, but you can't cook and at least with Duck I can help out with Avery." Bonnie looked at her house again and shook her head. She laughed. "What the actual fuck?"

Stumpy bumped his shoulder into Bonnie's. "Don't mean to point out the obvious here, but there is another housing option. You as much as admitted your life is more vibrant with her in it."

"She invited me to move in with her." Bonnie looked at Stumpy and shrugged. "I said no." Despite everything she laughed. It started small and then erupted into a full chested body shaking guffaw.

Stumpy joined her. "I don't know what other kind of sign you need, but I'd say the universe has spoken. Call the woman. I'll break the news to Duck."

Stumpy was right even if she didn't like it. Except part of her did and that was a problem. If this was Lionel interfering again his sense of humor needed some work. She seized the moment and dialed Grace. She didn't answer so Bonnie left a message. She hung up and stared at her phone as if it might come alive. "Holy shit." Bonnie resisted the strong desire to call right back and say it was all a joke. If she did that though, she knew she'd regret it and want to recant the recantation. That wasn't a merry-go-round she wanted any part of.

The longer she looked at the house with the wild branches and leaves sticking out from her roof, the more uncomfortable she became with what she'd set in motion. Was she wild to think that moving into the house she and Grace shared could possibly work? She knew it would entail plenty of temptation and reminders as to how much her heart had to lose. She was moving there, to live right down the hall from the woman she'd loved since before they could drive.

Living down the hall as roommates and friends couldn't be worse torture than what she'd put herself through the past fifteen years. Surely she could be satisfied with living under the same roof as nothing more than friends. At least she was pretty sure she could. How often did second chance love stories in real life end in happily ever after anyway? A stolen kiss or a searing look were all well and good, she and Grace could retreat to the safety of their homes at the end of the evening. But what happened when the only retreats were down the hall from each other? Bonnie put her head in her hands. Maybe a tree falling on her house was the least of her problems.

CHAPTER SEVENTEEN

Grace stood in the kitchen drinking coffee, in her pajamas. She was still getting used to not being alone for her first cup of the morning. Bonnie had moved in about a week prior. Truth be told, having Bonnie down the hall was harder than Grace had anticipated. She was only human, and knowing someone she found so damn attractive was one bed down had made for some interesting dreams.

Something was affecting Bonnie too because their interactions had been strained.

"I have an early day today so I'm taking my coffee to go." Bonnie's tone was curt and she looked flustered. She filled her to-go mug, grabbed a granola bar from a box on the counter, and rushed from the kitchen.

Grace put her coffee cup on the counter, dejected. They were still working out the roommate relationship and Bonnie certainly didn't owe her anything, but a "good-bye" would have been nice.

As soon as the thought floated through her mind, Bonnie popped back around the corner. "Your jammies are fantastic and I'll see you later. I hope you have a good day."

Grace looked down at her pajamas. They were damn fantastic. The button-up top and sleep shorts were covered in dapper looking hedgehogs in top hats. They'd been a gift from an influencer she'd had overlapping circles with a few years back. He'd faded from her life, but the pajamas remained a staple.

Almost as soon as the front door closed, Grace's phone rang. She half expected it to be Bonnie. There was no good reason she'd be calling, but Grace was still disappointed it wasn't her on the other end of the line. Luckily, it was Madison, who was almost as good.

"So, how was the first week of living together?" Madison didn't even say hello.

"How many times do I have to repeat, we didn't move in together. She moved here to live in a room in the house she half owns after a tree fell on her house. You can call us roommates, housemates, whatever you want, but we didn't move in together." Grace ground her teeth.

"Going that well, huh? Which nerve did I hit? 'I'd like to fuck her but can't,' 'This was the worst mistake of my life,' 'She's amazing and I'm going to pine in the corner,' or 'Why did I ever think she was attractive?' Is it one of those?"

Grace rolled her eyes even though Madison couldn't see her. "Is there a none of the above answer? We're both adjusting but it's been fine. The house isn't so quiet and that's very nice."

Madison snorted on the other end of the phone. "Nice. Fine. I know when you're lying, Gracie, but I'll let you keep fooling yourself a little longer. I'm planning a trip out there since you extended your stay. I want to see your Bonnie for myself."

"She's not *my* Bonnie, but you know that because I've reminded you over and over. I'm not falling into the trap again." Grace pinched the bridge of her nose. "I'd love to see you."

"And see me you shall. You're going to have to show me around your little village. You must know everyone by now." Madison sounded excited.

Grace didn't answer right away. She desperately wanted to lie and feed into Madison's assumption. Unfortunately, as soon as Madison set foot in Garrison, Grace's lie would be exposed.

"Actually, I've only met a handful of people. I've been busy with the house." It was a stretch of the truth. If you counted a handful as the folks Bonnie had introduced her to and the honeymooning couple, that put her close to a handful.

"You can't spend all your time alone with your father's things or with Bonnie and your complicated feelings for her. You extended your leave and aren't coming back here anytime soon from what I can tell. If you're trying to build a life there, you can't rely on her to be your end-all be-all. That's not healthy for any kind of relationship." Madison sounded worried.

"You're fretting for no reason. I'm not trying to build a life here. I have a life there. I only need a little more time to figure out everything here. I underestimated how much time it would take to take care of my father's affairs. That's all." Grace chewed her lower lip. Was that true or was she lying to herself? "I didn't want to interact with her at all when I got here, if you remember. It's sort of accidentally worked out this way, but she's not the only person I know here."

Madison carried on as if Grace hadn't interrupted her. "What you need is a hobby. Guitar lessons, LARPing, animal shelter volunteer, something."

"I could hang out in the bar a couple of hours a day. Nearly everyone in the village is in and out of there at some point." Grace didn't want to sign up for LARPing.

"Would you talk to anyone or simply smile and nod from your booth and never say a word?"

Grace could hear Madison tapping a pencil on her desk. She didn't want to answer Madison's question.

"Your silence speaks volumes, my friend. You were a social butterfly in LA. Beyond a butterfly. What is a group of butterflies called?" Madison was all business now.

"A kaleidoscope." Grace high-fived herself.

"Why do you know things like that?" Madison paused before diving back in. "You were like an entire kaleidoscope of butterflies before and now you're playing house with your ex-girlfriend and your social circle is down to less than the number of polka dots on my favorite velour pantsuit. You need a hobby and I'm coming out soon. Prepare yourself."

After they hung up, Grace couldn't stop thinking about a potential hobby, or Madison's pantsuit. She wanted to curse Madison, but she was right, Grace needed something that was all her own, even if she was only here a short while longer. It wasn't good for her to spend all her time alone in the house or waiting for Bonnie to get home so they could spend time together. She was a few polka dots short in the friend department. The most obvious solution she could think of was to call Ms. Babs. If anyone knew the underground hobby network in Garrison, it was going to be her.

Although she still had slight misgivings, Grace called Ms. Babs. As expected, she was a gold mine of information. She knew about everything from art galleries to zombie-themed paint ball fights.

No matter how hard Grace tried to explore all the options she'd quickly jotted down, the idea of a ceramics class tickled her fancy. She visited the website listed for the pottery studio and realized the class that best matched her skill and experience, both none, started this evening. Best of all, the class was only four weeks long and then cycled again so it wasn't a long term commitment.

Without overthinking, Grace paid her registration fee and sent in her paperwork. As soon as she was registered, she put her coffee cup in the sink and marched up the stairs to get dressed for the day. No matter what was on the agenda, aside from pottery, she felt ready to tackle it. Madison was right, as usual. Having something for herself to look forward to put a spark in her step.

Before going downstairs, she stopped at the closed door to her dad's room. She took a deep breath and opened the door. A wave of nostalgia and grief hit her along with the smell that was uniquely his. She wanted to flee from the room and the scent of him while at the same time never wanting to leave.

Sometimes lately it felt like she couldn't remember the sound of his voice or his laugh, but she didn't need to remember how he smelled because it was all around her. If she never changed a thing about the room, would it remain when she needed his comfort? Logically, she knew that it wouldn't, that in fact it might be gone the next time she opened the door, but being wrapped in it today was enough. On the heels of so much upheaval and her chat with Madison, having her father all around felt like a sign of approval from above. Maybe this was what he wanted for her, or maybe he was at least proud of the steps she was taking to find her way to home, wherever that was.

The selfish side of her wanted to keep the joy of feeling so close to him for herself. But she knew how much he meant to Bonnie too, and the idea of keeping this feeling from her felt cruel. She'd let Bonnie decide when she got home later.

She gently closed the door, kissed her hand, and pressed it against the smooth wood. She felt tears amassing, ready to fall in line and streak down her cheeks, but she didn't want to cry. Getting a moment where it felt like her dad was with her, living and breathing, instead of slipping further away, was joyous. She didn't want to fall into the sadness of grief now. She hustled down the stairs as fast as she safely could, as if she might outrun the feelings she knew could always find her.

What she needed was to get out of the house and focus on something else. Without much thought to destination or purpose, Grace locked up the house and took her car for a spin through the back roads of Garrison. It didn't take long to cover most of the village, but she expanded her area outside the village limits. Once her inspection was complete, she drove to the bar on Main Street. She could be social if she wanted. Time to prove Madison wrong.

After a couple of hours in the bar, Grace had made quite a few new acquaintances, with the potential for a friend or two. Despite more than one of her former classmates being there, none of them made a big deal about her presence or her strained past and present with the village.

Before she knew it, it was time to go to her first pottery class. She left herself enough time to get through LA traffic in her anxious anticipation so she was the first one to arrive by a large margin. By the time class started there were four more students, two Latina high school aged girls, an elderly white woman, and a frazzled looking white woman who was vaguely familiar to Grace, although she couldn't place her.

The other students were nice, focused on their work, and far more skillful than Grace at turning clay into something beautiful. Even when faced with her own inferiority, she found the experience invigorating. Even if she never made a passable bowl, cup, or figurine, her grief, confusion, and responsibilities didn't follow her in the door.

"Are you Grace Cook?" The familiar woman scooted her clay closer to Grace.

"I am. You look familiar, but I'm not very good with names and faces." Grace tried again to place the woman.

"It's been years. We had English and Calculus together in high school."

Grace looked at her one more time and it clicked into place. "Tanya? It's nice to see you. How are you?" It was nice to see her. Was it the magic of the pottery studio warping Grace's standoffish nature? But she wasn't usually standoffish. That part of her only came out to play in Garrison since she left after high school.

"I'm glad to see you back in Garrison. We all end up back here eventually, don't we? I tried but couldn't stay away either. I'm sorry about your dad." Tanya rolled another clay coil exactly like the instructor had shown them.

Grace looked at her own attempt at a coil. It looked like a lumpy pickle. She made another half-hearted attempt to get the clay to behave. "What made you come back?" Grace gave up on her coil and sat on her stool so she could more fully look at Tanya.

"Oh, lots of reasons, I think. I was living in Dallas and I didn't realize it, but it felt like the city was suffocating me. My husband and I started talking about having kids, and I imagined them growing up there." Tanya put aside her coil and sat facing Grace. "Garrison isn't perfect of course, but I liked growing up here. I guess I was called home."

A lump formed in Grace's throat. Suffocating. She never would have come up with that to describe how she felt in LA, but that was exactly the feeling. "I know that suffocating feeling." Grace poked at the pickle coil. "I've lived in LA a long time and it's certainly nothing like Garrison."

"You're home now though, right?"

Tanya didn't look nosy or overly curious. She looked like a fellow traveler encouraging Grace to finish the final leg of a grueling journey.

Grace hesitated. She chewed her lower lip. "I don't know." The admission surprised her. "I had no intention of staying when I came back for the funeral, but now I'm not sure. My life's still in LA, I'm only taking extended time off to settle my dad's affairs." Grace felt compelled to rush the last part out, maybe to make it true.

Tanya looked like she knew something Grace didn't. "Take your time, you'll know what's right when you need to." Tanya pointed to Grace's coil. "Do you need some help with that?"

"Yes, please. I fear I'm hopeless, but I'm going to keep coming back because it's so much fun." Grace handed over her malformed affront to clay coils.

Tanya showed her how to more easily roll the clay and they chatted while they both worked on their projects. By the end of class Grace had a few respectable coils and Tanya had formed hers into a very shapely bowl.

Grace promised to return the following week, and Tanya seemed genuinely happy to hear it. It was strange to feel so elated after playing with clay and having a perfectly normal conversation for an hour. Madison was right about the scale of her social interactions in LA, but twenty of them had a third of the nourishment and quality she'd gotten out of casual conversation with Tanya. But none of her relationships in LA had deep seated roots. Every relationship in Garrison was sprouted in her marrow. If anything should have felt suffocating, she'd always assumed it would be the small village, but now all she found was comfort.

On the way back to the car, Grace pulled out her phone and called Bonnie. "Have you had dinner yet?" Grace startled at how couple-ish and comfortable that question felt.

Bonnie's voice sounded inviting and provocative when she murmured "no." Grace was sure it was because Bonnie was still working and was probably jammed in a tight space or hanging upside down from the rafters or something, but it didn't stop her body from reacting. If Bonnie's feet were planted firmly on the ground, was that a voice reserved only for her? She knew she couldn't wish it to be so since she and Bonnie had decided those kinds of wishes shouldn't be part of their joint future.

"I'm picking up takeout. Can I tempt you?" Grace moved to a safer topic.

There was a long pause. "Always." Another long pause. "I'm starving. Where are you stopping?"

"Craving anything in particular?" After it was out of her mouth, Grace realized how her question sounded, especially coupled with the rest of the conversation.

"Are you teasing me?" Bonnie sounded amused, not angry.

"What would I have to tease you about?" Grace knew she was smiling like a goof. She was glad Bonnie couldn't see her. This banter had been missing since they'd started sharing the house and she hadn't realized how much she'd missed it. "I'm asking you about dinner."

"I guess you are. In that case, you choose. I'll eat anything." Was that regret in Bonnie's voice?

Grace couldn't help the "harumph" that escaped and her tightened grip on the steering wheel. "I hope you have higher standards than that. I'll be disappointed if I see that you don't."

"Are we still talking about dinner?" Bonnie's voice was soft.

"Do you still want us to be?" Grace's heart felt as though it was trying to escape her chest. It was certainly beating at a rate well exceeding what was displayed on the car speedometer.

"I thought we decided that wasn't a path we should tread." The regret was obvious in Bonnie's voice now.

Grace was silent while she fumbled for a way to answer. Yes, Bonnie had decided that. Did she still agree with her?

"Whatever we decided, I can care about you. I can want what's best for you." Grace pulled into the parking lot of the best pizza joint in northern Rhode Island. "We're having pizza, FYI. I hope that's okay."

"One of my favorite things." Bonnie sounded like a little kid being told Christmas was now a monthly event. "I'll have the table set and a glass of wine waiting for you."

The idea of Bonnie meeting her at the door, in her go-to after-work outfit of athletic shorts and a T-shirt, with a glass of wine and a smile, sounded like a daydream come true. The problem was Grace had been having a lot of those kinds of daydreams. Many more than she should be if they were going to continue a "friends only" relationship. Most friends didn't imagine scenarios including their friends greeting them in their after-work attire and that same attire strewn across the floor on the way to the bedroom.

Those frisky, unruly thoughts were always followed with the question "what's wrong with me?" but she knew, deep down, the answer was nothing. Nothing was wrong with her because she'd never stopped being attracted to Bonnie. She was the standard by which every woman in Grace's life had been judged since she'd left Garrison.

Spending time with Bonnie had guaranteed no one would ever live up to the standard she'd set, which was proving inconvenient. Surely Grace could be happy with someone in tier two. Except she hadn't been thus far and didn't see how she ever could be. Nearly four million people lived in LA and so far not a single one came close to meeting her expectations.

Except they were there and Bonnie was here. Bonnie meant the terrifying possibility of heart-crushing pain and rejection, again, but Grace was a different person now. Bonnie was too. It was easy to remember the shock and sadness that followed their breakup all those years ago, but not always how much they'd loved each other and why Bonnie had done what she'd done. She also had to factor in how much it would hurt seeing Bonnie with a girlfriend. A wife. Grace's stomach felt like it dropped from her body and her mouth felt dry.

Bonnie seemed to bring out strong emotions in her, no matter the context. Perhaps there was a downside to Bonnie living down the hall. If she brought home an overnight guest, Grace wasn't sure she'd handle it well. Nothing like being the clichéd crazy ex-girlfriend. The question was, should she take a risk and do something to address her feelings and if so, what the hell should she do?

CHAPTER EIGHTEEN

Stumpy and Carl pulled into the driveway and Duck, Candace, and Avery migrated across the field from their house. Bonnie watched from the porch as her friends arrived. Even her toes were tingling with excitement. As much as she loved the annual camping trip, there was something about prep day that she gleefully anticipated even more.

"Are we being invaded?" Grace joined Bonnie on the porch and looked at the coordinated arrival.

"No, it's prep day." Bonnie looked happily at the scene all around her. She was inordinately happy Grace was sharing the camping experience this year.

"So we're doing the invading?" Grace smiled over her coffee mug as she took a sip.

Bonnie was struck speechless by Grace. Her hair was loosely pulled back, but strands had escaped and were framing her face playfully. She looked content standing on the porch with her morning coffee, gazing at Bonnie as if there was nowhere else she'd rather look. It was heady and dangerous. Bonnie didn't look away. If they were alone Bonnie might have said something about how beautiful Grace was, but with an audience she was satisfied holding eye contact a little longer than normal and hoping Grace saw Bonnie's feelings shining in her eyes.

"Damn straight." Carl hollered Grace's way as he tossed gear from the truck, breaking the spell. "State park won't know what hit it."

Duck high-fived Carl and Stumpy as he parked the wagon he'd been pulling next to the truck. "That's what I like to hear."

Candace looked at Grace. "It's not like that." She turned to the three guys. "You're making Grace think this is something it's not. The biggest threat to the campground is Avery and a sleep regression. Bonnie, back me up."

Bonnie shook her head. "Candace, you know I cannot tell a lie, especially on prep day. Invasion begins in one week. Let the planning begin." Bonnie jumped off the porch and climbed into the back of Carl's truck, grabbing gear and handing it down to the other three.

She could hear Candace's exasperated exclamations to Grace. "I love those four like crazy, but I swear they stopped growing up when they were fourteen. Bonnie's as bad as the others, if that information is something that would be of interest to you."

"She's awfully cute though, isn't she? They all are."

"Hey, Bonnie." Duck stopped unloading and called over to her. "Grace thinks you're cute."

Catcalls rang out from all three of the guys. Bonnie looked at Grace who was turning a lovely shade of scarlet. Her phone rang before anyone could tease her further and she sprinted into the house to answer.

Bonnie wanted to check on Grace, but that might embarrass her more. Plus she was on the phone. Stuck in emotional limbo, Bonnie grumbled at Duck and continued unpacking.

"Everyone's favorite moment, tent time." Stumpy pulled a tent from its stuff sack and unfurled it on the lawn.

Carl joined him and the two set about erecting the tent. Duck and Bonnie worked on another. By the time they finished there were four tents dotting the lawn.

"I'll be right back for inspection. Go ahead and start without me," Bonnie called over her shoulder to Stumpy as she half jogged to the porch. Grace was back from her phone call and still looked a little embarrassed. She looked up at Grace from the grass. It felt very Romeo and Juliet. "Are you okay? Sorry about Duck."

Candace was loitering a few feet away, under the guise of keeping an eye on Avery, but she was clearly glued to their conversation. Bonnie waved Grace farther down the porch. It wasn't that Candace couldn't know her feelings, it was that she wanted Grace to know about them first.

"I don't think I'm supposed to say this, but I liked that you thought it. I'll work harder to go for something other than cute next time, but I'm not complaining that you were looking." Bonnie searched for nonexistent dirt under her fingernails.

Grace hesitated a moment, looking unsure. Finally, she crooked a finger, drawing Bonnie closer. Grace leaned over so she was close to Bonnie. "You want to know what I was really thinking?"

Bonnie nodded silently. Her heart rate sped up and her nipples twinged.

"I was thinking that you were hot as hell. Now get back to work so I can watch."

It wasn't only her nipples that were paying attention now. She was turned on and hard as a rock. Did Grace know what she did to her and her resolve?

Grace took Bonnie by the shoulders, spun her around, and gave her a little shove back toward the guys and tents. "You know where to find me. I want to see what else is going to happen to our yard."

Bonnie shook her head a few times on the way to the tents to clear out some of the fuzz Grace's declaration had introduced. It was good she didn't have to operate heavy machinery or perform surgery right now. Bonnie had assumed she was the only one developing any kind of feelings in their friendship, that their flirting was fun but didn't mean to Grace what it meant to her, but Grace just blew up those assumptions. What did that mean for them? Bonnie sighed, deflating. It didn't mean anything for them. Grace thinking she was hot didn't change a thing about their circumstances.

All the same, it was scary knowing it wasn't an unattainable fairy tale. Acting on feelings and desire introduced consequences and stakes. Stakes she'd been working on avoiding. But holy hell was Grace worth it if it was guaranteed to work.

"Stumpy, a friend of mine will be visiting during the camping trip. Is there room for her to come along? If not, I'm going to have to bow out this year." Grace was off the porch and walking with purpose toward Stumpy. She passed Bonnie and slid her fingers down Bonnie's arm and briefly tangled them with Bonnie's.

It was a fifty-fifty gamble whether Bonnie was going to go down in a heap where she stood and need resuscitation. How was Grace all of a sudden so forward and playing her so easily?

"The more the merrier." Stumpy sounded delighted. "We'll have to shuffle the tents a little, but that's not a problem. Runt, you're in with Carl and me, just like the old days. Grace, you and your friend get Green Machine there." Stumpy pointed to a bright green, medium-sized tent that could easily accommodated two to three people plus bags.

Grace looked at Bonnie. She looked disappointed.

"You'd better not jam us all into Tiny Terror." Bonnie tried to see Stumpy's list, but he pulled it from view. "I'm not sleeping in that tent with the two of you."

"Oh come on, Runt, you make such a good sandwich filling. Why won't you snuggle with me?" Carl came over and wrapped Bonnie in a bear hug. He lifted her off the ground and she kicked him in the knee.

"No, Avery gets Tiny Terror as her play tent. We're in Honey Pot. Candace gets the Mansion." Stumpy pointed to tents as he assigned them.

"What about me?" Duck raised his hands at his sides and fake pouted.

"Talk to your wife," Carl, Stumpy, and Bonnie all answered him simultaneously.

"What's the point of all this?" Grace walked over to Green Machine and peeked inside. "Don't you have to pack it all back up now?"

Bonnie joined her. "Yes, but this way we can check to make sure our equipment is in working order. No one wants to get to the site and realize there's a hole in your tent or the camp stove doesn't work. Plus, the tents get aired out and it's fun."

Grace crawled into Green Machine and lay down in the middle, staring up at the domed ceiling. "Do you ever sleep out in the tents to give them a test run?"

"Not usually." Bonnie smiled. Was she reading the look on Grace's face correctly?

"Would you reconsider? I haven't been camping in years. A test run might be a good idea." Grace sat up on her elbows. Her eyes were smoldering as hot and beautiful as the glowing embers of a campfire.

Grace's new forwardness was unnerving. It made Bonnie want to run to protect both of them. At the same time, Grace was not the kind of woman you walked away from. She'd done it once and it had nearly broken her. The feelings she'd been stifling were eating her alive. Why should she deny herself what Grace seemed to be offering? Except she had to and she'd made that clear to Grace.

"I think it might be better if you asked Stumpy or Carl to show you the ropes." Bonnie had trouble looking Grace in the eye.

"You're probably right." Grace crawled out of the tent and placed a gentle kiss on Bonnie's cheek. "I'm sorry I got carried away." Grace strolled back toward the house. "I need to call Madison and tell her to pack for the woods. Will you boys need lunch?"

"No, we'll probably go to the bar. That's our usual pattern on prep day." Bonnie was distracted by the kiss.

"Have fun." Grace waved and headed inside with Candace and Avery.

Bonnie returned to the guys, who'd been watching the entire interaction.

"I'm not an expert, but I don't think I look at my friends that way." Carl made a kissy-face.

Duck looked confused. "Yes, you do. Every time Stumpy walks in, that's exactly how you look at him."

"I do?"

"He does?"

Everyone looked at Duck.

"I can't be the only one who's noticed. Bonnie? Stumpy?"

They all shook their heads.

"Oh, come on. You all have eyeballs and, Carl, I know you spend a lot of time on your computer, but feelings still happen in that heart of yours, right?" Duck was more animated.

Bonnie saw red creeping up Carl's neck. He didn't look happy with the direction the conversation was headed. Stumpy looked uncomfortable too.

"I'm starving. Let's get lunch. We can test the rest of the gear after we eat." Bonnie climbed in the driver's seat of Carl's truck and waited for everyone else to join her. She had her own reasons for wanting to move on from the last five minutes.

"Why are you driving?" Carl looked at the open passenger door, his arms crossed.

"Because you drive too slow and I'm hungry." Bonnie motioned for them to speed up.

Carl shrugged and climbed into the back seat of the extended cab. Stumpy was next to enter and without hesitation climbed in next to Carl. Bonnie looked at the two in the rearview mirror behaving as they always did, and relief washed over her. She wasn't sure what she'd do if this group fractured.

They bickered and teased each other on the drive, while they waited to be seated, and until their food arrived, as they'd been doing their whole lives. Bonnie had always felt at home and complete with them, but since Grace arrived back in Garrison and their past was stirred up again, a small hole in her life had started to develop. She'd never been jealous of Duck and Candace, but now she wondered, was it possible she could have that too?

"What's got you down, Runt? From where I stood, your morning looked pretty good." Duck elbowed her.

Bonnie dropped her head onto the table. "That's the problem, it was good. Too good." Bonnie sat back up and looked at her friends. Maybe the answer to her conundrum was written on one of their faces?

"To recap, you have a super hot woman, who you've never gotten over, looking at you like clothes and an audience are the only thing keeping the two of you from a good fuck, and you're pouting about it?" Carl looked unimpressed.

"I'm sure it's more complicated than that, Carl." Stumpy looked from Carl to Bonnie, his face sympathetic.

"No shrink stuff, Stumpy." Carl wagged a finger jokingly in Carl's direction.

"Carl, my shrink stuff, as you call it, stays in the office when I leave every day. I have no interest in evaluating everyone's issues outside of times I'm paid to do it. Why doesn't anyone understand it's my job, just like any other? I can turn it on and off and leave it behind when I'm done for the day. I'm not psychoanalyzing everyone all the time." Stumpy's face was flushed.

"Whoa. I didn't mean to hit a nerve." Carl held his hands out in front of him in a peace offering. "For what it's worth, I've never assumed you were trying to figure out my deal. Who would volunteer for that?"

Stumpy looked like he was going to respond but then looked at Bonnie and seemed to change his mind. "Let's get back to Runt. She's having a crap day even though she was kissed and, from what I overheard, propositioned for a bit of solo tent time with her roommate."

"I've got no complaints about the kiss or the tent time invitation. It's all the rest that's got me twisted up. Grace was clear she was willing to go down that road with me again, but I said no." Bonnie scrubbed her face.

"Dude, what do you want?" Duck was hard to understand around a mouthful of fries.

"I don't know." Did you have to cross your fingers as an adult if you lied?

Duck scowled. "Bullshit. You know. I've never seen you act chickenshit. Why are you now? Grace deserves better than this version of you, that's for sure."

Bonnie looked at her friends, one after another. Stumpy and Carl didn't look like they disagreed with Duck's blunt assessment.

She swallowed, her mouth suddenly dry. "Is that the consensus of the league? That I'm a cowardly fool and don't deserve Grace?"

Carl whistled slowly.

Duck rolled his eyes.

Stumpy reached out and put his hand on Bonnie's shoulder. "No one said that, Runt."

"The consensus of the league is get your head out of your ass." Duck shoved another handful of fries in his mouth. "We care too much about you to not be honest."

"It's warm and snug up there. My head likes it right where it is. What happens if I do something about the way I feel, I take a shot at my second chance, and she decides I'm not enough for her? Or I blow it again? Or she goes back to her life in LA and I'm here with my life in tiny little pieces too small to put back together?" Bonnie snatched some fries off Duck's plate.

"If you leave your head up there too long, you never get a second chance." Stumpy looked like he was going to take Bonnie's hand, but swooped in to steal her pilfered fries instead.

What did Bonnie want between Grace and her? Flirting was fun, going beyond that was nerve-wracking. Bonnie didn't generally get nervous unless the stakes were high. They seemed to be reaching for the stars now.

"You're right. I was lying earlier." Bonnie plastered on a smile that she hoped projected more confidence than she felt. At least about her next move, she wasn't unsure of her feelings. "I might regret it, but I want more than an occasional peck on the cheek, but I only want it if we're going to have a real chance. That means we live in the same place."

"Then what are you waiting for?" Carl banged on the table with both hands. "Take my truck. Run home. Go get her. Convince her to stay."

"Whoa, dude, there's no other bar for miles. Don't get us banned from here." Bonnie put her hand over Carl's mouth. Stumpy and Duck each grabbed one of his arms. Bonnie noticed Stumpy's raised eyebrow as his hand wrapped around Carl's bicep. "I'm not running back there right now. I'm finishing my lunch and hanging out with my best friends."

"That's right, bros before—"

"Do not finish that sentence." Bonnie scowled.

"I wouldn't have. It tasted terrible in my mouth. I never would have disrespected Grace like that. I don't want you kicking my balls up into my chest to give me sexy man tits." Duck covered his nipples and gave a little squeeze.

"Candace would like you with man boobs." Bonnie pointed at Duck's chest. "Something to think about."

"As long as they didn't used to be my nuts." Duck broke into a ridiculous half smile. "We still want to make more little Candaces."

"Why are you rushing me out the door? Get home and start making babies. I want more nieces or nephews." Bonnie jokingly waved her hands at Duck to get him out the door.

Duck turned uncharacteristically serious. "It's been harder this time. It was so easy with Avery. It just happened with her. It's been months of trying and nothing. It's wearing on us both to be honest. Don't tell her I told you. She doesn't want anyone to know."

"Oh, shit. We're here for you, anything you need." Stumpy bumped shoulders with Duck.

"I keep thinking, what if all my boys are duds, you know? And the one that got us Avery was the last stud." Duck frowned and spun his beer glass.

Bonnie moved his beer when it threatened to slosh over. "Then you'll deal with it together, like you've done everything else. And like Stumpy said, we're all here for you, whatever we can do."

Duck nodded at each of them and took a big swig of his beer. He set it down then looked at Bonnie. "Let's get back to your sex life. More interesting than mine. You were about to run back and profess your undying love to Grace."

"That's not even close to what we were talking about." Bonnie took more of Duck's fries. She wanted to ask him more questions, but she knew he'd said all he was willing to share.

It wasn't long until they moved on to other topics. Bonnie didn't mind moving out of the spotlight. Although there was a part of her, maybe even most of her, that wanted to rush back to the house and talk to Grace, nothing much had changed in actuality. Maybe it had though because she'd said what she was feeling out loud. Perhaps that made the swirl of emotions she'd been wrestling with more concrete somehow. It sure felt that way. The question was, if Grace hadn't had the same epiphany was Bonnie willing to be the one to risk the first step down the path of no return?

CHAPTER NINETEEN

Grace paced at the bottom of the escalator outside the security gate at the one airport in Rhode Island. Despite knowing factually that Madison hadn't exited the plane yet, Grace was still worried somehow she'd missed her. She was waiting in the sole terminal at the airport, and although it wasn't large, it wasn't so small that it couldn't accommodate plenty of strangers, Grace, and her bundle of excitement and nerves.

Finally, Madison descended the escalator, dressed in her LA best, looking like a queen walking amongst her subjects. She squealed when she saw Grace and ran to her.

After a long, enthusiastic, loud greeting, Madison held Grace at arm's length and looked at her intently. "Gracie, you really are happy here, aren't you? You look like Bilbo without the weight of the ring."

Grace rolled her eyes. "You know I have no idea what you're talking about when you go full fantasy simile on me, right?"

"I know you're not going out every night and getting home when you used to. Don't you have time to read a book I've been bugging you about for years?" Madison put her hand on her hip and raised her eyebrow.

"Don't try and trick me. It's not one book, it's four if 'I'm going to do it justice.' You'd never let me stop without also reading the trilogy." Grace put her arm around Madison's shoulders as they walked to baggage claim. "How many bags are we waiting for?"

"Would you believe me if I said one?"

Grace shook her head laughing. "No way. I know you better than that."

Madison joined her laughter. "Fine, but I did well. I only packed two. And they're small. You said to pack for the woods, which ruled out most of my wardrobe. Who cares about my clothes though? I want to know about your Bonnie. Tell me everything."

"There's not much to tell." Grace frowned. "She's actually been a little skittish the last week. The initial weirdness at the house seemed to be settling, but now I'm worried I spooked her."

Madison hauled two bags, that Grace would never have labeled small, off the conveyor belt and they headed for the exit, each pulling one.

"What did you do, Gracie? Do you have a naughty side I've never known about?" Madison looked like she was going to vibrate out of her sky-high heels.

Grace felt like her face had become as hot as the surface of the sun. "I kissed her on the cheek and suggested I wouldn't be opposed to some pre-trip camping lessons. Just the two of us."

Madison raised an eyebrow as she loaded her bags into the back of Bonnie's truck. Grace had borrowed it anticipating Madison's baggage needs.

"Were you asking for help making a fire with two sticks or how to avoid poison oak?"

"Not exactly." Grace had a hard time not getting tingly in all the fun places thinking back to her blatant and suggestive flirting. "I suggested I might need help figuring out the tent."

Madison nearly spit out her sip of water. "Yes, zippers are very complicated."

"She seemed to be on the same page at first, but then said it wasn't a good idea. Since then, I don't know, it's been a little weird. I feel like she runs away from me every time we spend more than a few minutes together." Grace gripped the steering wheel tightly as she pulled out of the airport parking lot and headed for home.

"Do you want to zip her up in a tent and have your way with her?" Madison sounded confused. "I thought you were steering clear of Bonnie-shaped entanglements. All evidence to the contrary since you're now living together, but we can table that one for now."

Grace grumbled about the living together comment but didn't fight her on it again. The roommate argument didn't hold as much water with Madison since Grace had just confessed to inviting Bonnie to a tent sleepover.

"I thought flirting was harmless. We were both having fun." Grace's shoulders drooped.

"Flirting with the woman you were in love with for years, then avoided for even longer, and now own a house with? How is that working out for you?" Madison cupped her hand around her ear and held it closer to Grace. "I'm all ears."

"Easy for you to say, you've never met her. Once we get back to our place, you tell me if you would restrain yourself. Besides, you know what they say about hindsight." Grace batted her eyes at Madison.

"Blaming hindsight is for when you've done something dumb you wish you could have seen coming. Have you done anything to back up all your sexy talk and innuendos about tents?" Madison's eyes lit up when they pulled in the driveway, but she made no move to get out.

Grace turned off the truck and turned to face her. "No, remember, she shot me down. I felt kinda dumb and embarrassed even though I said I understood."

"Ugh." Madison flopped her head back dramatically. "It's a good thing I'm here or the two of you would mope alone in your rooms for the rest of your days. How was she looking at you when you asked her to fuck you on the lawn?"

"That's not the point." Grace tried to wave her finger at Madison to make a point, but Madison swiped it away.

"Of course it's the point. If you want her and she wants you, then get after it. Either agree to fuck and flirt and have fun and accept that it's going to hurt at the end when you leave or convince her you're staying."

"What do you want me to do, tell her what we have isn't working and strip her naked against the refrigerator?" Grace wished she didn't sound so unsure, even with her best friend.

Madison shrugged. "Sure, that sounds like a fun show. But it doesn't really matter what I want because I doubt I'd be invited. If you'd wanted me in your bed, you'd have asked a long time ago."

Grace was so startled her snap reply died on her lips. "Is that something you wanted? With me I mean?"

Madison winked. "There were a few drunken nights in college I wouldn't have said no, but that was a long time ago. All I want from you is the friendship we have and for you to figure out what makes you happy."

"What if she's not worth the risk? What if I get hurt again?" Grace leaned her head against the steering wheel.

"As you said, I've never met her, so I can't answer either of those, but you probably should before you zip in for an overnight camping lesson. Or at least answer whether scratching the itch you both clearly have knowing there will be pain at the end is worth it. Good sex with the right person can outweigh a lot of heartache." Madison looked around the truck. "Enough wallowing in this truck that is clearly not yours. If it belongs to her, I'm a little in love already. Take me to your Bonnie." Madison poked Grace in the side until she sat up and exited the truck.

As they approached the house and climbed the worn porch steps, Grace tried to see her house through Madison's eyes. Did she see all the work that needed to be done or the love that had seeped into every floorboard and joist? Could she see the care Bonnie had taken with every item on her list, or were those details only she could see?

"You might have shown me a picture once, Gracie, but this is beautiful." Madison shaded her eyes and took in the house.

"Yes, she is." Bonnie rose from the porch swing, looking directly at Grace.

Grace felt warmth spread through her chest. Her stomach did a little tap dance. How did she get Bonnie to keep looking at her like that? Like she was the only thing precious to her in the world.

"This tall drink of water must be Bonnie. I'm Madison. It is so very nice to meet you." Madison sashayed halfway up the porch steps and casually offered her hand to Bonnie.

With a smile, Bonnie took her hand and kissed it. Grace pictured ripping Madison's arm off and beating her with it. What was she thinking? Bonnie was off limits.

"I'll get your bags if you two want to get inside. I was in the mood for Arnold Palmers so there's some iced tea and lemonade in the fridge if you're interested." Bonnie hopped off the porch and toward her truck.

Madison leaned close as she and Grace ogled Bonnie's ass. "You did not tell me she was this level of hot. How do you let her walk around with clothes on? Could we bribe her to take some off?"

"Stop it, she'll hear you." Grace jabbed Madison in the ribs. "It's creepy to ask someone not to wear clothes all day so you can stare at them, by the way, at least around here. You can't get away with the same things you can back in LA."

"Fine, if you're not interested in her, let me know. I have no problem pinch hitting for the star quarterback taking a shot on the net with time running out to win the game." Madison threw her hands in the air like she'd won a championship.

"Don't you dare touch her." Grace looked at Madison to make sure she hadn't actually breathed the fire it felt like she was capable of. "And your sports, whatever that was, is a mess."

Madison looked like a cat who ate the canary. "Just friends, huh?" Madison put her arm around Grace and steered her inside. "How upset would you be if someone at one of our LA parties told you they were going to see if they could catch my attention?"

"So what? That's different." Grace shook Madison off and went to the kitchen for some lemonade.

"That's exactly my point." Madison was still looking around the living room.

"What's the point?" Bonnie was slightly out of breath, probably from carrying the bags up the stairs. A bead of sweat threatened to trickle down her cheek.

Grace stood paralyzed, a glass of lemonade in one hand, the pitcher in the other. The fridge door was still open, but she couldn't move to close it. All she could do was stare at Bonnie. She was so gorgeous, in her unique androgynous way, it made Grace's heart ache but also represented everything Grace had been avoiding for fifteen years. It didn't seem to matter. Her illogical, wild, adventurous heart was determined to follow its arrow, and that arrow seemed to point, without fail, in Bonnie's direction. Her brain didn't stand a chance.

"Hey, are you okay?" Bonnie looked worried. She darted quickly around the island, closed the fridge, and took the pitcher and glass from Grace and put them on the counter.

Grace balled her fists in Bonnie's shirt. She leaned her head on Bonnie's strong chest and took a deep breath. "Probably not." She looked up and met Bonnie's worried gaze.

Before Bonnie could ask anything further, Grace spun them and backed Bonnie against the fridge. She let go of Bonnie's shirt so she could cup her face as she kissed her. It was gentle at first, but as Bonnie seemed to get over the initial shock and they deepened the kiss, Grace wrapped her arms around Bonnie. She let Bonnie hold her and pull her close. "Just don't hurt me again."

It felt as if fifteen years of pressure was rapidly releasing as they kissed. They fought for supremacy and frantically sought more from each other. Grace was lost in the feel of Bonnie's lips. They were softer than she expected and, although familiar, still filled with the thrill of discovery.

Bonnie tasted of lemonade. Grace nipped at her lower lip, which made Bonnie's eyes widen in surprise. She smiled and tangled her hands in Grace's hair, teasing her tongue along Grace's top lip.

Grace was lost in the feel of Bonnie holding her, kissing her, and the way her own body was responding. She didn't hear Madison come into the kitchen until she gasped with surprise and then cried out with glee.

"Yes! I knew you were more than roommates."

Bonnie flew away from Grace, looking ready to bolt. Her hair was disheveled, and it looked like her emotions were just as wild. Before Grace could offer solace, Bonnie mumbled something unintelligible and shot from the room.

Madison looked chagrined. "Sorry. I didn't mean to spook her. I was excited for you is all."

Grace looked in the direction Bonnie had run. She yearned to chase her, but Madison was here, now was not the time. "We'll talk later. I probably shouldn't have done that, she'd been clear she doesn't want to pursue anything. I don't know what I was thinking, but it didn't seem like she minded."

Madison's eyes went huge and her mouth fell open. "Minded? Girl, I know for a fact I've never been kissed like that, but I would pay good money for someone to do it. If you'd kept at it much longer, I was going to get that lemonade and cool myself off."

"It's probably good you interrupted. I don't know if I would have stopped, but I do know I'm not ready for more than that, yet. I honestly forgot everything except her, even the fact that you were here." Grace shivered at the thought of "more."

For the rest of the day, Grace didn't have a chance to talk to Bonnie. She and Madison spent their time catching up and packing for the camping trip. Grace could hear Bonnie outside, banging around, hammering and sawing, but aside from a couple of trips in for water or a bathroom break, Bonnie seemed most comfortable outside and away from Grace and Madison.

Around dinner, Grace was surprised to hear tires on their gravel driveway. She peeked out the window and saw Stumpy and Carl piling out of Carl's truck. Madison joined her at the window.

"Who are those two fine looking gentlemen?" Madison gave a slow whistle.

Grace gave Madison a playful shove. "You're on the prowl over here? What about your wonderful LA life? It's very different in Garrison."

"Oh, I can see that already." Madison tackled Grace onto her bed and straddled her. She leaned over so their faces were close. "But clearly not all the beautiful people live in LA. How could I have missed that?"

There was a quick knock on the open door followed immediately by an abruptly halted boot tread.

"I didn't mean to. I should have." Bonnie was stumbling for words.

Grace tried to extricate herself from Madison who instead of getting up, turned on top of Grace to talk to Bonnie.

"Where have you been all day?" Madison seemed clueless to Bonnie's discomfort.

"Busy." Bonnie started to back out of the room. "The boys are here, I was going to see if you wanted to join us if I barbecued, but it looks like you're busy. We'll go to the bar."

"Madison, get up." Grace flailed once more and finally got out from under Madison.

Bonnie was already down the stairs. Grace took off after her. Madison was right behind her.

"Did she think we were, you know?"

"What else would she think we were doing? You were on top of me about an inch from my face. It probably looked like you were about to kiss me." Grace saw Carl on the porch when she hit the entry so she knew they hadn't loaded up to leave yet.

"But everyone knows I'm not a top." Madison sounded confused behind Grace.

Grace couldn't help it, she stopped and hugged Madison. "Never change, Maddy. But maybe next time wait until after I've talked to her to climb on top of me?"

"It's hard to restrain myself, but I'll do my best. Go find your girl. I'm going to chat up some handsome gentlemen who look like they could use the company." Madison smacked Grace's ass on her way out the door.

Grace looked around. Where would Bonnie have gone? She stepped out onto the porch. "Carl, is Bonnie out here?"

Carl pointed around behind the house. He didn't smile his usual greeting and his eyes were guarded. Yikes, if she didn't fix this, she probably had three lifelong enemies in addition to losing Bonnie.

Grace picked her way through the long grass behind the house. Bonnie was sitting on a bench overlooking farmland stretching below their property. "You know this used to be my dad's favorite place to sit in the afternoon."

"We used to sit out here a lot together before he got too sick." Bonnie looked like she was staring farther away than across the pasture in front of them.

Grace's heart clenched. Why hadn't she come home sooner? Why had she sacrificed those moments with him to chase a career and a life she didn't want? "Can I sit?"

Bonnie moved over but didn't look at her. "Why did you kiss me?" Bonnie did turn to Grace now. There was pain in her eyes. "Why did you ignore what I asked and kiss me like that, like you couldn't ever get enough, on the same day *she* got here?"

"Look at me so I know you're hearing me, Bonnie Whitlock. I know what it looked like upstairs, but that's not what was happening." Grace took Bonnie's hand.

"Yeah, right." Bonnie tried to pull her hand away.

"You don't know Madison, but she doesn't believe in personal space. She was at that moment yelling at me for not introducing her to you, Carl, and Stumpy sooner because you're all so damn good-looking." Grace scooted closer and tentatively traced her finger along Bonnie's temple, down her cheek, and along her jawline. "I told her I'd better not see her lay even a single finger on you."

It was subtle, but Grace saw a small smile at the corners of Bonnie's mouth.

"Then why is she allowed to lay her whole body and lips on you?" Bonnie turned fully to Grace. She captured her hand and entwined their fingers.

"Is that jealousy I hear?" Grace moved closer.

"Trying to understand the ground rules." Bonnie draped Grace's arm over her shoulder and pulled Grace into her lap. "If we try this, I'm not sure I'm capable of giving us anything other than my full effort. The idea of someone else touching you wrenches my insides."

Bonnie lightly bit above Grace's pulse point. Grace gasped and pushed her sex closer against Bonnie's stomach. "The only one I want touching me is you."

Bonnie growled against Grace's neck and kissed her way along her jawline to her lips. "Should I tell her?" Bonnie stood, taking Grace with her.

Grace wrapped her legs around Bonnie's waist and kept her hands on Bonnie's shoulders and the back of her neck. "Trust me. She knows. I swear to you, we are friends. That's all we are now, all we've ever been, and all we will be in the future."

The longer they kissed, the more Bonnie's hands wandered, the harder Grace found it to still her hips and not grind against Bonnie's abs to find some relief for her throbbing clit. Was she ready for this?

Bonnie broke their kiss gasping. She pulled Grace close to her and held her tightly. "I don't know how much more control I have left. I think we need to stop."

Even though she was more turned on than she could ever remember, Grace was relieved. She unwrapped her legs and returned to standing. She continued to hold Bonnie close another minute. "Thank you for listening to me and trusting me." Grace kissed her again, more chastely this time.

Bonnie sat again and motioned for Grace to do the same. "Where does this leave us?" She took Grace's hand and rubbed her thumb over Grace's knuckles softly.

"Madison suggested a path I hadn't considered before." Grace's heart thundered and her insides felt quivery. "Even if we know a separation is in our future, can we love every minute we have now?"

Bonnie took her hand back, leaned forward on the bench, and ran her hands through her hair. She blew out a breath. She stood and paced a few feet away. "I want to say no to try and protect myself, but who am I kidding? Whether I walk away right now or you leave to go home in a week or a month, the pain will be there. I might be delaying the inevitable, but I'd rather double the pain later than walk away now." Bonnie smiled and helped Grace to her feet.

They walked back to the front of the house holding hands. Grace's heart felt light as if something had finally clicked into place. She knew she needed to find out how much more leave she could take and the end of this time with Bonnie was going to break her heart, but right now, she was embracing the happiness.

CHAPTER TWENTY

Bonnie's alarm went off at four a.m. Normally, she'd hit snooze until she was in danger of being late, but today she sprang out of bed. It was the first day of the annual camping trip and Bonnie felt like an overtightened windup toy. Now that her feet were on the ground she was off to the races.

She got ready quickly and tiptoed down the hall. She hesitated outside Grace's closed door. If Madison weren't also sleeping inside, would she be able to resist sneaking in to steal a kiss? It had only been two days since Grace had driven her trepidation away with a kiss to end all kisses, but the shift between them felt real and powerful. What that meant or would look like once Madison left was still a question mark. It was probably good she was here and they had the camping trip. Bonnie was still wrapping her head around being able to kiss Grace whenever she felt like it. She'd been holding back her growing feelings. and now that she let them out to play it felt like they were growing fast and wild. It seemed like Grace felt the same. Left unsupervised, living together, who knew what kind of trouble they'd get themselves into.

Bonnie continued down the stairs and made coffee. The night before she'd written herself a checklist. She looked it over as she sipped her first cup. She made a few notes, adding things she'd forgotten to get on the list the night before, or questioning what got packed into which vehicle. She'd always been in charge of logistics, just like Stumpy and Carl were in charge of food.

She was so wrapped up in her final review she didn't hear Madison come downstairs.

"Is that communal coffee or do I have to arm-wrestle you for it?" Madison yawned and made a weak attempt at flexing her bicep.

Bonnie nearly jumped through the ceiling in surprise. "What are you doing up so early? Aren't you jet-lagged?"

"Most nights I haven't gone to bed yet." Madison poured herself coffee. "The anticipation of seeing those lovely friends of yours is too much for me. Who can sleep when they know those boys will be back?"

"Stumpy and Carl?" Bonnie tried to discern if Madison was joking.

"What kind of name is Stumpy? And who is Runt? They kept talking about him and I nodded and smiled like I knew what they meant." Madison pulled up a stool.

"I'm Runt." Bonnie pushed her list to the side. Apparently, she was as prepped for loading as she was going to be. "Stumpy's name is Eugene, but I don't think anyone calls him that except a few people in his family. I guess his clients know his first name isn't Stumpy, but I'm sure they call him Dr. Monroe."

Madison leaned her elbow on the kitchen island and her head on her elbow. Her elbow slid further along the slick island top until she was practically slumped across the granite. Whether it was practiced or accidental, Madison looked like she'd been posed that way instead to look her best.

"What's your deal with Grace?" Madison looked more awake now although she didn't sit up.

Bonnie barely contained the eye roll. "Is this the part where you threaten to break my fingers one at a time if I make her cry?"

"Do I look like a monster? I'd never do that to your sex life. Even if you're all alone those come in handy. I actually have a general, personal preference for nonviolence. Besides, why would I want to hurt you? She's happiest when you're around." Madison did sit up this time. "All I'm asking is what your deal is? Just fucking around? Looking for a wife to make baby Bonnies with?"

Bonnie got up and washed her coffee cup. "Until two days ago, having any kind of deal seemed like a fantasy. She said you were the one to suggest we embrace happy now, heartbreak later. Anything else that crosses my mind I think should probably be a discussion with her first."

"What discussion?"

For the second time that morning Bonnie nearly jumped out of her skin. This time Grace was the one to sneak up on her, but her protests evaporated when Grace snaked her arms around Bonnie's torso and she rested her head against the back of Bonnie's shoulders.

Grace kissed her between the shoulder blades, then reached around her for a coffee cup. "Good morning."

Bonnie wanted to pull Grace to her and give her a proper morning greeting, but she wasn't yet sure of the parameters of what they had started. Living together was a complication most people didn't have to deal with at this stage.

"No morning kiss? No breakfast in bed? Not even a gratuitous ass grab? This live action romance novel needs a few editorial notes."

Madison removed the empty coffee cup from Grace's hand and pulled her back to the entrance to the kitchen. "Turn back around toward the sink, stud. We're starting from the top."

"You're nuts, you know that, right?" Grace kissed Madison on the cheek. They were both smiling like they were sharing an inside joke. "Do as she says and it will be over soon." Grace motioned to Bonnie to turn around.

Bonnie complied. What in the world was Madison up to?

"You did great with the hug from behind, but you were too quick to go for the coffee mug. I'm here for the romance, I already have coffee. Bonnie, more smolder. Ready, go." Madison sat down again and clapped her hands once to set them on their way.

This time Grace's giggling gave her away so she wasn't able to sneak up on Bonnie. Bonnie turned to greet her. Grace still wrapped her arms around Bonnie, this time from the front.

She looked up, her eyes sparkling. "Good morning."

Bonnie leaned down and kissed her. She should have done it the first time instead of second-guessing herself. "It is now."

They continued to stare at each other. Bonnie wanted to steal another kiss. Grace looked like she was thinking the same thing.

Before either of them could act, Madison wedged herself between them. "You two nailed it the second time, but I'm afraid we don't have time for where that was clearly headed. I don't see a fire extinguisher around here and I'm not a firewoman. I know I said smolder, Bonnie, but you two can't burn down the kitchen."

"Madison." Grace's voice was full of warning.

"I want to go camping, Gracie. Look at this list." Madison snatched Bonnie's list off the island. "It looks like she has a lot to do." She plucked two items from the pantry and handed them to Bonnie. "Some breakfast. Off you go."

"You want me to eat uncooked soba noodles and breadcrumbs for breakfast?" Bonnie put the noodles and breadcrumbs back in the pantry. "Am I missing something here?"

Madison sat down heavily. Grace sat next to her. "No. I'm sorry I'm acting so strangely. Ever since college it's been 'Bonnie is the devil, we hate her,' no offense, Bonnie, and now you're kissing her every chance you get. And this house, this village, you, Gracie. It all fits, you're so…you. I couldn't be happier, but it means I'm not getting you back."

"Yes you are. Unless you hired my replacement, sold my things, and rented my apartment. I'm here for now, not for good." Grace looked over at Bonnie as she said it.

Was that regret in her eyes?

"Besides you're never going to lose me, so you won't need to get me back." Grace wrapped Madison in a giant squeeze.

"I'll let you two have a little time." Bonnie backed out the kitchen door. "I'll be outside if you need me."

She didn't want Grace to see how much it bothered her that a parting was in their near future. Despite what she'd said a couple days ago, happy then heartbreak wasn't what Bonnie wanted. Kissing Grace felt like an addiction she was happy to keep feeding. Maybe they'd have some time alone to talk, or spend time not talking, while camping. For now, Madison was right, she did have a lot to do.

Even though Bonnie had a system for loading the truck with the camping gear she was responsible for, it still took more time than she thought it would every year. By the time she was done, Stumpy and

Carl and Duck, Candace, and Avery were pulling into the driveway in two separate vehicles.

Bonnie ran to Carl's truck as it pulled in the driveway behind Candace's SUV. She jumped on the back bumper and banged on the tailgate. Stumpy climbed half out the window on the passenger's side and he and Bonnie raised a ruckus all the way down the driveway.

Grace and Madison were on the porch when Bonnie hopped off the back of the truck. Madison was warmly greeting Carl and Stumpy. Grace was looking sternly at Bonnie with a hand on her hip.

Bonnie grinned up at her. "Aren't you excited for the trip? Only thing missing is you and Madison and we're ready to roll out."

"As long as you don't fall under any trucks before we get on the road." Grace didn't look so peeved now.

"I was on the back. Worst that would've happened I would have fallen on my ass." Bonnie was still smiling. She probably would be until they were tucked in their tents tonight.

Grace climbed down from the porch and made her way to Bonnie's truck. "I guess I should ride with you and make sure that ass of yours is safe. I like looking at it and wouldn't want it to get into any trouble on the way."

"Don't leave without me." Madison hustled over and climbed into the cab of the truck. She rolled her eyes when both Bonnie and Grace glared at her for sitting in the middle. "I'm not risking the two of you causing us to drive off the road. I'm excited about camping. Carl promised to teach me to fish, and Stumpy and I are going to watch the sunrise tomorrow. Let's go." Madison waved them into the truck.

Bonnie didn't know someone outside the group could be as excited about the trip as they were. She'd been worried Madison wouldn't have a good time or that Grace had had to twist her arm, but clearly, she needn't have worried.

She helped Grace, who didn't need any help, into the truck, then ran around to the driver's side. The others were already pulling out of the driveway. Madison appointed herself master of the music and they jammed to eighties and nineties country, current pop hits, and the best of the eighties hair bands. They pulled into the group site at the campground blasting Twisted Sister, singing at the top of their lungs.

When the song was over and they piled out, all three of them were laughing. Ten eclectic songs and a lack of shame and the three of them were bonded and ready for the woods. Bonnie felt like she had a much better understanding of Madison and how she could innocently plaster herself on top of Grace, nearly kiss her, and not mean anything by it.

"You three know how to make an entrance." Stumpy gave a salute.

"You three are riding with me on the way home." Candace pointed to the three of them then to her SUV. She was getting Avery settled into a chest carrier.

"All right, Runt, put us to work." Stumpy unlocked the tailgate on Carl's truck and looked at Bonnie expectantly.

Bonnie nodded and walked the site slowly. She examined the picnic table placement and the areas where the ground was smooth and free of grass or other debris like rocks or stumps.

After she'd done her detailed inspection, she climbed onto the tailgate of her own truck and looked from a higher perspective. "Okay, the three picnic tables need to form a semicircle around the fire pit. Carl, Duck, can you move two over here?" Bonnie pointed to the right of the fire pit.

The boys sprang into action and the tables were quickly in place.

Bonnie looked at the site again and reevaluated now that the first move had been made. "Time for the tents. Avery's tent there" Bonnie pointed to a spot far from the road, fire, and back of the site. "Then one, two, three. The Mansion, Honey Pot, and Green Machine."

"Oh come on, you're putting us at the back in the cold." Carl grumbled. He looked like he wanted to stomp his foot.

"There will be three of us in that tent. How cold can it get?" Stumpy tossed the tent bag at Carl and grabbed a tarp and three sleeping bags from the truck. "Besides, you never stay in the tent anyway. Who knows where we'll find you in the morning."

"Spooning Runt, obviously." As soon as he reached the designated spot, Carl dumped the tent, rainfly, poles, and stakes on the ground. He and Stumpy got to work spreading the tarp and setting up the tent.

Grace didn't look pleased with Carl's declaration. If it were possible, Bonnie would bribe Stumpy to switch her to Grace's tent, but once Stumpy set the tents, he never rearranged.

Bonnie got the Green Machine and another tarp out of her truck. She motioned for Madison and Grace to follow. Bonnie wasn't surprised they were both naturals erecting the tent. She could have left them to it, but she loitered to be close to Grace. She couldn't help it, she craved the proximity. Even the space separating them now was enough to make her arms ache for her.

Grace looked up and blew her a kiss as if reading her mind. She said something to Madison that Bonnie couldn't hear, then came over to Bonnie. Grace draped her arms over Bonnie's shoulders and leaned her forehead against Bonnie's.

"When we're done unpacking, will you take me on a tour of the campground? Just the two of us?" Grace's hands began to wander. First, they ran up and down Bonnie's arms and over her back. Then they drifted lower to caress her upper chest. Before she moved to dangerous territory, Grace moved to tangle her fingers in the hair at the back of Bonnie's head.

Bonnie felt slightly dizzy from Grace's attention. "I'll take you wherever you'd like to go."

Grace's face lit up. "Such an open-ended, generous offer. You will be paying up on it."

She kissed Bonnie. It wasn't a gentle peck. It was a kiss of possession. It took Bonnie's breath away.

"How about after lunch?" Bonnie heard the stammer in her voice. How could Grace unravel her so completely? "There's still some unpacking to do and then Stumpy's going to be making lunch. Nothing should get in the way of Stumpy's camp cooking."

"Not even kissing?" Grace had a wicked grin on her face and she kissed Bonnie again.

"That's not a fair choice, but since you asked, kissing requires stamina if you're doing it right. Stamina requires sustenance. Food first, kissing second."

While Grace and Madison made their tent feel like home, Bonnie built the first campfire of the trip. Duck and Avery were playing in the smallest tent, Tiny Terror, which had been turned into a mini playroom just for her. Candace was hanging a tarp and hammock from two trees nearby, and everyone else was unpacking in the tents. She searched for a better descriptor, but contentment was the one she kept coming back to. Could this be her world?

Bonnie looked skyward and sighed. Was there another shoe up there, waiting to fall from the heavens and ruin this idyllic trip? She returned her gaze to more earthly pursuits. The fire danced and crackled as it tried to find its way against the wind and damp logs. Who made the rule that shoes had to fall in pairs? Why was happiness and contentment not enough for fluttering footwear? She sat and looked deeply at the flames. It was enough for her and that was all that mattered.

CHAPTER TWENTY-ONE

Grace opened her eyes and stretched now that the light was streaming into the tent more fully. She was only two days in, but the smell of the tent and the way the light filtered through the rainfly were now things she needed in her morning.

She closed her eyes again, content to doze a few minutes longer. She didn't hear movement at the campsite, although Avery had probably been up a while. She rolled on her side to get comfortable but bolted upright at a loud rustling sound just outside the tent door. Was it a bear?

She slapped her hand back to wake Madison, but her sleeping bag was empty. She must have gone out before the dawn with one of the guys to watch the sunrise.

"Grace, are you awake?" Bonnie whispered very close to the tent door.

After a deep breath or two to get her heart rate closer to something a cardiologist would approve of, Grace opened the zipper on the tent door and yanked Bonnie into the tent. Bonnie was clearly caught off guard and tumbled in, taking Grace down with her. They ended up tangled together, Bonnie on top looking down at Grace.

"Now this is a much more pleasant reality than worrying I was about to be mauled by a bear." Grace grabbed Bonnie's ass and pulled her tighter to her body.

"I didn't mean to scare you." Bonnie kissed Grace's neck, pulse point, jaw.

Grace rolled them so she was on top. She sat up, straddling Bonnie's lap. She captured her lips like they were hers forever. Bonnie seemed hungry for her, straining to reach her and deepen the kiss.

They were both gasping when Grace put a hint of distance between them. "You're forgiven."

Before she could continue, they were interrupted by Candace, calling out from somewhere in the direction of the fire pit. "I don't know how you two feel about an audience and hecklers, but you're about to have some."

Grace jumped off Bonnie at the same time Bonnie was scrambling to get up. "Out." Grace pointed at the door. Bonnie was smiling so Grace knew she wasn't upset at being shown the door so abruptly. Bonnie shimmied out the tent door and zipped it closed in record time. Grace pulled clothes from her bag and dressed quickly. She was out of the tent on Bonnie's heels before the rest of the group made it back to camp, although she could see them walking down the road nearby.

Bonnie was standing by Candace, awkwardly rubbing the back of her head. "I actually just stopped by the tent to see if she wanted to go for a walk."

Grace couldn't let Bonnie flounder alone. She approached and snaked her arms around Bonnie's waist and chest from behind. She rested her head on Bonnie's back.

"I get it." Candace looked full of amusement. "Roy came by to ask me the same thing once and poof, nine months later." She pointed to Avery.

"I can't poof, so no baby here." Bonnie pulled Grace's arms tighter around her.

Candace had started to walk back toward their tent but stopped, turned, and looked at Bonnie. "I never said the 'poof' was the part that made Avery. Sperm and an egg are all you need to make a baby. You need to work a little harder, Runt, if you don't know what I'm talking about." Candace looked behind Bonnie at Grace. "If she doesn't figure it out, don't wait around forever. You deserve more than a half-ass job."

"Do you hear that? I deserve the best you've got," Grace whispered in Bonnie's ear then walked away as the others came noisily back to camp.

Bonnie didn't let her get far. "Come on. I have a whole day planned for us and it doesn't involve being here." Bonnie held out her hand.

Grace was intrigued. She was happy to be anywhere with Bonnie, but it was especially sweet she'd planned an entire day for the two of them. Grace took her hand happily. Bonnie led her to the side of her tent and retrieved two backpacks. She handed the smaller of the two to Grace and kept the larger, no doubt, heavier, one for herself. Next, she picked up a fishing rod, tucked a small tackle box into a side pouch on Grace's backpack, and they were off.

"Where are you taking me?" Grace picked up their joined hands enough that she could see them better. Their hands looked like puzzle pieces that joined perfectly.

Bonnie grinned. She looked as happy as Grace felt. "You'll see."

They walked in contented silence for what felt like miles before Bonnie checked landmarks and veered from the main path straight into the woods. She didn't seem to be on any discernible trail. Grace held back. Bonnie was whipped around when their arms fully extended and Grace still hadn't moved.

"Trust me." Bonnie gave their joined hands a little jiggle. "We're almost there."

"Are you counting trees to know that? Everything looks the same." Grace was moving again, but her definition of fun in the woods stopped somewhere short of this.

"Trust me. It'll be worth it." Bonnie's eyes shone with excitement and something else Grace couldn't quite put her finger on.

Grace let out a dramatic breath and followed Bonnie. "It's hard to argue with you when you're hopping around like you have fire ants in your shoes."

"Better than my pants." Bonnie turned and winked. She stopped and held aside a last branch and ushered Grace onto a small beach along the lake, completely surrounded by trees.

Grace looked around in amazement. She would have had no idea this beach was here from the real trail they'd been on and no idea how to find it through the trees even if she did know it existed. The trees hung over the water as if providing a natural cabana for anyone lucky enough to find the sandy shores.

"How do you know about this place?"

Bonnie was back at the tree line across from where they'd broken through. It looked like she was searching for something. "We've been coming to this same state park for years. Over time we've explored about all of it. At least it feels that way. I found this place about seven years ago." Bonnie turned around with a rustic wooden table and two seats, which were chairs with backs and no legs. They were obviously homemade.

"Does anyone else know about this place?" Grace looked around again. The view over the water was so stunning it didn't look real. It was early still and the water was calm. It looked completely devoid of any ripples or disturbances. If she and Bonnie stood at the edge, would a perfect reflection greet them?

Bonnie shrugged. "No way to know, but Duck and I built this little table and these chairs pretty soon after I stumbled on this beach and they're always here when one of us comes for a visit."

Grace explored their personal oasis while Bonnie busied herself with the table, chairs, and something in her backpack. She was able to walk from one side to the other in about thirty-five paces. She kicked off her shoes as she passed Bonnie. The sand was unexpectedly soft between her toes. The only rocks she could see were closer to the water, where the soft lapping of water on sand was a peaceful backdrop to a beautiful morning.

"It's gorgeous, isn't it?" Bonnie stood beside Grace and looked out over the water. "I never get tired of spending time here, but now I'm afraid it's ruined forever."

Grace's stomach clenched. "What happened?" She searched Bonnie's face.

A strand of hair strayed across Grace's face. Bonnie tucked it behind her ear. "You happened." She cupped Grace's cheek. "This view, this place, it will never look as beautiful because you've been here, and I have a direct comparison. To me, nothing stands a chance next to you."

Bonnie was so earnest Grace couldn't help but be swept away. "Were you setting up something back there or am I allowed to kiss you for a very long time?"

"I've included plenty of time for kissing in our day, don't you worry, but I have breakfast for us now." Despite saying that, Bonnie stole a kiss, which quickly turned into much more than a passing peck.

Grace pulled away and pointed back toward the table and chairs. "Breakfast. Now. Or I'm not guaranteeing you won't start losing clothes."

Bonnie led them back where they'd left their backpacks. "All you had to do was ask." As she walked she stripped off her shirt and shorts.

It was all Grace could do to keep walking. Under her clothes, Bonnie was wearing a bathing suit consisting of boy shorts and a racerback bikini top.

"Are you really going to hang out like that?"

Bonnie looked at her innocently. She took a seat in one of the homemade chairs and indicated Grace should do the same. "Like what?"

"Naked, that's what. Have mercy on my blood pressure, woman." Grace took a seat and threw her head back dramatically.

"Does this help?" Bonnie moved from her chair and sat straddling Grace's hips, pinning her in her chair.

Grace shook her head, not trusting her ability to form words. Bonnie's breasts were partially uncovered and only inches from her. Her heart was pounding, and her clit was throbbing. She could see Bonnie's pulse point bouncing wildly as well.

Tentatively, Grace spread her hands across Bonnie's back. She felt goose bumps spring up under her touch. She got more confident as she continued her exploration. In high school Bonnie had always been strong, but this version of her was next level. Was it possible for Grace to come from the simple act of getting to know a deltoid or six-pack?

"This should be your house uniform." Grace kissed along Bonnie's collarbone toward her shoulder.

Although Bonnie's breasts were tantalizingly close, she was careful to avoid them. That was a line they'd both teased up against but neither had seemed willing to cross as of yet. It felt like once they did they were both accepting the heartbreak they knew was ahead.

"If this is the reaction I get from you, I'll consider it." Bonnie was breathing heavily. "But it would make power tools a bit more exciting than I like."

"You'd have to give up house calls too, I guess." Grace kissed her way back to Bonnie's lips.

"Really? Why?" Bonnie smiled against Grace's lips.

"Because I think I might want you for myself." Grace pulled away from Bonnie, suddenly feeling exposed and vulnerable.

"Hey." Bonnie ran her hand through Grace's hand and kissed her lightly. "Talk to me. I want you to want me. I didn't buy this bathing suit so Stumpy and I could compare tan lines." She climbed off of Grace's lap but pulled her chair closer so they were sitting right next to each other.

Grace pouted. Her emotions may have taken a more serious turn, but her body was still yearning for sexy Bonnie. She leaned over Bonnie and dragged the table in front of the two of them. She was hungry, might as well take advantage of the moment. She could also take advantage of the fact she had two hands and only needed one for eating. She traced her left hand up and down Bonnie's inner thigh, thrilling at the feel of Bonnie's muscles tightening with each pass.

"Since we broke up, you've been the woman every other woman was measured against. Now you and I are doing, whatever we're doing, and I don't have a comparator. It's scary and thrilling at the same time." Grace looked to Bonnie, searching for understanding on her face. "Especially since it's all so time limited."

"That's good?" Bonnie looked confused more than anything. She covered Grace's hand with hers and slowed the caress of her thigh.

"You were here when I was kissing you and accidentally admitted I want you all for myself, right?" Grace turned her hand and took Bonnie's hand in her own.

Bonnie glanced at their joined hands and looked relieved. "I recall something along those lines." She kissed Grace's knuckles. "But there's always the other part too. It was so easy to forget while we've been camping." Bonnie wasn't able to fully hide the sadness in her eyes.

Grace removed her hand from Bonnie's. "It would break my heart now instead of later, but I was the one who pushed when you asked me not to. If this is a bad idea, please tell me and it will be roommates only from now on." Grace's ribcage felt three sizes too small.

"If you hadn't started it, I would have. My resolve was paper thin. You're irresistible whether there's heartbreak ahead or not." Bonnie retook Grace's hand and kissed her knuckles. "How do you like Garrison, now that you're back and have commingled with us all a while?" Bonnie wasn't doing a very good job at looking casual.

Grace shoved a larger than necessary bite of food in her mouth hoping for an extra second or two to come up with an answer. "It's complicated" hadn't satisfied anyone since the first time someone strung those two words together. It wasn't fair of Bonnie to ask such a loaded question on the heels of talking about her future departure.

"I didn't think I'd love Garrison as much as I do this second time around. You, the boys, Candace and Avery, and my pottery class have been a big part of that."

That seemed to make Bonnie happy.

"Eventually though, we both know real life is going to come calling. My boss's flexibility is only going to continue for so much longer. I need to move toward wrapping up what I can with my dad's things. I haven't wanted to do that because of you and what we've started." Grace turned to Bonnie, hoping to see an answer she hadn't considered in her eyes or written on a sculpted thigh. Bonnie looked less sure of herself than she had a moment ago. "The one thing I know is I don't want to do anything that puts this day you planned, and the rest of this trip, in jeopardy." She motioned toward the lake.

"I guess we'll be fine then." Bonnie still looked a bit unsure.

Grace kissed Bonnie, then spun away from her, desperate to find the closeness and happiness they'd shared when they stepped onto the beach. She grabbed one last bite of the breakfast they'd shared and picked up the fishing rod. "Will you teach me to fish?" She held it up in front of her and Bonnie giggled. Grace looked down and realized how suggestive her pose was. She waggled the rod. "I hear you're good with one of these, can you show me?" Grace made her voice as low and seductive as possible.

Bonnie's body relaxed. "Anything for you." Bonnie retrieved the small box she'd packed from the backpack. "But I have to warn you, now is not the best time for getting any action." She quirked a sideways grin.

Grace raised her eyebrows and handed over the rod. "I didn't know there was an ideal time."

"In this case, since we're talking about fish, obviously, there is. Dawn and dusk work best for me." Bonnie loaded bait onto the hook and handed the rod back to Grace. "Do you know how to cast?"

"Do I get hands-on instruction if I say no?" Grace shivered.

Bonnie nodded seriously. "As your teacher, I feel it's my duty to give you the best instruction to make you successful. Hands-on teaching and learning are very beneficial, don't you think?"

Grace moved into Bonnie's personal space. "I encourage you to be very handsy." She kissed her and ran both hands over Bonnie's erect nipples, easily visible through her bathing suit top.

"Let's go, hot stuff, before we don't make it to the lesson at all. Sex on the beach looks glamorous in the movies, but sand chafing my lady bits doesn't sound sexy to me. Besides, after all these years, I don't want a frantic fuck on the beach." Despite what she was saying, Bonnie looked disappointed.

"I know you only half mean that." Grace kissed Bonnie again but moved farther away to give them both breathing room. In truth, she wanted to wait too. The buildup and anticipation had her practically on fire all the time. It was damn hot that Bonnie was so close, sleeping every night thirty feet away, but she couldn't have her yet. She'd never had this kind of extended foreplay, but she liked it, a lot.

"Come on." Bonnie took Grace's hand and led her to the water's edge. "Let's learn to fish."

True to her word, Bonnie was a hands-on teacher. Her teaching style might have been more of a hinderance to Grace's progress as a student, but Grace had no complaints. Bonnie pressed against her back, one hand over Grace's on the rod, the other wrapped firmly around her waist, was nothing to grumble about. They cast together that way multiple times, each time the line landing closer to shore. They were so wrapped up in each other it hardly mattered.

"Go sit and look beautiful. I'm going to try on my own." Grace untangled from Bonnie and pointed her toward the chairs farther up the beach.

Bonnie obliged and pulled more snacks from the backpacks.

Grace cast a few times, her single-minded focus allowing the line, baited hook, and bobber to fly far from the shore. Bonnie pulled the two chairs over and joined her. She brought snacks and water.

"Now what?" Grace looked at the floating bobber, cheerily rocking to and fro on the water's surface.

Bonnie extended her legs and stretched. She looked content. "Now we wait. It's called fishing, not catching. Let's see how the day goes."

Grace stretched back in her chair as well, grabbing a handful of chips from the bag Bonnie had packed. She absently crunched as she watched the bobber floating on the water. The longer she stared at it, the more she felt like the bobber, adrift in a strange lake with unlimited possibilities for a next direction.

How did Bonnie fit in if she opened up all possibilities? Was she the line holding her steady or was she the bait and hook dragging her down? Or the fish threatening to drag her under? Grace shook off those thoughts. Bonnie wasn't a weight. On the other hand, Bonnie meant Garrison, as Grace would never ask her to uproot from the community and family she had built for herself. Was she able to rule out a return to LA or anywhere in the country with a population greater than four hundred? What if she and Bonnie didn't work out?

A little voice in her head kept trying to point out that she grew up in Garrison, it was her town too. She was a homeowner. Hell, she had a regular pottery class. What more did she need to tie her to the community?

Bonnie was snoring softly next to Grace. She looked at her, unafraid of being caught. She was more beautiful than Grace had words to describe, and she had chosen Grace. The far side of the moon or tiny Garrison, she wanted to be where Bonnie was. Her heart knew it all along. Her brain needed to fall in line. She didn't need to fret alone. Anything that came up she and Bonnie could figure out together.

The bobber dipped under the water, first once, then again and again. Something was pulling on the bait below. Grace woke Bonnie and started reeling in her catch. She couldn't help but think, perhaps the weights and bait weren't about weighing her down. Weren't about control. Maybe they were a grounding force, a solid base that only gave her a shake when something big was happening. If she figured out why she'd been getting such a shake since she returned to Garrison, maybe all the pieces would fall into place.

CHAPTER TWENTY-TWO

Bonnie felt like a class A jerk when she declined Branch's invitation to join him for puzzles and snacks. He tried to hide his disappointment, but he wasn't able to. They'd been meeting regularly to work on his puzzles and shoot the shit, and today she was blowing him off. She felt awful. Except she had a damn good reason.

"I'll make it up to you next week, I promise. I've got a date tonight and I need to get home and shower first." Bonnie looked down at her filthy clothes.

Branch's eyes lit up. "Why didn't you say so? Get out of here, you smell like a sewer. Get her flowers, chocolates, and bring a ring, just in case the mood strikes you." He winked.

"It's a little too early for rings." Bonnie patted him on the shoulder as she packed up her tools.

"It's never too early if you know she's the one." Branch looked at her seriously.

Bonnie stopped packing and looked at him. Was she missing something? "I thought you never found your one true love and settled down."

Branch nodded absently. "Most of that is true, but you seem like the type that could be your own worst enemy and might need a reminder not to do something stupid."

"Like propose on the first date?" Bonnie laughed.

"No, like wait too long, get in your own way, and bungle it all up."

Bonnie paused, not sure what to say. Would she do that? She'd done it before. Finally, she found her voice. "Well, on that optimistic note, I'm going to head home and get ready for dinner."

Branch walked her to her truck and gave her a kiss on the cheek before she left. His stern words and tenderness had her off balance. Did he know something she didn't?

When she got back to the house Grace wasn't there. Bonnie's first thought was that she'd backed out and the date was canceled. She scolded herself. Grace had given no indication since their time on the beach that she was anything other than all in while she was still in town. They were both looking forward to their night out.

Her worries were assuaged by a note Grace left on the kitchen island. Candace had needed to run out on a quick errand and Grace was at their house while Avery napped.

"Get it together, Runt." She admonished herself all the way up the stairs and into the shower.

Bonnie had soap in her hair and her eyes closed when she heard a knock on the bathroom door.

"Mind if I come in?"

If she got her way, she and Grace would end up naked after their date so why not give her a sneak peek now? "Come on in."

She dipped her head back in the water and finished rinsing the shampoo from her hair. She nearly jumped through the roof when there were suddenly hands on her body. She wiped her eyes and opened them to find Grace, gorgeously naked in the shower with her.

"I couldn't wait, and you did say I could come in." Grace drew an intricate path along Bonnie's stomach.

"You're always welcome." Bonnie gasped as Grace moved closer to her nipple.

"I like the sound of that." Grace squeezed Bonnie's breast and teased her nipple, capturing her mouth at the same time. "And I love your body. You teased me with some of it at the beach, but I couldn't wait any longer for the rest."

Bonnie needed to get her hands on Grace too. She'd been taken by surprise, but she'd regained her footing. Bonnie flipped their positions so Grace was more fully under the water, the shower stream hitting her shoulders, running down and between her breasts and dampening her center.

She followed a trail of water down Grace's chest, then took her nipple fully in her mouth. Grace gasped and leaned into Bonnie's ministrations. Bonnie lavished attention on first one then the other, attentive to what made Grace moan or cry out in pleasure.

Finally, Grace pushed her away. "I can't, no more, it feels too good."

"I didn't know that was a bad thing." Bonnie stood and kissed her, turning her again, this time partially away from the water and walking her against the shower wall. Grace gasped as her back hit the cold tile. "Isn't feeling good the point?"

Grace was still breathing heavily and kissing Bonnie like she might never get another chance. She slipped her fingers into Bonnie's wetness and stroked her as she talked. "Yes, but you were going too fast. I'm not a prized pony to ride hard and fast. But I'm wound up now so you have to finish what you started." She put her hand on the top of Bonnie's head and pushed her down.

Bonnie put her hands on either side of Grace's body and traced her way down as she slowly sunk to her knees. Her heart and clit were pumping so wildly she hoped she didn't do anything embarrassing like come or pass out.

Once down, Grace tried to pull her forward, but Bonnie resisted. She wanted a moment to take in Grace's body, lithe, feminine, strong. Finally, slowly, she teased Grace's thighs apart and dipped her tongue into her wetness. A loud, low moan came from Grace and spurred Bonnie into more purposeful action.

She spread Grace wider and circled her clit firmly. Grace slapped her hands against the white tiles of the shower wall and moaned again.

"Bonnie, you know I don't like to be teased. Get on with it."

Bonnie's heart clenched. She used to know that, maybe a few other things were still true too. She slid her hands up the inside of Grace's thighs. She cupped her ass while she, for the moment, ignored Grace's plea and continued to tease her.

Grace's sounds of pleasure took on an undertone of frustration the longer Bonnie withheld the orgasm she was seeking. Grace had always liked to be treated like a queen and built up slowly, but once she was turned on, she was supercharged and impatient. More than anything else they'd done, it turned Bonnie on that she still knew Grace. She still knew how to give her the pleasure she wanted.

Bonnie didn't make her wait any longer. She sucked Grace's clit fully in her mouth at the same time she buried two fingers deep inside her.

Grace arched against the wall, rising on her toes and pulling Bonnie's head tight against her center. She matched the steady rhythm of Bonnie's thrusting. "Bonnie, you're the only one who makes me feel like this. Keep fucking me."

Bonnie did as she was told and within moments Grace collapsed onto her knees, joining Bonnie on the floor of the shower. They came together in a searing kiss, neither able to get enough of the other.

"I'm not done with you." Bonnie broke the kiss long enough to look at Grace and run her fingers through Grace's wetness.

"I haven't even started with you." Grace squeezed Bonnie's nipple.

Bonnie reached up and turned off the water. She helped Grace to her feet and got them each a towel. She was more than happy to towel off Grace, although she was fired from the job since she was distracted more than once.

"Get your sexy ass dry and in my bed." Grace pointed to the door of the bathroom and shooed Bonnie out.

Bonnie threw her towel on the ground and sprinted for the door. Grace was hot on her heels and caught her as they entered the bedroom. They tumbled onto the bed, tangled together. Before Bonnie could gain the upper hand, she was on her back and Grace was between her legs. It took a few beats for her brain to catch up to her body. She was halfway over the edge before she realized how close she was.

"Slow down, I want to feel you longer." Bonnie tried to wiggle away.

Grace let up and looked at Bonnie. "Not this time. I want you too badly. We have the rest of the night for slow."

She buried herself in Bonnie again and Bonnie gave herself over to the feeling of Grace driving her higher. She tumbled over the edge more ferociously than she could remember. Grace climbed up her body and snuggled into Bonnie's arms.

"You're amazing." Grace kissed sleepily in Bonnie's general direction. She missed her neck and ended up placing a gentle kiss under Bonnie's jaw.

"I l—" Bonnie stopped abruptly. "We missed our dinner reservations, maybe we should bring date night closer to home." What had she been about to say?

Grace sat up enough to look at her. "Isn't that what we've been doing?" She spun her finger casually around Bonnie's nipple.

Bonnie gasped. "I call uncle. You have to feed me first before you take me back to bed."

Grace laughed and increased her attention. "Except you're already in my bed."

"Next round's in mine." Bonnie flipped Grace so she was on top. "It's in your best interest to feed me first since I'm planning on it being a long night."

Grace pushed Bonnie off her and hopped out of bed. "What are you waiting for?" She pulled Bonnie after her and gave her a gentle push out the door toward her bedroom down the hall. "Pizza or something else?"

Bonnie leaned out the door of her room, a T-shirt half over her head. "Pizza is fine. It's fastest."

She watched Grace scamper down the stairs, wearing nothing but one of Bonnie's T-shirts and a thong. Her long legs looked like they went on forever. With each step, Grace's ass peeked out from under the tee. Bonnie had to steady herself against the doorframe. How had she gotten so lucky?

She wanted to lose herself completely in the feeling, it would be so easy, but she held back, just a little. Her heart was so far gone, maybe it didn't matter, but unless Grace changed her mind and decided to stay in Garrison, all of this was no better than playing make-believe. Despite the agreement they'd made she wanted Grace to build her life here, with her. Anything less than that now felt like too much to give up.

Bonnie pushed those thoughts aside. She knew what she'd signed up for. She and Grace could work that out later. Tonight was about the two of them, here and now. She ran down the stairs after Grace, suddenly desperate to kiss her.

Grace was on the porch, dragging the storage chest in front of the porch swing. Bonnie joined her and helped move the large chest. Grace darted back inside toward the kitchen. She returned with a glass of wine for herself and a beer for Bonnie. She'd also found a pair of shorts that didn't cover much more than just her underwear.

"I'll get plates." Bonnie returned with plates, napkins, and silverware. She also grabbed the only candle she could find, which was a sparkler birthday candle that, according to the packaging, wouldn't easily blow out.

Bonnie put everything down on the crate and returned to the kitchen for a tall drinking glass. Once outside again she exited the porch in search of loose dirt. She borrowed some from the flowerbed under the railing, filled the cup, and set it triumphantly on the crate. She set the candle in and held her arms out, proud that they would now have a chance to eat via candlelight.

The pizza arrived as Bonnie was congratulating herself on her creative candleholder. Grace kissed her cheek on the way to greet the delivery driver. Bonnie stared after her and she reconsidered if dinner was strictly necessary. Surely they could eat later.

Grace returned with two large pizzas and set them on the crate. She took one look at Bonnie and waved a finger at her. "Oh no. I see where your mind has wandered off to. All closed." She sat down on the swing and crossed her legs. "We're on a date, remember? You promised me a candlelight dinner." Grace pointed to the birthday candle in a glass of dirt.

"So I did." Bonnie lit the candle which did start fizzing and popping like a sparkler. She took a slice of pizza, leaned back on the swing, and opened her arms, inviting Grace to join her.

Grace wasted no time accepting the invitation. They ate like that, enjoying the closeness and silence, through two slices each.

"Garrison sure is beautiful." Grace broke the silence.

"I didn't used to think that, but now I agree with you." Bonnie looked around at their shared property. In the falling darkness, it was truly stunning.

"Are you talking about your parents? What changed?" Grace rolled her head on Bonnie's chest until she could see Bonnie better.

Bonnie nodded. "Yeah, they were kind of the worst, but I'm not inviting them to date night dinner. As for what changed, would you like to guess what turned my life upside down over the course of the last few months?"

"Unless you have other life events you're not telling me about." Grace grabbed Bonnie by the earlobe and shook gently. "And you better not have a secret wife and family you visit three days a week."

"Not a chance." Bonnie was horrified at the thought. "The only change has been you. If I'm being honest, I like what you've done. I like the woman I am when we're together."

"I'm very fond of the woman you are." Grace deposited both of their empty plates on the crate, tucked her feet beneath her on the swing, and snuggled into Bonnie's arms.

Bonnie laughed. "Fond of me? You sure know how to turn a girl's head."

Grace looked up at Bonnie and gave her a light punch on the shoulder. "Don't forget it. It's a high honor."

"I'm duly honored." Bonnie schooled her face into what she hoped was a look of reverence.

Grace sat up and pulled Bonnie into a searing kiss. "Anything else you're willing to duly do?"

Bonnie stood and held her hand to Grace. "What'd you have in mind?"

"Everything." Grace stood and jumped into Bonnie's arms.

As they stumbled into the house, kissing and pulling off clothing, Bonnie was sure she was dreaming. How had she gotten a second chance with the love of her life, even if it wasn't meant to last? Could this be what Lionel had wanted for them? To close the open wound and find a way to say a proper goodbye? Bonnie refused to believe that. There was too much still sparking between them and like their candle, Bonnie didn't think it was easily extinguished.

CHAPTER TWENTY-THREE

G race slammed her laptop closed and blew out a loud breath. Slamming her hands down on the table and throwing something large through the window sounded more satisfying, but since she was a grown-up, she settled for dramatic sighs and aggressive laptop closing.

"You all right, sweetheart?" Bonnie walked through the dining room and kissed the top of Grace's head.

Despite her bad mood, the term of endearment wasn't lost on Grace. Bonnie seemed unaware she'd used it, but it hit Grace right in the heart. It also made her frustration more acute.

"Sweetheart? I like how that sounds on your lips." Grace looked at Bonnie and her stomach did a familiar and exhilarating flip. She did like the sound of it, but it also brought a tinge of sadness.

"I like how it feels on my lips." Bonnie took Grace's hand and placed a kiss on top. "So what had you grumbling and trying to break your computer?"

Grace leaned her head back and looked at Bonnie standing over her. Bonnie looked worried. Grace had caught her with that look a few times lately. She wondered what it was Bonnie wasn't telling her.

"You can take your pick, probate delays, Madison missing all of us, more frequent check-ins from my boss." Grace nearly opened her laptop so she could slam it shut again.

"They've finally realized you're indispensable at work, huh?" Bonnie wasn't able to hide her anxiety.

"Is that what's had you in a state for the past week?" Grace studied Bonnie's face.

Bonnie looked away and didn't answer immediately. Grace couldn't blame her, she'd been feeling it too.

Grace stood and pulled Bonnie into her arms. Bonnie felt like she was wound tight enough to pluck like a guitar string. "Talk to me, Bonnie. Whatever it is, there's nothing we can't deal with together."

"You're going to be late to pottery." Bonnie pointed to the clock on the wall behind the table.

Grace released Bonnie and crossed her arms. "No way, you don't get out of talking to me that easily. What's going on?"

Bonnie looked taken aback. "Maybe saying goodbye to you is going to be harder than I realized and I'm not ready. It's hard for me to hear you talking about your boss wanting you back sooner when all I want is for you to stay longer."

"Is that what all this's about?" Grace ran both hands through her hair. "It's not all that easy for me either you know. I'm not eager to run to the airport but I don't know if I'm going to have a choice pretty soon. I'd bring you with me but you'd hate LA and every root you've ever planted is in Garrison."

"I know, I know." Bonnie looked dejected. "I'm being silly." She kissed Grace and shooed her toward the door. "Enjoy your pottery class."

Grace mulled over Bonnie's confession on the drive to her class. If she was honest with herself, she was having a harder and harder time finding any appeal to returning to LA, but that's where her job, her life, and house was. No, she corrected herself, her apartment was there, her house was in Garrison. If only she could figure out where she felt at home.

When she arrived at her class, Tanya was getting out of her car. She waved and waited for Grace.

"Half the reason I come to this class is so we can chat every week." Tanya had an infectious smile and much more pottery skill than Grace, but they did spend most of their time chatting.

"All that's missing is a glass of wine or two." Grace opened the door for Tanya, and they made their way to their table and got out their supplies.

Tanya's eyes lit up. "Do you think anyone would notice if we brought some in in water bottles?"

"Should we try next week and see?" Grace whispered behind her hand as if that would ensure their plan would never be overheard. Tanya nodded, a sparkle in her eyes. "So, tell me how your hot handywoman is doing. I have to live vicariously through you. My husband and I have kids so we're lucky if we both make it to bed at the same time without one of us falling asleep on the couch. I don't know how families with more than two children have the energy or time to keep making more."

From her time with Tanya, Grace knew how much she loved being a mother and how devoted she was to her kids. Gentle complaining might be fun, but she knew Tanya wouldn't change a thing about her family.

"An hour ago, I would've said everything with Bonnie was perfect. But then she got a little too real about my eventual return to LA and now I'm not sure." Grace pounded her fist into a piece of clay.

Tanya stopped what she was doing and turned to face Grace completely. "Not sure about her? Not sure about the two of you? Not sure about where her head's at? I need to know what we're talking about here."

Grace looked up abruptly and stopped what she was doing as well. "How I feel about her and us isn't in doubt. But my boss is checking in constantly now and his last email said he needs me back in the office by next week or he's going to have to let me go. He's been supportive of my time off, but I don't blame him for needing me back. I'm out of family leave and one of our busiest times is coming up."

Tanya nodded, her eyes understanding and kind. "Have you told Bonnie?"

Grace shook her head. "I was going to when I got back tonight. But then before I left she was telling me how hard it's going to be for her when I leave and how she wants me to stay longer. We were both so willing to accept heartbreak as the end result of all of this, but now that the end is here, I don't want to pay up."

"Why do you have to? A job is just a job. Or what about remote work?" Tanya pushed her clay aside and focused completely on Grace.

"Being seen on the scene is part of my job. It can't be done remotely. Garrison isn't exactly a marketing Mecca." Grace looked down at her laughable attempt at an animal figurine.

"Sounds like an opportunity, if you're looking for a reason to stick around." Tanya raised an eyebrow and went back to her clay.

For a long time, neither of them said anything. Grace mulled over what Tanya said. Was there an opportunity in Garrison? It sure didn't seem like it and if there was, it would look nothing like what she did now.

"I don't feel very comfortable in LA. I've never been sure that it feels like home." Grace poked at her clay without looking at Tanya.

Tanya nodded. She rolled a piece of clay back and forth between her fingers, making a perfect sphere. Finally, she put the ball down and looked at Grace. "Remember how I said my husband and I moved here because of the experience I had growing up in Garrison? Well, he'd never lived anywhere tinier than a small city."

"Whoa, I bet Garrison was a big adjustment." Grace made a half-hearted attempt to shape her clay into the week's assignment before shoving it aside.

"You have no idea." Tanya looked like she was revisiting memories both good and bad. "For close to six months, I woke up every morning expecting that to be the one where he said he couldn't take it anymore and he had to move, with or without me."

Grace felt like a cartoon character with her eyes bulging four inches out of their sockets. "That's incredibly stressful. I guess he never decided to flee?"

"Oh no, he loves it here. Turns out he was made for small town living. My point is he didn't know he'd found home until he had no desire to run back to the city he'd always known." Tanya shrugged. "It might be worth considering why you keep extending your leave."

Grace frowned. She stayed so she could take care of things for her father's estate. But that didn't explain the pottery class. Or redecorating the house. Or Bonnie. Grace wagged her finger at Tanya. "I paid a lot of money for a therapist in LA, but all this time, I should have been coming to you, in your office at the back of a pottery studio, where I could pay you nothing and drink wine in water bottles."

Tanya held up her water filled water bottle and she and Grace clinked plastic. "Only want you to consider all your options, which in this case means not being afraid to follow your heart. You seem like the type who lets your head get in the way too often."

On the drive home Grace mulled over what Tanya said. Was there more to her desire to extend her work leave than she was willing to examine? At the moment, that felt less important than breaking the news to Bonnie that she had to leave in a matter of days. The thought turned Grace's stomach. Why had she been so stupid to come back to Garrison and kiss Bonnie Whitlock?

Bonnie was on the porch, swaying lazily in the swing, when Grace pulled in the drive. Grace subtly banged the steering wheel. Of all the days she could have used a moment to collect herself before seeing Bonnie.

"How was class?" Bonnie handed Grace a glass of wine and patted the seat next to her on the swing.

Grace sat and allowed herself to melt into Bonnie's embrace. What would it be like to never picture an end to evenings like this? To never feel the pressure of an end date or an expiration? She shook herself out of that wishful thinking.

"Class was good. Tanya suggested we sneak booze into class next week." Grace leaned her head back and stole a kiss. "We do need to talk about earlier though."

Bonnie looked embarrassed. "I'm sorry. I shouldn't have asked about Garrison or made a thing about your boss getting in touch. Of course they want to know when you're coming back. I'm sure you're as amazing at your job as you are at everything. They miss you. I get it."

Grace shook her head. "You have nothing to apologize for. I needed to tell you this but we didn't have much time and then you were asking about Garrison and I got annoyed. I have to go back by next week or I lose my job."

Bonnie stood so abruptly Grace almost tumbled out of the swing. As it was, its motion was sent into a twisty pattern that mirrored Grace's jangling nerves. "So soon?"

Grace reached out and pulled Bonnie back to sitting. They sat silently, only tension and sadness filling the space between them. Finally Grace tentatively reached out and took Bonnie's hand. "I don't want to leave you."

"Then don't." Bonnie looked at her with unshed tears in her eyes. "We've, you've started building a life here. Stay."

"I can't." Grace was barely able to choke the words out above a whisper. "I have to go back to real life in LA. What I've been building here isn't that. It isn't real."

Bonnie stood again and took the first few steps toward the front door. She turned and indicated between the two of them. "It could be you know, if you wanted it to be. It felt real to me." She turned again to go inside.

"Where are you going?" Grace's insides felt like a flock of thousands of birds had taken off in unison, wild, chaotic, and a little frightening.

"Talking about how this would end and actually getting to this point are very different beasts. My broken heart and I need a little time to comfort each other. I'm going up to my room." Bonnie attempted a smile that was more forlorn than anything.

Grace jumped up and followed. She stopped Bonnie and cupped her cheek, ran her hands across her shoulders. "What can I do to help? I don't have to leave for a few days." She wanted to pull Bonnie close but the usual welcome was missing.

Bonnie looked into the living room in the direction of the photo of the two of them from high school. "Let's talk again in the morning. Tonight I think I need to spend some time wrapping my head around your leaving." Bonnie looked like she regretted every word as it came out of her mouth.

Grace's heart felt like it was being ripped to shreds with the hand tiller in her gardening tools. She sank to the floor and pulled out her cell phone. There were two choices in front of her and since neither involved Bonnie, she wasn't excited about either, but calling Madison sounded more appealing than ugly crying alone on the floor.

Madison answered on the first ring. "I heard. What are you going to do?"

Grace pulled the phone away from her ear for a moment to stare at it in disbelief. "What do you mean you 'heard'? And what do you mean what am I going to do?"

"Please, you know what I mean. If you didn't, you'd be in bed with her, not calling me. Stop stalling. Talk." It sounded like Madison was drumming her fingers on a hard surface. She must have recently gotten her nails done because they were tapping out an impatient rhythm beautifully.

"I've been summoned back and it's either return now or never come back. The news is hard for Bonnie and me. She needs some space tonight and I called you so I don't lose it sitting here alone in the entryway. I should probably at least move into the living room." Grace butt scooted into the next room and leaned against the couch.

"Okay." Madison dragged out the word. "So I ask again, what are you going to do?"

Grace rested her head against the couch and looked up at the ceiling. "I don't understand what you're asking. I'm coming back."

"Why?"

"Why does everyone keep asking me some version of that?" Grace didn't mean to snap at Madison.

"Gracie, I love you, I really do, but I feel like you're smart enough to already know the answer to that question. How many years have you been looking for a woman to live up to your version of the perfect woman?" Madison had her no-nonsense voice working overtime.

"Since I got to LA. Fifteen years." Grace sighed.

"Fifteen years you've given LA to produce the perfect woman and no luck. You get back to your adorable teacup sized village and within ninety seconds, your perfect woman, right there. And now, you're returning to LA, the land of fifteen years of futility, for a job. A job you are equivocal about at best I might add. Have I missed anything?" Madison waited an uncomfortably long time for Grace to say nothing. "Does that answer your question?" Madison's voice was now soft and kind.

"Maddy, LA is my home. I can't ignore that. I have a whole life there that I put on hold, but I have to restart. Bonnie and I agreed. We said we'd be together while I was here and then that would be it. We knew going in. So why is it so hard?" Grace couldn't help the tears now. She got up and walked out to the porch. The slight breeze cooled the lines streaking down her face.

"Gracie, honey, LA might be your physical home, but I suspect it's not your heart's home. Do you love her?"

Grace pictured the way Bonnie's eyes softened before she kissed her and how she looked fresh from completing a project around the house, triumphant and sweaty. Or the care she took on anything she did for Grace. "Yes." Her heart filled with the affirmation.

"Yes. I knew it." Madison sounded as happy as Grace felt. "And do you love your job?"

Grace hesitated. "Sure, I guess so."

Madison whistled low. "Gracie, I can't tell you what to do, but you might want to think about how you answered and what's going to make you happy. If you come back, I'll be at the airport with bells and pompoms to pick you up. I miss your face. If you aren't at the airport, I'll use my pompoms to cheer you on from afar."

Grace sat on the porch swing until long past the point it got too chilly to be outside. She wanted to go up and knock on Bonnie's door and try to make it right, but she'd done nothing wrong. She turned Madison's words over and over, then mixed them with Tanya's. Could she be happy here? It wasn't simply leaving her job and moving to be with Bonnie. Choosing Garrison after it had rejected her felt like burying a part of her past she'd never moved past. Except maybe she had. Maybe that was the real inheritance her father had left her. He'd given her the gift of the town that built her through the stories she'd heard about him and how he lived here in the village. Could she be happy with a similar, quiet life? What about a job? It wasn't fair of her to even consider Bonnie's offer to stay if Bonnie was the only reason. That wasn't fair to either of them but right now she couldn't see a way to build a life for herself that would fulfill the parts Bonnie couldn't. She still had a few days before she had to be back. Hopefully a definitive answer would present itself before she made a decision she and Bonnie would spend another fifteen years regretting.

CHAPTER TWENTY-FOUR

B onnie rolled her beer back and forth between her hands and sighed loudly.

"Okay, that's enough. I can't stand it anymore." Duck grabbed Bonnie's beer bottle and drank it all.

"What the fuck, man?" Bonnie started to stand, but Carl and Stumpy held her down on either side. Bonnie shook them off but sat back down.

"Time for you to grow a pair of tits, or ovaries, or Fallopian tubes, or lady balls, whatever you want to stop being such a damn coward." Duck slid Bonnie's empty bottle to the middle of the table where the empties went.

"What are you talking about?" Bonnie's stomach felt jumpy. She didn't like where this conversation was going.

"He's talking about Grace and you know it." Stumpy patted her arm supportively.

"We're past the time for coddling, Stump. She needs the truth now." Carl held up the beer bottle Duck finished "You've been wasting good beer, sighing so much it's making dinner miserable, and it's impossible to have a conversation with you because your head is elsewhere."

"You can fix all your problems by admitting what you need to do and getting on with it." Duck flagged the waitress and ordered another beer.

"Come on, it can't be that bad." Talking about Grace made Bonnie's chest ache even more acutely.

"It's actually worse." Stumpy returned his hand to her arm. "It's time for you to step up if you're serious about making a life with Grace."

Bonnie crossed her arms and frowned. "I asked her to stay. I'm serious. She still left."

"And you stayed." Stumpy's eyes were kind and without judgment.

Bonnie stomach knotted. "I didn't know losing her again would hurt so damn much. I don't know what to do. What if I fuck it up?"

"You're fucking it up now." Carl sounded exasperated. "Look, I'll show you what you do. Grace, I'm sorry I took so long to say this." Carl glanced at Stumpy. "But I love you. I want to give us a real chance, so please tell me what I should do next."

Stumpy looked dumbfounded. Duck looked triumphant, and Carl was making aggressive eye contact with Bonnie. Bonnie wanted to look at Stumpy, get a better read on his reaction, but Carl looked like he was holding onto her as a lifeline, and she couldn't let him down.

"Hey, Runt, wasn't there something you wanted to show Duck in your truck? Something that just came into the shop maybe?" Stumpy did catch Bonnie's eye and he nodded toward the door.

"Right, come on, Duck. Maybe you can give me more advice on how to unfuck my life while we're out there." Bonnie didn't want to leave, her love for her friends and desire to watch the drama unfold pulled her back to her seat, but she respected Stumpy too much to ignore his request.

Bonnie and Duck walked in silence to the parking lot and over to Bonnie's truck. She pulled down the tailgate and they both sat, staring straight ahead, processing.

"Did that happen, for real?" Duck found a rock in the truck bed and, since Bonnie had backed into her spot, there was plenty of pasture for him to fling it.

Bonnie jumped down and grabbed a pile of rocks. "I think so. What's Stumpy going to say?"

Duck threw another rock, this one landing past Bonnie's. As with most things, it was now a competition. "Depends on if Carl's his type I guess. He's pretty private about what kind of dude he finds attractive."

Bonnie aborted her toss midway sending her rock flying way off course. "Wait a minute. You're saying Stumpy's gay? And Carl? Why do you know that and I don't?"

"No one can keep a secret hidden from Candace." Duck collected more rocks. "That's how I found out about Carl, although Candace swore me to secrecy since it wasn't her news to share. Stumpy told me himself. He doesn't want anyone to know since he already has trouble with his practice and people feeling comfortable around him." Duck looked sad. "Not only would he be the village shrink, but he'd be the gay village shrink."

"I hope they work out." Bonnie looked toward the door to the bar. "They deserve a happily ever after."

Duck looked at her pointedly. "Carl risked a lot going after his. She mean enough to you to do the same?"

"Yes." Bonnie didn't hesitate.

"What are you waiting for?" Duck jumped off the tailgate, slammed it shut, and dragged Bonnie to the driver's side door. "Get your ass in the truck and go get your girl. I'll wait for the other two or call Candace for a ride."

Bonnie climbed into the truck and hung out the window. She clasped hands with Duck. "Thank you. What if I'm not made for the big city? What am I going to do without you all?"

"We'll never be that far away." Duck hugged her through the open window. "She's worth it. We can help you with the logistics here, go do your romantic thing now."

"I have one stop to make and then I'm going to win her back no matter what it takes. Let me know how it goes with those two." She nodded toward the bar.

Duck waved as she pulled out of the parking lot. Turning left would have brought her back to the house so she could pack for the airport, but she turned right. She needed to talk to Branch. If anyone knew about relationship pitfalls it was the ninety-four-year-old who dated a lot but never settled down.

She pulled into the driveway and laughed when she saw him in the front yard, waving his cane at the squirrels trying to grab a snack from the bird feeder. He looked her way when she killed the engine and got out of the truck.

"You don't usually come visit me at this time, or do I have my days and times mixed up?" Branch came across the lawn, using his cane to threaten the squirrels as much as he used it for walking.

Bonnie felt a little silly now that she was here. She should have at least called first. Branch looked her over and waved her inside.

"Looks like you better come on in. Whatever it is seems to be serious. One of two things can inspire that look, death or women. I'm hoping you're not here to tell me a friend died, although at my age, most of my friends are dead already."

Bonnie followed Branch inside and helped him settle into his favorite recliner in the living room. She retrieved lemonade from the fridge for both of them. She put hers down on the end table out of fear of spilling. Her hands were shaky, and she was having trouble sitting still.

"Aren't you a fart in a mitten today. Let's hear it." Branch folded his hands and waited.

"You said you dated a lot but never found someone to share your life with, the love of your life?" Bonnie leaned forward from her perch on the couch.

Branch wagged his finger. "No, I said I wasn't any help with women. I never said I didn't find the love of my life."

"I'm not sure what that means." Bonnie frowned.

"Evelyn Cooper. I would have done anything for her. She was the one, but I screwed it up. I always screwed it up." Branch looked deep in his memories.

"How did you screw up? How did you make it better?" Bonnie scooted to the edge of her seat.

"If we're going to talk about this kind of thing, we can't be drinking lemonade." Branch hoisted himself from his chair and rooted around in a short cabinet tucked under the window. He returned with two shot glasses and a bottle of whiskey. "Put your keys in the bowl on the counter, then you pour."

Bonnie did as she was told. She took a look at the bottle as she poured. The whiskey was expensive and tasted like it. She let it coat her throat and warm its way down.

Branch let out a contented sign. "Ahh. Now we can get started. Like I said, I always screwed up with women. I thought I heard them, but I was never listening. You can't be a good listener if you're waiting for your turn to talk or thinking about ways to solve a problem in your head while someone's talking. I learned the hard way, not everyone needs their problems solved. Sometimes they need someone to listen."

Bonnie thought that over. Since Grace told her she had to go back to LA, Bonnie hadn't truly listened to her thoughts and feelings about it. She'd shut down and nursed her own feelings. She was ashamed at how selfish she'd been, Grace must have been hurting too. It wasn't her fault her job had put her in that position.

"The other thing I learned which might be important to you." Branch pointed to Bonnie. "Given that you're a strong, independent, capable woman, I'd expect you to want a partner who's the same. Grace is probably still brilliant and driven like she was in high school. She's not going to settle for an unequal partnership. Back in my early days, men were the decision makers, the money managers, the caretakers, but that doesn't work now. If you decide you're going to tell Grace what to do or make all the decisions about something, you're going to find yourself out on the streets." Branch held out his shot glass until Bonnie poured for both of them.

"So I shouldn't sell our jointly owned house and decide to move to LA without talking to her about it?" Bonnie poured another round.

Branch saluted her with his shot glass and tipped it back.

Over the course of the next hour, she and Branch talked about Grace, Evelyn, and the mistakes they'd both made. They also took at least another shot, but Bonnie wasn't sure if one more had also slipped in.

Eventually Branch stood, swayed a little, and declared. "We have to get you to Grace. Go fight for Grace, and for Evelyn."

Bonnie leapt up at his rallying cry, ready to run to Grace and plead for another chance. She was willing to grovel if needed. As soon as she was on her feet however, she realized she was in no shape to drive. Branch offered to drive but he wasn't any more fit than she was.

Eventually, she called Duck. Fifteen minutes later, Candace, Avery, Duck, Carl, and Stumpy pulled into Branch's driveway in Candace's giant SUV.

"Did everyone have to come?" Bonnie squinted at her friends.

"Yes." Avery jumped and gave a small cry when all of them voted affirmatively with a united voice.

"Let's go, Romeo. The record should reflect I don't find drunken groveling to be sexy, but all the boys say to go for it, so Avery and I are outvoted." Candace waved Bonnie over to the car. "The airport express is seeing you off. Hopefully you sober up on the way across the country."

"You're not going without me." Branch lurched after Bonnie.

Duck cursed and jumped out of the car to help Branch in.

Bonnie laughed as Candace gently banged her head against the wheel. "I love you, Candace." Bonnie blew her a kiss.

"Save it for Grace. Your charm won't work here." Candace smiled despite her stern tone. "Everyone buckle up, bus is pulling out. Someone make sure our two intoxicated friends are well secured, and no puking in my car."

"I need underwear and headphones. Can we stop at my house?" Bonnie tried to point in the right direction but ended up poking Carl instead.

The drive wasn't long, but Bonnie's head was spinning, and she was a little queasy. It didn't help that she was all the way in the back of the SUV sandwiched between Carl and Stumpy.

"Are you two okay?" Bonnie looked from one to the other then held her head in her hands to keep everything from spinning.

"Better than you, lover boy." Stumpy ruffled her hair laughing.

"What the hell were you thinking getting drunk with Branch Tucker of all people? We would have been happy to drown your sorrows with you." Carl leaned in to kiss her cheek.

Stumpy followed his lead and they each kissed a side and smushed her two cheeks together for much longer than she was comfortable with, which was to say they did it at all.

"Yuck, get off me." Bonnie flailed around until they backed away. "Ooh, you know what we should do? We should call Madison. I bet she'll want to come with us."

Stumpy tried to grab Bonnie's phone, but she was faster. "I don't think that's a good idea, Runt.

"Too late, already dialing." Bonnie smiled and waved so enthusiastically she dropped her phone. "Oops, sorry, Madison. We'll get you. Candace, don't put on the brakes or Madison is going to come flying your way."

Candace looked in the rearview mirror at Bonnie. "Zip it back there. I'll stop this car whenever I need or want to. I'm not taking driving suggestions from the cheap seats. Bonnie, think sobering thoughts. Madison, whichever seat you're under, hello. I hope you can hear me."

Bonnie listened carefully. "I hear her. Carl, by your foot."

Carl dug around until he found the phone and said hello to Madison. Bonnie tried to grab it from him, but he turned away from her and spoke quietly for a few minutes. Bonnie tried to reclaim her phone multiple times but was unsuccessful. Finally, Carl turned back toward Bonnie. "Runt's drunk and she's going to fly to LA to try to convince Grace to take her back. We're all along to see her off. Wanna come?"

"Bonnie, I asked you before camping what your deal was. You never answered me. Have you figured out your shit? You're awfully cute, but if you haven't gotten your shit in order you're going to end up hurting her." Madison had lost her merry tone.

"Where are you?" Bonnie turned her head, or the phone, she wasn't entirely sure since everything was a little spinny. "I don't want to hurt her. I didn't ever want to hurt her." Bonnie had found some of the sobering thoughts Candace recommended.

"I hope you'll keep your promise even after you sober up. Hand me over to Stumpy, I need a word." Madison's tone was lighter again.

As soon as Candace pulled into the driveway and the car was mostly parked, Bonnie unbuckled and climbed over the middle row and shot out the door. It took a few tries to get the front door unlocked and open, but once she did, she took the stairs two at a time so she could pack a carry-on with the essentials.

"I'm looking at flights for you." Duck shouted from downstairs. "Are you okay flying in the overhead bin?"

"Just get me there, Duck." Bonnie leaned against the doorframe to her bedroom.

Bonnie looked down the hall at the room Grace had called hers a few days prior. What would home look like in LA? Would Grace want her to stay? Anxiety surged. She tried to tamp it down, but it was stubborn. The alcohol wasn't helping her manage her emotions. Grace was worth it, but how was she going to manage without her friends? Without a job? Her whole life?

She shoved the final article of clothing and her toothbrush into her suitcase and zipped it closed. Getting it and herself down the stairs in her current condition proved a challenge, but she made it in one piece.

Her friends were all gathered at the dining room table. She parked the suitcase by the door. "Duck, did you find a flight for me?" She glanced into the dining room.

Duck looked at the computer then to Candace then Stumpy. "Still working on it."

Something seemed off about Duck's response, but Bonnie couldn't pull it from her brain. Damn Branch and his whiskey. She cut a shaky path to the living room and picked up the picture of Grace and her from high school. She knew the way she was looking at Grace in the picture was the way she still looked at her. Lionel would be proud of what he accomplished from beyond the grave. The letter was on the mantel next to the picture. She whispered a thank you to Lionel, although perhaps it was premature. Grace had to want her to stay in LA for Lionel to get everything he wanted.

Bonnie looked at the letter again. "Lemonade." She practically shouted.

"No, young buck. We were drinking whiskey." Branch steered himself to the couch and sat down heavily.

Bonnie shook her head and then thought better of it. "No, Lionel hid money for lemonade somewhere in the house. For Grace and me to have together. I have to find it and bring it with me. I need help looking." She called into the dining room. "I have to find lemonade money before I can go. It's hidden in the house."

"How much do you need? I can spot you." Branch checked his pockets. "Well, looks like I forgot my wallet. Guess I better help you search."

"I don't think Grace is going to like us poking through all her things." Duck carefully lifted the top off an art piece.

"Did he give you a clue? Are we looking for an easter egg?" Carl looked in the fridge and pulled out a soda.

Bonnie stood in the living room looking around at her friends' half-hearted search attempts. She had no idea where to start herself but felt desperate to find the money. Without it her plea to Grace felt incomplete. Maybe her sober self would find the idea silly, but in this moment, she couldn't leave without Lionel's lemonade money.

"Please, I need to find it. I need to find that money so I can take Grace out to get lemonade." Bonnie felt like she could cry which was almost as embarrassing as getting drunk with Branch.

"I know where it is."

Bonnie froze. She didn't want to turn around because as long as she kept her back to what she could have sworn was Grace's voice, she could pretend she was standing behind her. Finally, she worked up the nerve to turn around.

"Hi." Grace gave a little wave.

Bonnie took a step to Grace and stopped. "What are you doing here?"

Grace looked unsure, a mixture of hopeful and scared. Bonnie understood that feeling. It resonated in her bones. As soon as she saw her, Bonnie felt like her heart was trying to escape her chest and flee to Grace. Like it was searching for reunification with the only thing in this world that could make it whole, but she was confused and needed Grace to explain.

"I'm here to talk to you." Grace looked at the roomful of their friends. All eyes were on them. "Maybe somewhere private."

Bonnie knew she'd do anything for Grace, and that included heeding Branch's advice and truly listening. Grace was here and that had to mean something. Bonnie extended her hand and Grace took it. They walked hand in hand out the back door into the yard to the bench overlooking the field beyond their property. Bonnie loved staring at the wide-open farmland; it always represented possibility in her eyes.

They sat together, having closed a three-thousand-mile distance, with fields of possibility as far as the eye could see. Bonnie turned to Grace and waited. When she started to talk, Bonnie listened.

CHAPTER TWENTY-FIVE

Grace took a few minutes to enjoy the feel of Bonnie's hand in hers and the smell of open space and clean air. This moment was so different from all the ones she'd experienced from the time she told Bonnie she was leaving. She'd missed Bonnie desperately.

Grace leaned in to snuggle closer to Bonnie but recoiled from the smell coming from her. "Are you drunk?"

"Yes, but it was an accident." Bonnie gave a lopsided grin. She looked handsome and roguish.

It infuriated Grace how much she wanted to kiss the smirk off Bonnie's face. "Did you mistake bourbon for root beer? Trip into a vat of tequila and the only way out was to drink your way to safety?"

Bonnie made a face. "I don't like tequila."

"What's going on, Bonnie? Why were you running around the house drunk looking for lemonade money and a suitcase?" Grace folded her arms across her chest and shoved aside all the emotions fighting it out for supremacy. She couldn't untangle them easily and she wanted to focus on Bonnie.

"I went to talk to Branch and he thought a little whiskey would help us solve my problems." Bonnie looked at Grace earnestly. "You remember when a tree knocked my house down?" Bonnie continued after Grace nodded. "Well, inside it looked like one of those fake rooms in furniture stores to sell you table lamps you don't need. Everything was white and cold and just, nothing. I didn't even have the table lamp. That's what my life is like without you in it."

"Am I a table lamp in this analogy?" Grace couldn't help teasing.

Bonnie paused and considered. "I don't know. I lost myself. All I know is you make my life better. That's what Branch helped me get at. He knows a lot of things about women. It turns out I knew a lot about what I wanted with you, even though I didn't know it."

Grace frowned. What was her life coming to that her relationship was hanging on the advice of a geriatric, recovering homophobe who was a confirmed lifelong bachelor? "Should you trust the kinds of things Branch knows about women?"

"Branch doesn't know anything about keeping the woman you love, but I have a few ideas." Bonnie turned and swung one leg over the bench so she was fully facing Grace. "Grace, I'm sorry I let us get to a place where we could break each other's hearts again. I'm sorry I put pressure on you, even a little about moving to Garrison. Most of all, I'm sorry I let you get on that plane alone, again. If you'll have me, it will never happen again."

Grace stared at Bonnie. What was in Branch's magic whiskey? Her hands tingled and her lips felt warm and swollen. Was Bonnie really offering to move to LA to be with her? Grace frowned.

"Am I wrong? Did I say something wrong?" Bonnie looked worried. "I love you, Grace. I want us to have the chance to be together in LA."

Grace took a deep breath. She'd flown all the way out here, there was no going back now. "What if I don't want us to be together in LA?" Grace turned so she was also straddling the bench and facing Bonnie. She moved closer.

Bonnie's expression dropped and she looked like she was fighting tears. "I understand. I guess I misunderstood what we had."

"No, you didn't. You didn't let me finish. She slid closer until she was invading Bonnie's personal space. She kissed below her ear, then down her neck. "I said I didn't want us to be together in LA. What if you don't have to worry about me falling asleep anywhere but in your bed, here in Garrison?"

Bonnie's eyes had gotten big at the first kiss on her neck, but they nearly bulged out of her head at Grace's suggestion. "If you're not being serious, please don't mess with me, Grace."

"I would never. I love you too much to be cruel." Grace draped her arms over Bonnie's shoulders and kissed along her jawline. "It took me too long to see it, but Garrison is where my home is. You're where my home is."

A slow smiled spread across Bonnie's face. "You love me too?" Grace rolled her eyes but there was no malice behind the gesture. "Did you hear any of the rest of what I said?"

"Of course I did. You're going to tell me where that lemonade money is and we're going to toast your dad for being right all along. You're moving to Garrison and I love you and you love me." Bonnie had a big goofy grin on her face like she couldn't contain all the happiness residing inside.

Soon Bonnie and Grace were both laughing, hanging on each other and trying to keep from tumbling off the bench. Bonnie did lose her balance and pulled Grace closer. Instead of focusing solely on preventing a fall, Grace pulled Bonnie to her swiftly and kissed her like she might not get another chance. Bonnie melted into the kiss, and they began vying for power and control of the kiss.

Grace was about to suggest they pause long enough to go inside when she pulled away abruptly. "Do you smell smoke?"

Bonnie looked like she was in a haze of lust and brain fog. "Smoke, yes. Smells like a campfire."

"Come on, let's go see what's happening. It smells close by." Grace pulled Bonnie to her feet.

They jogged hand in hand to the front yard. Grace's heart was racing from the knowledge she and Bonnie were going to be okay and the unknown of what they would find on the other side of the house.

When they turned the corner, they did find a large fire, but not one out of control or threatening. Instead a big group of people, including all of their friends, were seated around an inviting fire pit well away from the front porch.

Grace gasped and pulled her hand from Bonnie's. She stopped and put both hands over her mouth. Bonnie must have thought something was wrong because she turned to comfort her. It was in fact, quite the opposite. Grace shook Bonnie's shoulder excitedly.

"The boys got tired of listening to me whine so we built this last weekend. The yard needed it." Bonnie shrugged.

Grace heard a familiar squeal and braced herself. As soon as she got close enough she leapt into Grace's arms, wrapping her legs around her waist. "You look happy. You're happy, right?"

"What are you doing here?" Bonnie looked confused.

Madison finally hopped down and looked back and forth between Grace and Bonnie. "I came to make your life very painful if she asked me to." Madison squeezed Bonnie's shoulder, hard.

Bonnie buckled under Madison digging deep into a pressure point in her shoulder. She looked like a small child trying not to cry so an older kid doesn't have a reason to make fun of you.

"Enough, Madison. You know how much that hurts. This is the happily ever after part. You missed your moment."

Bonnie gasped when Madison released her. "Remind me not to do anything to piss you off if that's only show and tell." Bonnie bent over with her hands on her knees. She shook out her left arm, perhaps wondering if it would ever feel the same.

Madison leaned over and smiled. "I could make you feel that all over your body."

"I thought we weren't doing the 'I'm going to break your kneecaps if you hurt her' routine. Don't you believe in nonviolence?" Bonnie stood and rotated her shoulder.

"What the fuck would I want your kneecaps for? Non-violence sure, but I believe in her happiness more." The look on Madison's face was priceless.

"Easy, girl. Bonnie's not going to hurt me." Grace put her arm around Bonnie and kissed her cheek.

Bonnie slid her arm around Grace's waist. She swallowed hard. Grace could feel her vibrating ever so slightly. Was it because of nerves? Love? Something else?

Grace felt a little wobbly from the overwhelming love she was feeling, free from the uncertainty and rancor of the recent past. Grace's stomach did a quadruple axel and stuck the landing. Grace smiled at Bonnie. She could see the love shining back at her in Bonnie's eyes.

She held out her arm to Madison. "Care to join in the fun?"

Madison hesitated a moment, then took Grace's offered arm. They walked, arm in arm, or arm around waist or shoulder, back to the bonfire.

"Runt, did you get the girl?" Duck looked up from letting Avery lick tiny bits of marshmallow off his fingers.

"She sure did." Grace kissed Bonnie in a way that left no doubts about the way they felt about each other.

"You moving to LA?"

Everyone around the fire was serious and silent. Even the flames seemed to slow their dancing while the question hung in the air.

"She is not. Her girl is moving to Garrison." Grace warmed at the loud cheering that arose around the fire.

She and Grace squeezed onto a log on one side of the fire. Madison rejoined Stumpy and Carl on the other side. Grace couldn't help but notice how close they were sitting and the frequent glances and quick smiles they shared. What had she missed in the last couple of days?

"Runt, we dug in your cabinets and found all the fixings for s'mores if you want some. Otherwise, Carl and I will eat them all." Stumpy looked at Candace glaring at him. "Definitely *not* eat them all is what I meant to say." He looked a little sheepish.

"I have a better idea." Candace jogged across the lawn toward her house and returned a few minutes later with a few staples from the kitchen and two plastic circles about the size of a soccer ball with openings about the diameter of an orange. "Here's a recipe for you lot to follow, then start kicking."

"Kicking? Do you know what she's talking about?" Grace looked at Bonnie and the rest of the group around the fire.

"Ice cream!" Carl, Stumpy, Duck, and Bonnie simultaneously jumped to their feet.

They scrambled over and around the assembled logs, chairs, and guests to get to Candace. Grace laughed watching the four of them elbow and crowd their way around the new treasure like they'd been doing since they were kids. She stood and joined Madison and Candace. Despite the sugar from the marshmallows, Avery was nodding off in her stroller, oblivious to the chaos. Nothing in LA had ever felt so comfortable, like a pair of sneakers molded perfectly to her. How could she not have seen Garrison had always been her home?

"Look at those four, will they ever grow up?" Candace shook her head as if annoyed, but she was smiling fondly toward Duck and the others.

"I hope not." Grace felt like little heart emojis were probably shooting from her eyes as she looked at Bonnie. "I love her exactly as she is."

"Love, huh? You two worked out the distance for good?" Candace gave her a hug. "I'm so happy for you. Are we going to still be neighbors?"

Grace nodded. "I'm moving home. It's hard not to fall in love all over again with Garrison. Especially when the only woman I've ever loved lives there too."

Madison pulled Grace and Candace into a group hug. "I love when we reach the sappy part of an evening. But how can you say there's only one woman you love?" Madison stepped back and pouted dramatically."

"Been in love with, is that better?" Grace pulled Madison close and gave her a sloppy kiss on the cheek.

"Much. You're in marketing, you know how important words are. One in or out is smiles or shit piles." Madison winked at Candace.

Grace playfully wagged her finger Madison's way. "I'm not in any business anymore. I quit remember?" She jumped out of the way as one of the spheres Candace brought out careened toward her ankles.

Bonnie ran past, doubled back for a kiss, then continued pursuing the runaway container. She was out of breath and a little sweaty and from where Grace was standing couldn't have been sexier if she'd spent hours trying.

"Ice cream will be ready soon." Bonnie pointed at the red plastic ball.

"If you say so, hot stuff. You've made me a promise and I expect you to keep it." Madison blew Bonnie a kiss.

Bonnie caught it dramatically and held it close to her heart before running back dribbling the ice cream maker like a soccer ball. She seemed to be feeling much better after her drunken afternoon.

"If ice cream comes out of that thing and it's not covered in dirt and rocks, it will knock my socks off." Madison watched Bonnie and the boys kicking the two balls around vigorously.

"It'll be the best ice cream you've ever had, you'll see." Candace nodded knowingly. "And I for one can't wait. I didn't have any cravings with Avery, but this one is making Roy go on plenty of late night snack runs." Candace looked from Grace to Madison with a shy smile.

"Are you serious?" Grace barely contained the squeal of delight. She gave Candace an enormous hug. "Are you finding out boy or girl?"

Candace smiled widely and looked lovingly from Avery to Duck. "We are. The anatomy scan is next week. We wanted to wait until at least then. It was so hard to get pregnant this time the pregnancy felt delicate, even though everything's been fine. That's why we've kept it to ourselves until now. Roy's going to tell the others tonight."

"Thank you for telling me. Best news of the night." Grace's chest felt warm and full. The day had started out bleak and was ending filled with love and joy.

Grace watched Bonnie with Duck, Carl, and Stumpy, kicking the ice cream spheres around the yard, Branch and Avery cat-napping slightly away from the action, and Candace and Madison chatting happily. If she'd had any remaining doubt that this was where she belonged, it all evaporated.

She'd never felt more at home, surrounded by love, by Bonnie's love, and the wonderful friendships she'd found since coming home. As soon as the thought formed it was chased away by the reality that a Madison sized hole would be torn in this momentary utopia at any moment.

"When do you have to leave, Maddy? This is too perfect. I don't want you to ever go back."

"Okay." Madison shrugged.

Grace was sure the world stopped for a moment. "What do you mean 'okay'?"

Candace looked like she knew a secret Grace didn't.

"It means you're a bad influence on me and I quit my job before we came here. Turns out I think village life suits me. Carl said I can stay with him for a while until I find a place, and we get our business set up, but he also knows the owner of the house Bonnie used to rent and it should be tree free and back in rental shape shortly. Apparently, it would be very Rhode Island of me to move into your girlfriend's old house."

"Who has a girlfriend?" Bonnie appeared with an armful of ice cream bowls.

"You do." Grace took her bowl from Bonnie and kissed her. She couldn't get enough of her. The days they'd been apart had been torture.

"Hey, you two, tone down the heat, I don't want to eat ice cream soup." Candace shooed them farther away.

"What do you mean by 'business,' Maddy?" Grace stayed close to Bonnie as she ate her ice cream.

Madison's eyes lit up. "First, remote work is a thing so we can do a lot of what we did in LA from here. Second, there are some great places to visit and shop at in Garrison. All they need is a little more marketing exposure. My goal is to get at least one product from our village featured on one of the national Christmas shopping lists next year." Madison was ticking things off on her fingers while she talked.

Bonnie cocked her head. She looked interested. "I'll be your first client. I'd love to expand my business."

Stumpy and Carl swung by with their ice cream. "Me too. It might be best if I wasn't the village shrink." Stumpy looked around and shrugged sadly.

"I have an idea about that." Madison's eyes twinkled mischievously. "Therapy can be done in person or remotely, right?"

Stumpy nodded, looking skeptical.

"I happen to know a whole town that could use a good therapist. It's also impossible to see anyone out there. What do you say you expand your licensure and we work on setting you up with some referrals from well outside Garrison?" Madison raised an eyebrow.

"I'm your guy." Stumpy grinned.

"I thought you were my guy." Carl pulled Stumpy into an enthusiastic hug from behind and gave him a kiss on the cheek.

They both blushed adorably and sprung apart before looking at each other shyly. "That's different." Stumpy smiled at Carl.

Grace tried hard not to stare. She'd have to get some more information from Bonnie later. She hadn't been gone that long but too much had happened without her. She wouldn't be making that mistake again. She was home to stay. Grace took Bonnie's hand and led her back to the fire.

Bonnie sat in a low lawn chair next to the fire and pulled Grace down onto her lap. "I'm sorry I pulled away from you when you said you were going back to LA." Bonnie slid the hair out of Grace's face and tucked it behind her ear. "And most of all for staying away so long. I should have talked to you that night and followed you onto the plane when you were leaving."

"Next time we'll both do better." Grace put down her bowl and nuzzled into Bonnie's neck.

"What do you mean 'next time'? Isn't it all sunshine and roses from here?" Bonnie's chuckle sent a happy vibration through Grace's chest.

"Of course, what was I thinking." Grace sat up and kissed Bonnie a little more thoroughly. "We'll never disagree on anything again. Except maybe on what color to paint our bedroom."

Bonnie raised an eyebrow. "Our bedroom?"

"Are you planning on separate bedrooms and sneaking down the hall to see each other like we might get caught?" Grace sat back and looked at Bonnie. Could Bonnie tell she wanted to go upstairs and test all the beds, couches, and surfaces in the house to find the single best place to have sex?

"As hot as that sounds, you in my bed every night sounds better." Bonnie was flushed and breathing a little more heavily than usual.

"Do you think anyone would notice if we slipped off now?" Grace bit down gently on Bonnie's ear.

Bonnie looked around Grace and her eyes got wide. "I think they might."

Grace turned around. All of their friends were staring at them. Spontaneously, they started clapping.

"Thought we were about to get quite a show," Stumpy said. "You two are a fire hazard."

"We were ready to cover Branch's eyes though, don't worry." Duck pointed to Carl and himself.

"Are you two staying or should we alert the fire department that this bonfire might get out of hand?" Candace's eyes were sparkling with shenanigans and firelight.

Bonnie looked at Grace, clearly letting her make the decision.

"Depends on if there's more ice cream."

Their bowls were refilled, and they scooted their shared chair closer to the fire. Grace didn't miss Stumpy and Carl subtly holding hands in the dark space between their two chairs. It felt like love, of all persuasions, was in the air and for the first time since she was a child, she could say there was nowhere else she'd rather be.

"Your father must be awfully proud of himself looking down at us now." Bonnie squeezed Grace tightly. If there's a way to say 'I told you so' from Heaven, I'm sure he'll figure it out."

Grace laughed. "He will, but I'm glad he was right. You're everything I want. Garrison is what I want. Tanya said Garrison is the perfect place to raise a family."

"I think Tanya's a smart lady. I think she's right and I want that. A family. With you."

Grace couldn't see Bonnie's face, but her words had been quiet and a little shaky at the end on her last sentence.

"Let's make an entire soccer team. I want a herd of little Bonnies running around." Grace took Bonnie's hand.

Bonnie kissed her cheek sweetly. "I love you, Grace. You never told me though, where did he hide the lemonade money?"

Grace looked up to the sky and pictured the twinkle in her father's eye shining down on her a million times over in every distant star above. "It's in the framed picture of us. It's the only place he would have left it. It's the only place we would have looked if this worked out."

If she could see into her body, Grace was sure she'd see puzzle pieces all falling perfectly into place. All of the nagging uncertainty, the doubt, the heartbreak that had never fully healed were gone. She was home.

"I love you, Bonnie. I've never stopped loving you. Or Garrison. I should have known that you were here waiting for me in the town that built us."

About the Author

Although she works best under the pressure of a deadline, Jesse Thoma balks at being told what to do. Despite that, she's no fool and knows she'd be lost without her editor's brilliance. While writing, Jesse is usually under the close supervision of a judgmental cat or two. *The Town That Built Us* is Jesse's ninth novel. *Seneca Falls* was a finalist for a Lambda Literary Award in romance. *Data Capture, Serenity*, and *Courage* were finalists for the Golden Crown Literary Society "Goldie" Award.

Books Available from Bold Strokes Books

A Second Chance at Life by Genevieve McCluer. Vampires Dinah and Rachel reconnect, but a string of vampire killings begin and evidence seems to be pointing at Dinah. They must prove her innocence while finding out if the two of them are still compatible after all these years. (978-1-63679-459-4)

Digging for Heaven by Jenna Jarvis. Litz lives for dragons. Kella lives to kill them. The last thing they expect is to find each other attractive. (978-1-63679-453-2)

Forever's Promise by Missouri Vaun. Wesley Holden migrated west disguised as a man for the hope of a better life and with no designs to take a wife, but Charlotte Rose has other ideas. (978-1-63679-221-7)

Here For You by D. Jackson Leigh. A horse trainer must make a difficult business decision that could save her father's ranch from foreclosure but destroy her chance to win the heart of a feisty barrel racer vying for a spot in the National Rodeo Finals. (978-1-63679-299-6)

I Do, I Don't by Joy Argento. Creator of the romance algorithm, Nicole Hart doesn't expect to be starring in her own reality TV dating show, and falling for the show's executive producer Annie Jackson could ruin everything. (978-1-63679-420-4)

It's All in the Details by Dena Blake. Makeup artist Lane Donnelly and wedding planner Helen Trent can't stand each other, but they must set aside their differences to ensure Darcy gets the wedding of her dreams, and make a few of their own dreams come true. (978-1-63679-430-3)

Marigold by Melissa Brayden. Marigold Lavender vows to take down Alexis Wakefield, the harsh food critic who blasts her younger sister's restaurant. If only she wasn't as sexy as she is mean. (978-1-63679-436-5)

The Town that Built Us by Jesse J. Thoma. When her father dies, Grace Cook returns to her hometown and tries to avoid Bonnie Whitlock, the woman who pulverized her heart, only to discover her father's estate has been left to them jointly. (978-1-63679-439-6)

A Degree to Die For by Karis Walsh. A murder at the University of Washington's Classics Department brings Professor Antigone Weston and Sergeant Adriana Kent together—first as opposing forces, and then allies as they fight together to protect their campus from a killer. (978-1-63679-365-8)

A Talent Within by Suzanne Lenoir. Evelyne, born into nobility, and Annika, a peasant girl with a deadly secret, struggle to change their destinies in Valmora, a medieval world controlled by religion, magic, and men. (978-1-63679-423-5)

Finders Keepers by Radclyffe. Roman Ashcroft's past, it seems, is not so easily forgotten when fate brings her and Tally Dewilde together—along with an attraction neither welcomes. (978-1-63679-428-0)

Homeland by Kristin Keppler and Allisa Bahney. Dani and Kate have finally found themselves on the same side of the war, but a new threat from the inside jeopardizes the future of the wasteland. (978-1-63679-405-1)

Just One Dance by Jenny Frame. Will Taylor Spark and her new business to make dating special—the Regency Romance Club—bring sparkle back to Jaq Bailey's lonely world? (978-1-63679-457-0)

On My Way There by Jaycie Morrison. As Max traverses the open road, her journey of impossible love, loss, and courage mirrors her voyage of self-discovery leading to the ultimate question: If she can't have the woman of her dreams, will the woman of real life be enough? (978-1-63679-392-4)

Transitioning Home by Heather K O'Malley. An injured soldier realizes they need to transition to really heal. (978-1-63679-424-2)

Truly Enough by JJ Hale. Chasing the spark of creativity may ignite a burning romance or send a friendship up in flames. (978-1-63679-442-6)

Vintage and Vogue by Kelly and Tana Fireside. When tech whiz Sena Abrigo marches into small-town Owen Station, she turns librarian Hazel Butler's life upside down in the most wonderful of ways, setting off an explosive series of events, threatening their chance at love…and their very lives. (978-1-63679-448-8)

Broken Fences by Jo Hemmingwood. Former army sergeant Seneca Twist has difficulty adjusting to civilian life until she meets psychologist Robyn Mason and has a place to call home. (978-1-63679-414-3)

Never Kiss a Cowgirl by Ali Vali. Asher Evans dreams of winning the National Finals Rodeo in Vegas, and Reagan Wilson wants no part of something that brings back the memory of what killed her father. (978-1-63679-106-7)

Pantheon Girls by Jean Copeland. Cassie Burke never anticipated the detour life was about to take when a meeting with a prospective client reunites her with a past love and reignites the star-crossed passion they shared twenty years earlier. (978-1-63679-337-5)

Roux for Two by Aurora Rey. For TV chef Chelsea Boudreaux and hometown boy Bryce Cormier, love proves as tricky as making a good pot of gumbo. (978-1-63679-376-4)

Starting Over by Nance Sparks. Jennifer has no idea if she can mend Sam's broken soul after the sudden loss of her wife, but it's never too late for starting over. (978-1-63679-409-9)

The Accidental Bride by Jane Walsh. Spinsters Miss Grace Linfield and Miss Thea Martin travel to Gretna Green to prevent a wedding, only to discover a scandalous passion—for each other. (978-1-63679-345-0)

Three Wishes by Anne Shade. A magic lamp, a beautiful Jinni, and a cursed princess make for one unbelievable story. (978-1-63679-349-8)

Undiscovered Treasures by MJ Williamz. For Cyl and her friends Luna and Martinique, life's best treasures often appear when you're not looking. (978-1-63679-449-5)

Curse of the Gorgon by Tanai Walker. Cass will do anything to ensure Elle's safety, but is she willing to embrace the curse of the Gorgon? (978-1-63679-395-5)

Dance with Me by Georgia Beers. Scottie Templeton mixes it up on and off the dance floor with sexy salsa instructor Marisa Reyes. But can Scottie get past Marisa's connection to her ex? (978-1-63679-359-7)

Gin and Bear It by Joy Argento. Opposites really can attract, and as Kelly and Logan work together to create a loving home for rescue cat Bear, they just might find one for themselves as well. (978-1-63679-351-1)

Harvest Dreams by Jacqueline Fein-Zachary. Planting the vineyard of their dreams, Kate Bauer and Sydney Barrett must resist their attraction while battling nature and their families, who oppose both the venture and their relationship. (978-1-63679-380-1)

The No Kiss Contract by Nan Campbell. Workaholic Davy believes she can get the top spot at her firm if the senior partners think she's settling down and about to start a family, but she needs the delightful yet dubious Anna to help by pretending to be her fiancée. (978-1-63679-372-6)

Outside the Lines by Melissa Sky. If you had the chance to live forever, would you take it? Amara Rodriguez did, and it sets her on a journey to find her missing mother and unravel the mystery of her own heart. (978-1-63679-403-7)

The Value of Sylver and Gold by Michelle Larkin. When word gets out that former Boston homicide detective Reid Sylver can talk to the dead, the FBI solicits her help on a serial murder case, prompting Reid to assemble forces once again with Detective London Gold. (978-1-63679-093-0)

When It Feels Right by Tagan Shepard. Freshly out of the closet Marlene hasn't been lucky in love, but when it comes to her quirky new roommate Abby, everything just feels right. (978-1-63679-367-2)